Books by Joy Collins

Second Chance 2007
Coming Together 2009 (co-authored with Joyce Norman)
I Will Never Leave You 2017
No Other Choice 2021

No Other Choice

Joy Collins

Desert Spirit Press

Arizona

Author's Note

Desert Spirit Press, LLC
www.DesertSpiritPress.com
DesertSpiritPress@cox.net

ISBN:
978-0-9889850-5-6

Printed in the United States of America
First Edition

Author photo: Photography by Leanna
http://photosbyleanna.com/

To John
For always believing in me
For always loving me
Still

Acknowledgements
○३

It has taken me several years to write this book. Not because it was a particularly hard book to write. No, life just got in the way.

I started this book back in 2008. The story kept evolving as stories are wont to do. My husband helped me with the plot and had several good suggestions. Then, in May of 2010, he died suddenly, and my world turned upside down.

It took me quite a while to be able to reclaim my life. In the beginning, I could barely read, let alone write.

When I finally came up for air, I wrote *I Will Never Leave You*, a memoir of our life together and what I experienced after John's death. It was very well received and for a while I thought I would write a companion book to it. A workbook, if you will, expanding on what I had learned about metaphysics and spirituality since John's passing.

But that never felt right. I had said all I really needed to say about that. Anything beyond that needed to be left to the experts. And I don't consider myself one.

So, I decided to go back to my first love - fiction.

And then life hit again. This time, the whole world was involved. The COVID pandemic turned everyone's life upside down, mine included. I experienced a phenomenon that was not unique. Many of us who lost loved ones and were now gripped with the isolation caused by the pandemic experienced feelings of loss all over again. Once again, sadness and an inability to concentrate overwhelmed me. Writing was the last thing I wanted to do.

But I got through it. I had help. And gradually, slowly, things changed. Not only did life start to feel better but I was able to write again.

I have many people to thank for helping me through that time and I want to acknowledge them here along with those who helped make this book the best it can be.

I want to give a huge shout out to my therapist Carolyn Settle MSW. I had been in therapy with Carolyn since John's passing. Our in-person sessions turned into Zoom meetings and were a lifesaver that I clung to in those first few months. She is retired now but I am grateful for all the years of care that she gave me.

Carolyn referred me to two other women who helped me as well.

Thank you to Dr. Elissa Katz who made Bach flower remedies that worked wonders. And who listened to my worries with a kind ear.

And thank you to Dr. Amy Novotny, founder

of PABR® Institute, who, believe it or not, was able to perform physical therapy via Zoom and helped me learn to breathe in a way that calmed me. Our sessions helped me so much and will continue to do so.

Thank you to my beta readers Cathy Marley, Kathy Harris, Stephani James, Cynthia Flowers, and Claudia Flowers. They helped make this book so much better. They caught things I never would have and made suggestions that were priceless.

A special thank you to Cathy Marley for her afternoon phone calls.

Thank you to Tim and Lew Toettcher for the groceries and the calm words and for agreeing to be there for me no matter what.

And finally, thank you to my husband John who continues to show me every day that he is still with me and looking out for me. Our love continues to grow.

And just like Charlotte and some of the other characters in this book, I have learned that life throws you curves but you just have to put one foot in front of the other and do the best you can with what you have.

There is no other choice.

Joy Collins
May 2021

Prologue

ೞ

He followed the blue sedan from two cars lengths back. He did not want her to see him until the last minute. He knew the terrain ahead and knew his opportunity would come. He had to be careful. His plan was only to scare her and her nosy doctor friend. But they had to pay.

As he made his way along the open road into Fountain Hills he was momentarily confused when she did not turn where he expected. He was afraid she would get into a residential area and spoil his plan.

She kept on driving past and through Fountain Hills and it was then he realized she was heading farther out. He would have to move quickly. He had no idea where this was going to go. As soon as they made it into open desert again, he would take his shot.

The blue car was directly ahead of him now. There were no other cars between them. There was now hardly any traffic.

It was now or never. He sped up until he was right at her rear bumper. He saw her look into her rear-view mirror.

Scared, bitch? Good.

He tapped the accelerator and gently hit her bumper. She immediately swerved to her right. Probably thinking he would pass her.

Guess again.

He hit her car again. The road they were on was only two lanes, one in each direction, but he could see there was no traffic coming in the other direction. There was a dry riverbed to the right of the blue car with an embankment leading down into it.

He moved into the left lane. He knew he had to move quickly. He didn't want to risk oncoming traffic and get hit himself.

He swung his car sharply to the right, hitting her car on the driver's side door. She looked over at him, panic on her face.

He hit her again.

She swerved to her right to try to get away from him and lost control of the car. He watched as her car went down the embankment and stopped halfway down after hitting some rocks. He smiled. The car wasn't visible from the highway.

No one had seen what had happened.

Things had turned out even better than he had expected.

He moved back into the right lane and kept on going.

Chapter One

⚘

Several months earlier…

"That's my house! I don't want him to buy me out." I slapped my hand on the hard polished conference room table and felt a stab of pleasure when Peter flinched.

I knew I was supposed to keep quiet, but the words tumbled out of my mouth before I could stop them. My attorney, Tom, placed his hand over mine, a sign he wanted me to quietly shut up. He whispered "Charlotte" so only I could hear it. An older man and usually very patient, his jaw twitched in frustration. I knew he wanted to say more. He had earned the gray at his temples by guiding a boatload of prospective ex-wives, myself included. Just prior to the meeting, he had told me how important it was for me to keep silent during these negotiations and to let him handle everything.

But seeing Peter across from me in Tom's conference room just made me want to reach over and slap him. I wanted to wipe that smug look off his arrogant handsome face once and for all. How did twenty years of marriage come to this?

"Mr. Hobson is prepared to buy Mrs. Hobson's portion of the equity in the house and offer her a more than fair settlement." Peter's attorney adjusted his glasses and carried on as if I had never spoken. He had heard ex-wives complain before.

I glared at Peter. "How can you do this to me?"

Peter avoided my gaze.

Coward.

"That's *my* house," I repeated.

Tom patted my hand, attempting once more to rein me in. I pulled my hand out from under his and placed it in my lap. I stared at the jacket of my suit and counted the buttons.

I had tried to dress so perfectly for this meeting. I wanted to make Peter regret ever leaving. Cocoa-colored suit to complement my brown hair. Moss-colored blouse to bring out my hazel eyes. I had worn the suit hoping to look competent, but I was sweating now under its weight and my emotional state, and I felt like a wet rag. None of the windows in the room opened. It was fifty-two degrees outside, but it felt like a hundred inside. I had worn my high-heeled black boots to make me look taller than my five foot four inches. Now they were also making me sweat and, since I was sitting, they were doing nothing to improve my height anyway. I obviously had not thought this through. I could smell Peter's cologne from where I sat, and it was making me ill.

Tom looked at Peter's attorney and smiled. "What Mrs. Hobson means is that she is prepared to buy Mr. Hobson out, that she desires to do so, and is asking for a realistic amount of time to accomplish this. I think under the circumstances that this is a reasonable request."

I saw Peter's face react when Tom said "under the circumstances" and I knew he understood what was being implied.

Good, you bastard. See if Bianca is worth losing the house.

Peter's attorney removed his glasses and turned slightly toward his client while he whispered something in his ear. I tried not to remember how it used to feel to be that close to Peter, to have him whisper my name as he caressed my cheek and pushed a strand of my curly brown hair behind my ear while he nibbled it. I had hated my long hair, but Peter loved the way it fell off my shoulders when we made love. He had begged me never to cut it. I was wearing it short now and hoped he got the message.

Peter tugged at the knot of his red silk tie. I knew that gesture meant he was losing his patience. I also knew that tie. I had bought it for him on our last happy Valentine's Day.

He shook his head repeatedly while his attorney whispered some more. A sheen of sweat formed on his upper lip.

"Fine. Three months." Peter looked directly at me and pointed. "Three months and not a day more."

His attorney squirmed in his seat. I guessed Peter was not performing as he had been instructed, either.

"Three months is very generous," Tom said

19

before I had a chance to jump in. "In three months, Mrs. Hobson will either secure financing to buy out Mr. Hobson, or she will accept her share of the equity from him. I'll make arrangements for the house to be appraised and get the numbers to you."

He looked over his papers and stood. "I think everything else is worked out satisfactorily. I'll have my secretary get the rest of the finalized property settlement written up and over to your office by the end of next week." Tom shook the other attorney's hand. "Call me, Richard, if you have any other questions."

A few minutes later, Peter and his lawyer left, and I started shaking. "I'm sorry, Tom. I know you said to keep quiet, but I just couldn't bear the thought of him getting my house. He knows how much that house means to me. He is just doing this for spite. He can have any house he wants. Just not mine. Not with her."

Tom sighed. "Well, we bought some time anyway."

"Right. Now I'll get a mortgage and that will be the end of it." Optimism replaced the anxiety I had felt all day at the prospect of these negotiations.

Tom poured himself a glass of water from the carafe on the credenza. "It may go to him anyway if you can't raise the money." He raised his glass to me. "Do you want some water? It's stifling in here."

I did not trust a glass in my shaking hands. "No, I'm fine," I lied. "What do you mean 'it may go to him anyway'?" A knot started to form in my stomach. "Why won't I qualify? I have a job."

"And bills. That house and its upkeep are expensive, and your job may not be enough to support it." Tom sat next to me again. He placed the glass on a coaster and turned in his seat to face me. "Charlotte, listen to me. It is going to take a lot to buy Peter out. Your house has appreciated tremendously over the last few years. We talked about this. You might be better off taking a lump sum from him and getting a smaller place for yourself."

I stood finally and walked to the window. Tom's suite of offices was on the third floor and looked out over a large parking lot. I could see my silver sports car where I had parked it just a little while ago. It now felt like years ago.

"I don't want a smaller place. I want my house." I heard myself and knew I sounded like a whining little kid, but I didn't care. "This is too much. Peter cheated. Let him make all the changes." I felt the sting of tears and swallowed to keep from crying.

"Have you heard back from the bank yet?" Tom knew I had applied for a new mortgage a few days before.

I turned to face him. "Not yet. I'll give them a call and see what's up." Maybe he was right. Maybe they had not called because the news was bad.

Tom gathered the papers of my file from the conference room table as he prepared to leave. "Let me know as soon as you hear anything. In the meantime, I'll have Gwen write everything else up and send it to you to look over before I ship it off to Peter's attorney."

Tom stopped and smiled. His eyes crinkled and I could imagine him with his grandchildren. The man oozed compassion and friendliness. "It's going to be okay, Charlotte. You're doing fine.

Divorce is never easy."

I shook my head. "Not for me, that's for sure. I never expected to be here."

"No one does. That's what keeps people like me in business. Go home. Get some rest. See a movie. Do something fun. Get drunk."

I stared at him.

"Okay, forget the drunk part. That's for men. But do something nice for yourself today. Buy shoes. My wife always buys shoes when she's depressed."

"I can't afford shoes now."

An older woman with a gray bun stuck her head in the door. "Mr. Ryan, your four o'clock is here."

Tom nodded. "Thanks, Gwen. I'll be right there."

I stuck out my hand. "I won't keep you any longer. Thanks for today, Tom. Talk to you later this week."

I thought about what Tom had said while I rode the elevator down to the lobby. Maybe he had a point. Maybe the bank would turn me down for a mortgage. Then not only would I feel the anger from Peter buying my house, but I'd also have the humiliation of him knowing I couldn't raise the money. Damn! I should have just let him buy me out. Make him think I didn't care. Move on, that's what my friends were telling me. Maybe rent an apartment for a while.

But a decent apartment anywhere here in Nassau County was going to be just as expensive as a house. Maybe more.

Damn it! Damn it! Damn it!

Why was this happening? I kept going back to the same thought I had been having ever since I had found out about Peter's affair. I had been fighting the idea that things were not right between Peter and me for some time. Marrying a divorced man with custody of his child was never easy but after a few years, I felt I had finally carved out my own place in his world and his daughter's. Even though we never had children of our own, I had thought my life with Peter was good.

We both loved Beth. We bought our dream house together. We wanted the same things. It wasn't perfect but it was good.

Then, Peter started working late.

Or so he said.

He took up coaching sports – or so he said.

He wanted to give back to the community, he said. Besides, it was good for business. I had thought he was interested in the local girls' volleyball team. Instead, he had been interested in the volleyball coach - who was only a few years older than her students.

And now he wanted to move his love nest into my house. Substitute Bianca for me and everything would go back to the way it was. No muss, no fuss for Peter Hobson, asshole extraordinaire.

Well, it wasn't going to happen. Not if I could help it. The bank was just going to have to loan me the money. So what if I was approaching fifty and in debt up to my eyeballs? I was healthy, I had a job. Maybe I could pick up extra shifts at the hospital. They were always looking for nurses to work overtime.

The elevator doors opened, and I found myself looking straight at Peter and Bianca.

Bianca tried a half-smile, but I shot her my most scathing look, and she quickly lowered her gaze and studied the floor.

"This is awkward." Peter tried to smile. "I forgot something in your attorney's office. I was going …I didn't think…."

"You're right," I said. I looked at Bianca. "You weren't thinking."

I pushed past them before they could see how much I was shaking. I didn't remember walking to my car but found myself gripping the steering wheel minutes later. I turned the key in the ignition and drove out of the parking lot. A light rain started, and I turned on the windshield wipers as I turned right and headed for the highway, taking me back to the house that was, at least for the time being, still mine.

Easing onto the highway, I cranked the radio on full blast. I drove home while The Pointer Sisters sang, "Jump For My Love".

Chapter Two

൜

The rain was coming down in earnest by the time I got home. I flipped on lights as I walked from the garage into the laundry room and then into the kitchen. This house was still my refuge, the one spot in my life where I felt I could close the door to Peter, work, banks, and decisions. I knew I should probably check the day's mail, but it was raining too hard to attempt the walk out to the curbside mailbox. I wasn't in the mood for reality, anyway. After seeing Peter and Bianca, I craved an escape. I poured myself a glass of wine and curled up on the sofa with the novel I had checked out of the library the week before.

The rain's intensity had increased. The steady patter on the windows and the wine soon had their effect. After a couple of chapters, my eyes grew heavy, and my head drooped.

But I was suddenly startled awake by the sound of the doorbell. The rain was coming down in rivers now and the sky was dark. I thought I heard thunder in the distance. I got up and peered out the side window next to the front door. A man I didn't recognize stood there. He was wearing a dark-colored raincoat and had his hat pulled down over his eyes. The rain ran in streams off the hat's brim and onto the floor where it pooled at his feet. I should have been afraid but, oddly, I wasn't.

I opened the door a crack, leaving the chain on. "Can I help you?"

"Charlotte, it's me. Luke. I have been looking everywhere for you. Can I come in?"

Luke! It couldn't be! I had not seen him in decades, not since he broke off our engagement. I undid the chain and swung the door open. Rain whipped around the doorway and pooled in the foyer. I didn't care. It was Luke. I stared at the man who had torn my heart to pieces all those years ago.

"Luke? How did you find me?"

Luke said nothing but he immediately walked into the foyer. He took off his hat and coat and let them fall to the floor. I looked into his face and was amazed that he hadn't aged at all. His eyes were still the same chocolate brown that went straight to my soul. His lips curved into a sweet smile that showed the dimple that I loved, and he hated. As I reached out with my fingers to touch his lips, he took me in his arms and kissed me. His tongue brushed my mouth. His hands caressed my chin, my cheek.

I quickly leaned into him and returned his kiss. The years between us miraculously melted away. "I missed you so much," he whispered gruffly into my ear. He kissed my neck and I felt little shivers of pleasure run right down into the pit of my stomach – and elsewhere.

"I want you so much, Charlotte," he said. I felt his embrace tighten. His hands were working their way under my sweater.

And then the phone rang.

I sat up and touched my lips. For a few seconds, I had no idea where I was. I could still feel Luke's mouth on mine, but I quickly realized with a pang of immense sadness that it had been a dream. Luke was nowhere in sight. I looked at the front door. It was still bolted shut. The chain was untouched.

I was alone.

The phone next to the sofa rang a second time, a third. I finally grabbed it.

"Hello?"

"Charlotte? Where were you?" It was Aunt Camille, calling from Arizona.

"I was sleeping." The cobwebs were slowly leaving me, but I was having trouble shaking the feeling of being in Luke's arms. This wasn't the first time I had dreamt about him. Ever since the break-up with Peter, Luke had been invading my sleep on a regular basis.

"Sleeping? Are you okay?"

"I'm fine. Everything's okay. What's up?" I was awake now. Luke's kiss was fading.

"I just wanted to know how your appointment with the lawyer went."

"It wasn't an appointment, Auntie. I had a meeting with Peter and his attorney to go over the settlement." I sighed. Aunt Camille's memory was getting spotty, and I often had to remind her of something many times. While I loved her dearly, repeating myself every time we spoke was wearing on my nerves, especially today.

"Oh, that's right, dear. You told me that

before. I swear, this memory of mine." She laughed. "Well, what happened? Is he going to give you the house?"

"No, Auntie. I told you. I have to buy out his share. I have to get another mortgage and give Peter his portion of the profit."

"That doesn't seem fair to me."

"I agree with you. After what he pulled with Bianca, I don't think he deserves a penny. But the law says he's entitled to his share."

"Are you going to do that? Buy him out, I mean?"

"I want to, but I don't know if I'm going to be able to. I may not qualify for a mortgage."

"Well, you know what I want you to do."

"I know. You've been pretty clear about that, Auntie." Ever since Peter and I had split up, Aunt Camille had been waging a one-woman campaign to convince me to move out to Arizona and live with her.

Actually, it was a two-woman campaign. My best friend lived in the same town as Aunt Camille.

Hannah Lee Myers and I had first met in grammar school in Astoria, Queens. We were desk-mates in Sister Mary Ida's first grade class at St. Francis of Assisi parochial school. First day, right after roll call, she whispered to me how she hated her name. I guess her parents had listened to one Peter, Paul & Mary song too many and thought Puff's hometown made a good child's name. Personally, I think they were smoking some funny stuff when Hannah was conceived.

At any rate, Hannah and I had held hands as we lined up two by two to go to the bathroom on that day and we have been best friends ever since.

We shared giggles over boyfriend crushes and tears over lost loves. We went to the same high school and double dated for the Senior Prom. Our paths diverged after graduation. She stayed in New York City and got her degree in business at Hunter College while I moved away to study nursing at Penn State University in Harrisburg, Pennsylvania. After graduation, we picked up where we had left off. I moved back to New York City and worked at Lenox Hill Hospital on a cardiac telemetry floor while Hannah managed her father's dry-cleaning business in Queens. We double dated again. Hannah teased me about dating my doctor (the Luke who was now haunting my dreams) and she took up with Sean, an attorney.

When she married Sean, I was her Maid of Honor. When Luke broke our engagement, Hannah was there and sat up nights with me when I thought I wanted to die. But about a year later, Hannah and Sean moved to Arizona where he started his own firm. Aunt Camille was already living out there and I was sorely tempted to follow them both. But, by that time, I had already married Peter and he wouldn't hear of it.

Now, the thought of living in Arizona was once again very appealing but I just wasn't ready. I had too many loose ends in New York to settle first.

"Well, I think you should consider it," Auntie said. "Besides, when I have my surgery, you'll have to come out here."

"Surgery? What surgery? What's going on?" Aunt Camille was always worrying about her health but as far as I knew, she was fine.

"Well, you know how I get so out of breath. My friend Myra told me that her friend Carla's husband had the same problem, and he went to this doctor, and he put sticks in his heart, and he breathes just fine now."

"Sticks?" I couldn't imagine what she was talking about and then it hit me. "Stents? Auntie, did he have something put in to keep his artery open? That's a stent. Not a stick."

"Sticks, stents, I don't know. All I know is that he's better than ever now. I think I should have them, too."

"Auntie, that's serious business. Please promise me you won't do anything like that without talking to me first."

"Well, if I need them and you're not here, I'll just have to make that decision on my own."

"That's blackmail."

"Charlotte! That's a terrible thing to say."

I sighed. "Like you aren't above that. I'm going to hang up now and make some dinner. I'll think about coming out there – for a visit – and let you know soon. Maybe I can get some time off from work. Promise me you won't do anything until I call you."

"Well..."

"Promise me, Auntie. Please."

"Okay. But you call me. Soon."

"I will. I give you my word."

I put a mug of water in the microwave to heat for tea. I was worried about Aunt Camille. I hated that she was so far away. Aunt Camille had raised me after my parents were killed by a drunken driver. I was three years old when it happened, and I barely remembered my parents now. In fact, I suspected what little memories I did have were likely from my Aunt Camille telling me about them. Auntie was my mother's older sister. She and Uncle Bob never had any children. They had lived in a small apartment in Manhattan and after my parents' accident, they uprooted themselves, settled in my parents' home and took over my care without missing a beat. They were the only family I had and when Uncle Bob died when I was in college, I was devastated. Aunt Camille trudged steadfastly on. She continued to work as a secretary. Soon after, she decided the New York winters were too cold. By that time, I was living on my own. Auntie knew I didn't need her anymore and she wanted to fulfill her lifelong dream of owning a home in Arizona. That was a few years before Hannah and Sean moved out there. Some days, I wondered if God was going to move everyone I loved to Arizona.

The microwave beeped and I put a tea bag in the water and dialed Hannah. I hadn't spoken to her in a couple of weeks, and I missed her. I knew I could depend on her to check up on Aunt Camille for me. I didn't trust Auntie in the least.

The phone was answered on the second ring.

"Hello? Rafferty residence," said a young girl.

Hannah's twelve-year-old twins sounded exactly alike, and I always got them mixed up. I had given up trying to tell them apart. I just took a wild guess and hoped for the best.

"Frances?"

"No, this is Gloria," she giggled. The twins loved to fool people. "Who's this?"

"Gloria, you sound so grown up." She giggled again. "It's Aunt Charlotte, honey. Is Mommy there?'

"Aunt Charlotte!" She screamed into my ear, and I had to pull the phone away to keep my eardrum intact. "Are you coming out to see us?"

"No, sweetie. Well, maybe. I don't know

yet. Can I talk to Mommy?"

"Yeah, hang on. I'll get her." She dropped the phone on the counter. I heard "Mom! Phone!" yelled so loudly I had to pull the phone away again. A few seconds later, a breathless Hannah came on the phone.

"This is Mrs. Rafferty."

"Hannah, it's me. Charlotte."

"Charlotte!" Hannah yelled almost as loudly as her daughter had. "Are you coming out here?"

"Slow down. You're as bad as Gloria."

"Well, it's been too long. I miss you."

"I miss you, too. What's up?"

"Not much. I told the twins I would take them shopping for new bathing suits and they're standing here staring at me. Just a minute." Hannah's voice sounded a little farther away as she told the twins she would be with them soon, but she needed them to let her talk to Aunt Charlotte for a few minutes. I could hear whining in the background. "If I hear another whine, there will be no shopping at all." Sounds of running feet and the door slamming. "Ok, I'm back. That should give us fifteen minutes of peace."

"Hannah, it's only the end of April. It hardly seems time for swimsuits."

"For you, maybe. This is Arizona. It will be a hundred degrees by the end of the month. Be thankful you live in a normal place."

"I may not be for long."

"What do you mean?"

I told her about the meeting with Peter and his lawyer and the deadline they had given me. "My attorney seems to think I'm going to have trouble getting a mortgage on my own. That wasn't the worst of it, though. On the way out of the building, I ran smack into Peter and Bianca."

"Ouch. That must have been more than uncomfortable."

"Actually, it wasn't as bad as I thought it would be. I was shaking but I don't think they noticed. They seemed as upset about it as I was."

"And how did Miss Bianca look?"

"Like the slut whore that she is."

"Don't hold back, Char. Tell me how you really feel."

"Okay, maybe not so much whore as trollop."

"Much better. Trollop is in these days, I hear. But getting back to the house issue. Maybe you should re-think this. Do you really need that big house, Charlotte? Maybe you should let Peter have it."

"You sound like my attorney and Aunt Camille. She wants me to move to Arizona and live with her."

"Well, you know how I feel about that. I'd love to have you here with me. Maybe you should consider it. Maybe not live with Aunt Camille. I can't see you doing that. But get your own place. Start over fresh."

"I don't know. Starting over somewhere where I don't know anyone is frightening."

"You know me. You know Camille."

"That's different. Here, I know all the doctors. I have seniority on my floor. I'd be starting at the bottom again at an Arizona hospital. Besides, my pride won't let me give up without a fight."

Someone yelled "Mom!" in the background and Hannah said, "Charlotte, I gotta go. The girls are getting restless."

"I understand. Just one more thing, though. I

need you to do me a favor. That's really why I called."

"Sure, hon. What do you need?"

"Will you drop by Aunt Camille's house sometime soon and check up on her for me? She seems to have it in her head that she needs heart surgery."

"What?" Hannah laughed. "Is that the disease of the week?" Hannah knew all about Aunt Camille's hypochondria.

"I guess. One of her friend's husbands or somebody had sticks put in his heart and she's convinced she needs them, too."

"Sticks?"

"I think she meant stents. It's a valid cardiac procedure but I doubt she needs it."

"I remember. The doctor talked to Sean about that as a possibility when he had his episode."

Hannah's husband Sean had developed chest pain the year before while he was working night and day preparing for a big malpractice trial. Hannah had dragged him off to a cardiologist. Luckily, everything turned out all right. It was just stress.

"Maybe if she insists on needing surgery you can take her to Sean's cardiologist for me. I know it's nothing, but she'll probably need a doctor to tell her that. What was his name? Maybe I can call and talk to him ahead of time."

"Who...his name...I can't remember right now. I'll look it up for you some time."

"You can't remember the name of your husband's cardiologist? That's not like you."

"Charlotte, I think I hear the twins calling me again. Look, I'll call you soon when we can have a nice long chat. Maybe make plans for you to come out here."

"Okay…are you all right? You sound funny all of a sudden."

"No, I'm fine. I really have to go, though. Love you, honey. Gotta run." The line went dead.

I stared at the phone for a few seconds and then shrugged. I should have been used to Hannah's abruptness. It was just part of her energy. She had been this way for as long as I had known her. Life was too short for Hannah. She was always in a hurry to cram more in.

But this had seemed like more than that. As if mentioning Sean's cardiologist had upset her. Maybe it was my imagination. Maybe thinking about Sean being mortal was something Hannah wasn't prepared to think about. I decided to let it go.

As luck would have it, I needed to work overtime the next day so checking up on my mortgage application didn't happen, although someone from the bank named Mrs. Crandall left a short message, the tone of which left me thinking the worst.

I finally made it to the bank the following week. I sat across a desk from a young woman whose nameplate read Carol Gibbons and within two minutes, she destroyed my life. Tom's words had been prophetic.

"We can't approve your mortgage, Mrs. Hobson."

"I'm not sure I understand. I'm a nurse. I make a good income. In fact, I was just promoted to management. I got a raise."

"I understand that, Mrs. Hobson. But in order for you to buy out your husband, you have to give him his half of the equity. Your house has appreciated quite a bit since you bought it. You would have to pay him a lot of money. How are you going to come up with that much cash without taking out a mortgage to cover it all? Then, you have to make the payments on that."

My blank stare must have scared her. She sighed and turned to the computer on her desk. "Look, let me run the numbers and show you." She did some quick calculations and then turned her monitor to me so I could follow while she explained.

"You currently still owe about $100,000 on your mortgage. Your house is now worth about $550,000 in today's' market which is nice until you have to pay your ex. Subtract the balance of your mortgage, divide by two and you owe your husband roughly $225,000. Unless you have that amount of cash somewhere, you will have to take out a mortgage to cover that amount plus what is still owed on the house before he can assign ownership to you. So, you will need a mortgage with a principal of about $325,000. At your salary, you can't afford that monthly payment plus all the other expenses that you will have. Insurance, taxes. What about repairs? Eating? It just doesn't add up. Our bank can't issue a mortgage to you under these circumstances. As I'm sure you're aware, we are being more careful these days. I'm sorry."

I looked down at my hands in my lap and squeezed my fingers. I was *not* going to cry in front of this woman. "Isn't there anything I can do?"

"I'm afraid not. There is only one other possibility, but I don't recommend it."

"Anything. What?"

"Is there someone who could sign for this mortgage with you? Someone whose income could cover it?"

My hopes fell as soon as she said that. I thought of Aunt Camille. She had enough money stashed away that she could loan me what I needed to buy Peter out so that I wouldn't even have to get a new mortgage but that would mean I would owe her. I wouldn't think of asking her. Worse yet, she would just use that as an excuse to resurrect her plan to have me move to Arizona and live with her. No, asking Aunt Camille was out of the question.

"No, that plan won't work." I rose, shook the banker's hand, and thanked her for her time.

"I'm sorry to be the one to have to tell you all this, Mrs. Hobson. If it's any consolation, you're not the only woman who has been in this position. I've seen this happen all too often. I know it doesn't help to hear that. But look at it this way - if you don't buy your husband out, he will either buy you out or you will sell the house. And if he offers to do that, I would take it if I were you. You'll get half the equity which is quite a bit. Then you'll have all that money to start a new life with, debt free. Think about that. It's a good position to be in."

She had a point. And, if I wasn't so stubborn, I would probably agree with her. But my heart didn't want to be debt free. It wanted to be in my house, alone, without Peter. Even if it meant drowning in debt. I wanted him to lose something like I had lost something. Everything.

I stopped by Tom's office on the way home. Might as well tell him now that things weren't going to work out. He wasn't available but his secretary agreed to pass on the information.

"Tom had asked me to send this packet of information out to you but you might as well take it as long as you're here," Gwen said. She handed me a large manila envelope. "It's the proposed property settlement aside from the house. Tom said to look it over and let him know if there are any changes before we send it to Mr. Hobson's attorney." An entire marriage shoved into an 8 x 11 envelope.

I stopped on the way home and picked up some frozen potpies for dinner. The envelope lay on the seat beside me all the way home. I didn't have the heart to open it in public. I knew I would just start crying again. I needed to be alone, preferably fortified with some wine.

One glass of wine later, the papers were strewn over my kitchen counter. A few had even been thrown across the room, in a fit of frustration. Our marriage had been reduced to who gets the china and the silverware and...and...and. I hated that Peter had so callously destroyed our life. I wanted to make him pay. I wanted him to cry and have sleepless nights the way I did. I thought we had been in love. I thought he cared about what we had. Now, I doubted it all. I wondered if he had ever loved me. If he did, would he have thrown it away so carelessly? Maybe all he ever wanted was just a mother for his child. Peter, the long-suffering divorced father, just wanted me to fill in the empty slot left by Sheila when she had run off with her boss. I remembered Hannah's warning. How she tried to tell me I was just stinging from Luke's abandonment and should be careful, that I shouldn't jump into a relationship with Peter so quickly. I wished now I had listened to her.

I threw a potpie in the microwave and hit the timer. I was getting tired of frozen dinners. I used to enjoy cooking. It just seemed silly now to cook a nice meal for one person. While I waited for my frozen food to thaw, I dialed Aunt Camille's number. I needed to make sure she hadn't made an appointment to have any "sticks" put in her heart since we had spoken the week before.

"Hannah called me a few days ago," she told me. "She talked to me about going to her husband's doctor. I might do that. Or I could go to Myra's friend Carla's husband's doctor."

My head was spinning trying to follow that line of relationship. "Aunt Camille, we don't even know who that is. I work with doctors all day long. Please trust me on this. They are not all the same. I want you to be seen by somebody good. Sean's doctor seemed very thorough. And he didn't rush Sean into surgery, either."

"How do you know anything about him? You don't know who he is – do you?" I thought I was picking something up in Auntie's voice that sounded a little like fear, apprehension.

"No, but I trust Hannah. She's no dummy."

"Right." Whatever I thought I had heard in her voice was gone. "Well, I think if I need surgery, I should have it."

This conversation was getting out of hand quickly. "We don't know you need surgery. What kind of symptoms are you having?"

"I get short of breath. I sleep late. My eyes are blurry."

"Fine. You used to smoke, you're getting older, and you need a stronger eyeglass prescription."

"You think you're so smart, don't you?" I could tell she was enjoying this, but she knew enough not to push it. "Okay, I'll call Hannah and see what we can arrange. But if he can't get me in soon, I'm calling Myra."

"Fair enough."

"Let's change the subject. Did you hear

anything from the bank?"

I was tempted to lie to her. I hated admitting defeat but there was no point in putting off the inevitable.

"Yes, I did, Auntie. It doesn't look good. I can't qualify for a loan. Unless I can come up with some way to buy Peter out without getting another mortgage, it looks like he's going to get the house."

Aunt Camille was silent on the other end for a few seconds.

"Auntie? You still there?"

"Yes, I'm here. I was just trying to think of something to say that didn't include a bad word."

"Bad words are fine. I've been saying them all day."

She hesitated again. Then, "Look, I have some money stashed away. More than I'm ever going to need. Why wait until I'm dead for you to get it? It's yours. Now. Buy out the son of a bitch. I want you to be happy."

Auntie's language side-tracked me for a second and then realization – and temptation - set in. This could be my ticket to everything I wanted. It was an offer. Not a loan. No strings. But guilt was also strong. "Oh, Auntie. I can't do that." Inside I was screaming *Yes!* and pumping my fist in the air but I just didn't feel right taking the money without a fight. I had to look humble.

"Sure, you can. In fact, I insist that you do. I'll make the arrangements. There's just one thing…"

Here it comes. I knew there was a catch.

"What is it?" I had a feeling I knew what was coming.

"I want you to come out here and give Arizona a try first. Give me two weeks and then tell me that moving here isn't right for you. If you can do that, the money is yours and you can have your house free and clear. What do you say?"

Two weeks in Arizona with Aunt Camille trying every day to change my mind? I could outlast her. I knew I could. And then everything would be the way I wanted it. Well, not exactly the way I wanted it but good enough.

"Deal."

Chapter Three

ଓ

I knew Aunt Camille was smiling at the other end of the phone. She smelled victory. Little did she know the full depth of what I would do to keep my house. No matter what she did, I was not going to cave. The house was as good as mine. Peter and Bianca had better start looking for another love nest.

"Auntie, you're going to have to give me a few weeks to schedule the time off. It's not easy getting two weeks off in a row at the hospital."

"Take all the time you need, Charlotte. I'll be here."

"I know that, and you can wipe that smug grin off your face, too. All I'm agreeing to is coming out to Arizona for a visit."

"Visit, schmisit. You'll be living here before you know it."

The following morning, I approached my nurse supervisor.

"Marge, I know this is short notice, but my aunt is ill, and I really need to be there for her. She might need a cardiac catheterization." I picked a procedure I knew she would understand. I felt guilty using my aunt's health like that and hoped karma wouldn't get me in the long run.

"I know how much your aunt means to you, Charlotte. But this is really a bad time."

I had been named Nurse Manager of the unit only two months before, a position they created as a way to eliminate Head Nurses for all three shifts, the hospital's attempt at saving money.

"I know and I wouldn't ask if this wasn't important. But she's all I have. Especially now." Marge knew all about my divorce. I gave her my saddest look. "I have to be there for her."

"Okay. I guess we can work this out somehow." She agreed to give me the first two weeks of the next schedule off. That meant I could be in Arizona by the middle of June. I did a quick calculation and realized that – given the two weeks I would need to survive Auntie's plan – I would have my money in plenty of time to meet Peter's deadline.

Excited, I placed a call to Tom during my morning break.

"Forget the message I left you yesterday about the bank's loan refusal," I said as soon as he got on the phone. "I'm going to be able to get the money to buy out Peter after all."

"Is someone co-signing the loan for you?" he asked.

"Better than that. My aunt is giving me the money outright. I should have the money by the end of June. Maybe we should let Peter's attorney know."

Tom hesitated a little before answering. "I don't know, Charlotte. Let's wait until you actually have the check in hand. Sometimes, these deals fall through. Better to be safe than sorry."

"Okay, I'll play it your way, but I know this is going to work." I refused to let his cynicism get to me. He was a lawyer. He had to be skeptical. I knew I was going to make this work.

I told Tom when I was going to be out of town. "I won't go into the details but it has to do with the plan to get the money for the house."

"Fine, just let my secretary know where we can reach you."

I phoned Aunt Camille that night after I got home from work.

"Everything is all set, Auntie."

"We're going to have so much fun," she said. "I can't wait to see you again. It's been too long."

"I'm looking forward to seeing you, too." It was true. I missed her. Regardless of the reason, it was time I went out to see her again. I felt guilty that she had to dangle a check in front of me to get me out there, but I would make it up to her. We would have a wonderful visit.

The next few weeks flew by. Between working and getting the little details taken care of to prepare for my trip, I hardly had time to think about Peter and all the chaos that the divorce was causing. My only focus was on seeing Auntie. Despite her ulterior motives, I was really looking forward to seeing her. She had always been there for me and I loved her dearly. It was going to be hard to disappoint her, but I knew living in Arizona was not something I could ever do. I was an East coast girl, through and through.

Before long, I was sitting on a Southwest Airlines early Monday morning flight to Phoenix. Due to a storm in Pennsylvania, the first hour of my flight was turbulent. Breakfast had been a hurried affair before I left the house, and my stomach was rolling now right along with the plane.

I tried to read the in-flight magazine to distract myself but after a few pages, I gave up, shoved it back in the pocket of the seatback in front of me and stared out the window at the hills below instead. In between the clouds, I could see patches of green fields. My thoughts drifted to Luke as we flew over his home state, and I wondered if he still lived there. After our break-up, I had heard from another doctor that Luke had moved to a town outside of Philadelphia. I never heard from Luke, never heard anything about him after that short piece of news from his co-worker, never knew the full story of why he ripped himself from my life. I may have desired him in the sexy dreams that still invaded many of my nights, but during my waking hours, I was still angry. I would never understand how he could have claimed to love me so much and then just vanish like that. I knew, despite my dreaming about him, that I would never want him back. But I was curious about him, nonetheless.

I thought about those last couple of months when we were together. Somewhere in there, there had to be a clue about why he left me. I had done this many times the first few weeks after our break-up and I found myself doing it again since the dreams had started.

When Luke's last year of residency was ending, he had planned to take a fellowship in cardiac surgery at Jefferson Hospital in Philadelphia. He wanted me to move there with him but wasn't promising marriage. I wanted to go but didn't feel right uprooting myself without the guarantee of something more.

"I'm just not ready," was all the answer he would give me. I knew his parents' divorce bothered him greatly. His father was an orthopedic surgeon and his practice had often taken him away from Luke, his mother, and his older brother. Apparently, after twenty-five years, his mother had had enough. The divorce was bitter and drawn out. Luke was in college by then, but the break-up of his parent's marriage had still upset him deeply. His greatest fear, he had told me, was turning into his old man.

"Charlotte, I love you. Isn't that enough for now? My fellowship is going to consume me day and night. That's no way to start a new marriage."

No matter how I argued that I would be fine, Luke would not budge. After one brutal argument, we decided to break it off. He left right after that to interview in Philadelphia. I didn't hear from him again until a couple of weeks later. When he called me and asked to have dinner, I knew everything was going to be okay. I loved Luke. If he wanted to move to Philadelphia and live on the street in a refrigerator box, I would have done it. Being separated from him like that had made me realize that nothing else mattered except that we were together.

We had dinner and I thought things looked hopeful. He held my hand during dinner; we took a long walk afterwards. He told me about Philadelphia and where we would live, and we started planning the future again. I deliberately avoided mentioning marriage. When we made love that night, I felt the world shift back into place.

Then, weeks later, he became moody again and we fought. I consoled myself by thinking that if I waited it out, he would open up to me when he was ready.

But he didn't. His residency ended. He vacated his apartment and I never heard from him again. One of his old colleagues told me he had heard Luke had taken a cardiology fellowship at Jefferson. I thought it odd that he didn't go for the cardiac surgical fellowship he had wanted but, in the end, it didn't matter. He was gone, out of my life for good this time.

I cried. I threw things. I drank. I slept the weekends away. Thank God, Hannah was there for me through it all. Eventually, I came out the other side. I vowed never to care about someone again. But I met Peter a few months later and before I knew it, he asked me to marry him. I didn't love him as I had loved Luke, but I figured what had that gotten me? Why look for that again? Peter said he loved me, and he offered me a marriage and a ready-made family. I decided it was enough. Too bad, it wasn't enough for him.

"Pretty, isn't it?"

"What?" I jerked my head to my left, startled out of my reverie by the woman sitting in the middle seat. She was tiny, looked to be in her mid-fifties, with short bleached blonde hair. She had been reading a copy of the National Enquirer and listening to music on her headphones. I had paid her little attention the first part of the flight.

"The scenery below is pretty," she said. Her voice told me she smoked too many cigarettes.

"Yes, I guess it is."

"I'm going to visit my sister in Arizona. You?"

"My aunt."

She extended her hand. "My name is Marsha." Her grip was firm for such a small woman.

"Charlotte. Nice to meet you."

"This your first time in Arizona?"

"Oh, no. I've been here before, several times."

"Me, too. I've been coming here ever since my sister moved out in the early eighties. It was still the old west back then. I've seen it change a lot over the years. Gotten real big city lately. Phoenix isn't what it used to be. Then again, in some ways, it will always be the old west. What other place can you still carry a concealed weapon?"

"I guess." Marsha was turning into one of those airline passengers that I hated to be seated next to. Lots of meaningless chatter. I really wasn't in the mood.

"My sister is even thinking of running for City Council. Illegal immigration is getting to be a hot topic. Everybody has an opinion these days. The coyotes are smuggling people in left and right. And charging those poor people an outrageous amount of money to do it."

"What?" I was sure she had lost it now and I was sitting next to a bona fide crazy woman. How could coyotes – the dogs of the desert – be smuggling illegal immigrants into the United States? I knew dogs were smart but that was ridiculous. She was even pronouncing it wrong. She put an accent on the end, saying it coyoté. I had a bizarre image in my head of coyotes driving a truck through the desert, a sort of Arizona version of those velvet pictures of dogs doing stupid things. "How can coyotes do that?"

"Not coyotes. Coyotés. That's what they call the men who smuggle the illegal immigrants. It's big business. And dangerous. Many of the illegals are left to die in the desert. The Arizona heat is deadly."

"Can I offer you a drink?" The flight attendant interrupted Marsha's tale of the desert and I used that as an excuse to extricate myself from her. I didn't want to hear about people dying in the desert. After I drank my juice, I excused myself and actually managed a short nap.

The thud of the wheels hitting the tarmac jolted me out of my sleep. I sat straight up and forced my brain awake as I watched the buildings of Sky Harbor International Airport glide by. Somewhere in one of those buildings was my best and dearest friend. I was going to need her to get me through the next two weeks.

I stood as soon as the seatbelt light went off. I needed to stretch my legs and I was anxious to get off the plane. People around me were doing the same, clicking on cell phones, grabbing bags from overhead compartments. The plane was still gliding into place at the terminal, but the aisles were already crowded.

New security measures prevented people from greeting loved ones at the gate so I knew I wouldn't see Hannah until I reached Baggage Claim. I arrived at the luggage carousel within minutes and jockeyed for a position next to it so that I could see my bag the minute it jumped out of the chute.

I scanned the crowd while I waited for the conveyor belt to start up, but Hannah was nowhere in sight. Late as usual. Suddenly, a loud buzzer sounded, piercing the chatter of conversations around me and everyone surged forward. The belt started to move, and bags spewed forth from the elevated chute in the center. I jostled myself between two businessmen in suits when I saw my green bag emerge. Grabbing it with both hands, I hoisted it off the belt and plopped it on the floor. Extending the handle, I quickly wheeled it away from the crowd and looked for Hannah again.

I saw her then. Her red hair was longer than it had been the last time I had seen her. She had tried to sweep it back from her face with two combs, but they were losing the fight. Golden red strands were flying all over but on Hannah it looked good. She was wearing white shorts, a pink short-sleeved top and sandals. I felt overdressed in my long pants, cotton sweater and pumps. I always forgot how much hotter – and casual – it was in the southwest.

Hannah scanned the crowd, looking for me and I waved to catch her attention. She was breathless by the time she reached me. I hugged her with an intensity that surprised me. I really needed to be here with her.

"God, I've missed you," she said.

When we released each other, Hannah pointed to my shoes and pants and laughed. "I hope you brought some summer clothes. I haven't worn trousers in three months."

"I brought lots of shorts."

"Great." She looked at the bag on the floor. "Is that it?" She looked around me. The conveyer belt was still going around with luggage on it and people were dragging suitcases off.

"Just this one."

"You're kidding, right? I'd need that just for shoes."

50

"I'm not planning on doing anything fancy while I'm here. Just visit with you and Auntie. Then it's home and back to the real world."

"Hm. We'll see."

"What's that supposed to mean? Did Auntie get to you already?"

Hannah rolled her eyes. "Let's just say we have plans for you, dahling."

"Forget it. I'm stronger than both of you put together."

"So you've told me. But I may have an ace or two up my sleeve."

"I'm not sure I like the sound of that." By now, we were walking to the parking garage.

"Oh, you'll like it. Trust me."

"Okay, now you have my attention."

"Uh-uh. No more from me." We were at her car by then and she had the trunk open, and my bag safely stowed. She slammed the trunk closed. "Let's get you home."

Hannah didn't mention another word about my moving out to Arizona the rest of the car ride to Auntie's house. Instead, she filled me in on the twins and Sean and her new business. Hannah had recently opened a catering business that was doing very well.

"I have plenty of work. I've hardly done any advertising. Most of my clients are coming to me by word of mouth. In fact, if I get any busier, I'm going to have to hire some permanent helpers."

"That's great, Hannah. What does Sean think about all this?"

"He's thrilled. It keeps me busy but I'm still able to stay home and be there for the twins when they get home from school or cart them around to their various activities. I swear their social calendar is worse than mine."

I envied Hannah. She had it all. A loving husband, a wonderful home, the kids, her business. It was what I had hoped my life would have been as well. It was definitely what I had imagined it would be if I had married Luke. It was what I had expected when I married Peter. Sometimes, life just sucked.

"Hey…where'd you go?" Hannah snapped her fingers. "Earth to Charlotte."

"Sorry, I was distracted."

"I could see that. Anything you want to share?"

"No - I was just thinking about how things didn't turn out quite like I had hoped."

"You mean with Peter?"

"Peter." I hesitated. "Luke."

Hannah considered that for a moment before she answered. "Do you still wonder what happened to him? Luke, I mean. You know – the one that got away. The what if's?"

"You watch too much TV, don't you? Yeah, I've wondered about him. Now and then. But what good would it do me, anyway? He made it pretty clear when we broke up that there was no hope for us. Why pour salt in that wound? I'm over him. That was ages ago." I hoped I sounded more convincing than I felt. My body surely didn't think it was over, not if my dreams were any indication.

"People do things for different reasons and then things change."

"What's that supposed to mean?"

"Nothing, just me being weird. Let's change the subject. Do you have any plans for the next couple of days?" Hannah eased the car off the highway on to Shea Boulevard, the road that would lead us into Fountain Hills and Auntie.

"No, I thought I'd hang out with Aunt Camille and just relax a bit. I do want to take her to her doctor and get her checked out. She's still on a kick to get her heart operated on and I want to see for myself what's going on."

"I know. I talked to her about that, and I was going to take her to see Sean's doctor like you asked, but then you said you were coming. So, I decided I'd wait until you got here and then you could decide."

"Good idea. But I'm going to take her to her family doctor first. I'm not involving a cardiologist unless she needs it. You know if I take her to one he's just going to want to run a bunch of tests and I'm not sure she needs all that stress."

We had reached the outskirts of Fountain Hills by now. The streets of Scottsdale had changed into the open hills of Auntie's and Hannah's hometown and the views were breathtaking. As we turned off Shea and drove the last mile to her house, I could see why she and Hannah were so smitten with this part of the country. Saguaros dotted the hills on both sides of the road as hawks flew overhead, looking for lunch in the washes below.

Hannah had Siri place a call to Auntie and told her we were almost there.

We rounded the bend to Auntie's house, and I sat straighter in my seat. It was going to be so good seeing my beloved Auntie again, no matter what underhanded things she was planning for me.

Within seconds, I saw Auntie's house. It was almost indistinguishable from those of her neighbors. All the houses on her street had tile roofs and stucco walls. Auntie's house was a one-story home with an attached garage off to the right. The front yard boasted a large saguaro cactus in the middle that dwarfed my aunt who was standing in her driveway as we drove up. Her short gray hair had been recently permed and curled around her face. Pale blue shorts showed off her skinny legs with their knobby knees. It was obvious she had aged since I had last seen her, and I again felt guilty that it took her bribe to get me out here.

I jumped out of the car as soon as Hannah hit the brakes.

"Okay, you can let go of me now," Auntie said as we hugged. "I think you broke a rib." At five feet even, she was just a little shorter than me. I rested my head on hers and hugged her closely. But she was laughing, as happy to see me as I was to see her. "Come on inside. It's too hot to be standing out here like this."

Hannah grabbed my bag out of the trunk and followed us into the house.

I looked around. The living room looked just as it had when I was there last. The large room opened up onto the back deck that overlooked the pool below. There was a small fountain bubbling in the corner of the deck next to a bird feeder. Several birds were eating while others bathed and splashed in the fountain.

Sam, Auntie's aging Golden Retriever ran up to me. He sniffed my shoes, and I patted the top of his head. His muzzle had gotten grayer, but his eyes were still attentive and his tail was still in perpetual motion. I saw Buster, her orange cat, lurking in the dining room to my right.

Auntie had set the dinette table for lunch. It was next to a large bay window and the bougainvillea outside it were in gorgeous bloom. "Can you stay, Hannah? I set a place for you."

"I wish I could but I have to get some trays

ready for an event I'm catering tonight." She hugged me. "I'll call you later tonight." Hannah turned to me as she placed my bag on the floor. "Let's plan on going out for lunch and doing some shopping tomorrow. We can talk more then."

"You got it."

After Hannah left, I watched Auntie while she made lunch. Sam took his place under the dinette table in the kitchen and went to sleep. Buster headed for Auntie's bedroom and didn't reappear.

Despite her claims to the contrary, Auntie seemed to be doing fine. She walked around the kitchen with more energy than I was feeling these days and I didn't notice any shortness of breath despite her earlier claims to the contrary. Still, I was glad I was here to take her to the doctor myself. I couldn't face the thought of losing her.

Auntie placed sandwiches on two plates and set them on the dinette table.

"So," she said, taking a seat opposite me. "Is there anything special you want to do while you're here?"

"No, my plan is pretty simple. Just visit with you, and Hannah and her family. I do want you to see your doctor to make sure everything is okay. Then I'm getting back on the plane and heading home."

"I don't want to waste time in doctor's offices while you're here. I can do that after you go home."

I pointed my sandwich wedge at Auntie. "No, that's not what we're going to do. That was part of why I agreed to this plan of yours. I want to speak to your doctor myself and make sure nothing is going to be done that isn't necessary."

Auntie put her head down and was quiet for

a minute. Then, "My friend Kitty's daughter is selling her house and I thought we'd go look at it."

The change in subject jarred me for a moment. "Why? Are you thinking about selling this place?"

"Noooo...I thought maybe you would want to see what kind of house you could buy if you moved here."

"Boy, you don't waste any time, do you? What was that - a new land speed record for coercion?"

"You aren't buying, just looking."

"And if I look, it implies I might buy. Auntie, I told you when we set this arrangement up that I had no intention of moving here."

"You also said you would let me try. What can it hurt? We're just looking at a house."

I sighed. "Okay, on one condition. You let me take you to the doctor while I'm here and you get a complete check-up."

Auntie smiled. "I'm way ahead of you. I have an appointment with my doctor for tomorrow morning and the real estate agent is meeting us after that."

I shook my head and listened to Auntie chuckle. The next two weeks were going to be a battle of wills.

Chapter Four

ભ

Sonoran Family Medical Clinic was in a small squat building in the center of Fountain Hills. The waiting room was crowded but the receptionist recognized us as soon as we walked in. She nodded to Auntie as we approached the front desk.

"Just have a seat, Mrs. Monti. The doctor is running a little behind."

Auntie patted the young Hispanic woman's hand. "This is my niece that I was telling you about."

The woman looked up and smiled weakly at me. It was early in the day, and she already looked weary. "Nice to meet you."

I dragged Auntie over to some seats as far from some sneezing children as we could get and settled in. After thirty minutes of flipping through month old magazines, we were ushered into a small room in the back. The nurse took Auntie's blood pressure and pulse, confirmed her medications, and left us alone again after more promises that the doctor would be with us soon. By this time, my patience was wearing thin.

"Do they always keep you waiting this long?" We were seated in two small plastic chairs placed side by side next to a utilitarian-looking green metal desk. A wheeled stool in front of it was obviously waiting for the doctor. The nurse had shoved Auntie's chart in a rack on the outside of the door, which was probably a good thing. If she hadn't, I would have been leafing through it.

Auntie patted my knee. "It's okay. It won't be much longer. But maybe I should let Sally know we're going to be late." Auntie dug her cell phone out of her purse and punched in some numbers. "Sally? Hi, it's Camille. Listen, I'm running late at the doctor's. We're probably going to be another forty-five minutes or so. Will we still be able to see that house this morning?" Auntie nodded while Sally spoke. "Good. See you then."

She clicked the phone closed. "We're in luck. Everything is still on schedule."

"Oh, goodie."

A tall young-looking woman rushed into the room. She was wearing a white lab coat, her long blonde hair swirled into a tight bun. She looked up from the chart in her hand and extended her hand to Auntie.

"Hi, Camille, what brings you here today?"

Aunt Camille grabbed my hand and squeezed. "I've thought about your suggestion to have a full cardiac work-up and I want to do that now while my niece is here."

Dr. Kramer looked straight at me and offered her hand. "Joan Kramer. Nice to meet you." Her handshake was firm and strong. Without waiting for me to answer, she looked back at Auntie. Dr. Kramer apparently didn't have time for small talk. "Is it all right with you if I speak in front of your niece about your symptoms?"

Auntie nodded. Dr. Kramer scooted the stool over and sat directly in front of both of us.

"Your aunt came to me a couple of months ago complaining of shortness of breath. Her EKG was non-specific but I couldn't rule out some possible changes. I know you're a nurse, so you understand that with her history of smoking, it's important to do a thorough workup. I'd like to refer her to a cardiologist I know in Scottsdale for an exam and a possible cardiac catheterization. But Camille was reluctant to do that before now."

I reached for Auntie's hand and felt it tremble ever so slightly. The full impact of her fears suddenly hit me. Despite Auntie's bravado, she was really scared that something was wrong. All her talk about "sticks" had obviously been brought on by real symptoms.

"I totally agree with the idea of a work-up, Doctor Kramer, but I'm not sure we need to rush into a cardiac cath just yet. Those aren't without risk, either."

"Agreed, but I trust this doctor's opinion. I've referred many patients to both him and his partner and I've been pleased with their work." She pulled the stethoscope off from around her neck. "Let me take a listen."

Dr. Kramer listened to Auntie's heart and lungs. Despite her abrupt manner, I had the distinct impression she really cared about her patients. She patted Auntie's shoulder when she was finished. "Your breath sounds are a little diminished but no more than they were before. Your last chest x-ray was fine. Why don't we have my office manager make the appointment for you with Dr. Farrell? Tina might be able to speed things up since I'm sure your niece won't be here for very long." She smiled for the first time and looked straight at me. "Or did I hear Camille say that you were moving here?"

"Only in Auntie's dreams."

A few minutes later, we were standing in front of Tina's desk listening to her haggle with her counterpart at Dr. Farrell's office.

"Yes, I understand but it's imperative that we get this patient in as soon as possible." Tina listened and nodded. "Let me check." She put her hand over the phone's mouthpiece. "Camille, can you make an 11 o'clock appointment tomorrow? They're going to squeeze you in."

"We'll be there," I said before Auntie's mouth was even open to answer.

"They'll be there," Tina said to Dr. Farrell's office manager. "Thanks. I'll take care of the paperwork on this end." She hung up and grabbed a business card from a stack on the desk. "Let me give you a copy of Dr. Farrell's card." She flipped it over and wrote a date and time on the back. "If you need directions, just call his office. His staff is very helpful. His partner's information is on there, too, in case you need it." She held the card out to me, but Camille snatched it from her hand.

"Thanks, Tina." Camille threw the card in her purse. "I'll hang onto that so it won't get lost. We really need to go now. We're going to miss another appointment." Camille practically dragged me out to the car.

"What was that all about?"

"Nothing. I just don't want to keep Sally waiting anymore." In lightning speed, Auntie was in the driver's seat of her car and buckled in. "Let's go. I'm not getting any younger."

Sally was not what I had expected a real estate agent to look like. The ones I had dealt with back east had been all business, suited up, briefcase in hand. Sally was my age, wearing what was apparently the Arizona uniform: shorts, sandals, huge shoulder bag slung over her arm. She was standing outside a large sprawling stucco-ed home when we drove up.

"Hey, Camille," she hugged Auntie as soon as we exited the car and then extended her hand to me. "I'm Sally. Nice to meet you. Let's go in, shall we? You're going to love this house."

"You know, Sally, I'm not sure what my aunt has told you but I'm only looking at this house to please her. I'm not planning on moving to Arizona and I feel bad wasting your time like this."

Sally looked at Auntie and something went between them that I didn't get. She pulled a sheaf of papers out of her purse, placed them on a clipboard she also pulled out of her bag and looked at the first page. "I understand what you're saying but it never hurts to look. This house just came on the market, and I need to look it over before I show it to anyone else anyway. So, in a way, you're helping me as well. It's okay. I have the time. Let's start with the kitchen. That's always my favorite."

She led us to the back of the house and to a kitchen made in heaven. New appliances gleamed. Windows overlooked a large deck with a pool beyond. From the dinette windows, I could see views of the mountains in the distance. I immediately pictured myself having coffee in the morning on the deck and then I caught myself. I was falling into Auntie's trap.

Sally was looking at her clipboard. "This house is a real bargain at this price. Homes in Fountain Hills don't last long and this one is priced just right to sell."

I could hear the pitch winding up and rolled my eyes at Auntie. "Well, I'm sure someone will snap it up in no time."

Sally's cell phone chirped. She pulled it out of her purse and looked the caller ID. "My son." She pressed a button.

"Hi, Chuckie." She shook her head as he talked. "No, I told you that before. No off campus. You stay there for lunch. Yes, I know I'm mean. So, sue me. I love you anyway. Gotta go. I have a client. See you after school." She clicked the call off and then pressed another button. "Just checking to make sure the little bugger is where he said he was. I have a tracking device on his cell phone so I can see where he is. It's a parent's ideal toy." She studied the screen. "Good, he's at school. He gets to live another day." She showed me the screen. "This is a special service I signed up for. Many of the parents have them on their kids' cell phones now. It's the best thing since Big Brother."

I looked at the screen she offered and saw a grid with a flashing red dot on it.

"That's amazing. Does he know you have that?"

"Oh, yeah. That was the deal when we got the phone for him. I can also monitor who he calls, place restrictions, you name it. I know he wants to be independent, but I have an obligation to keep him safe." She shoved the phone back in her purse. "Well, let's get back to this house, shall we?"

We walked through the rest of the house. She pointed out special features along the way and I had to guard myself against falling in love with the house. It was more tempting than I had anticipated. And more affordable than my home back east.

When we were done, I thanked Sally and then settled back into the car with Auntie. She smiled to herself as we drove back to her house.

"What are you looking so smug about?" I asked. "That was clearly a waste of time."

"No, it wasn't. Today is only day one. I still have thirteen more to go."

I groaned and released my seat back so that I could pretend to sleep. "Actually, it's only twelve. Wake me up when we get home."

Hannah picked me up fifteen minutes after we arrived back at Auntie's.

"You survived the morning," she said, as she started her car's ignition. "Have you bought a house yet?"

"Don't you start. It was only by sheer force of will that I don't have a deed in my name already. She really is pouring on the ammunition. But I'm tough. I can outlast anything she can throw at me." I clicked my seat belt into place. "But now I deserve some fun. Where are we off to?"

"I'm taking you to a sandal sale at the best mall in the world in Scottsdale and then I'm treating you to lunch. How does that sound?"

"It sounds wonderful. Drive on."

Two pairs of new sandals later, Hannah and I were seated at a table inside the Mexican Grill at Scottsdale's Fashion Square Mall. We had just given our lunch orders to the waitress.

Hannah took a sip of her iced tea. "You're coming to dinner tonight, right?"

"I wouldn't miss it for the world. I can't

wait to see the twins. They must be getting so big by now."

"You don't know the half of it. I can't keep up. They're into everything, too. Soccer, horseback-riding lessons. Before I know it, they'll be dating. Sean is getting gray just thinking about it. He doesn't want his little girls to grow up." Hannah had her children late in life after many trips to fertility specialists. She might complain but I knew she loved every minute of motherhood.

"I'm glad Peter and I didn't have any children. It would have made this whole divorce mess so much harder. As it is, I can't believe I'm not going to have anything to do with Beth anymore."

"Why? She's old enough to make her own decisions." Beth was in her mid-twenties and married.

"I know but it will be a loyalty issue for her. I told her I wanted to keep in touch, but she didn't sound like she felt comfortable with it. I know Peter is pressuring her. I can't put her in the middle like that."

"Well, life isn't over, you know. There's still time for children. You could adopt."

I gave Hannah what I hoped was an "Are you crazy?" look.

Just then the waitress arrived with our food.

"Here we are," she said as she placed our salads in front of us.

Halfway through hers, Hannah put her fork down and took another swallow of tea.

"Tell me how it went at the doctor this morning."

I told her about the doctor's take on Auntie's EKG and how they had us scheduled to see a cardiologist the following day.

"Some Dr. Farrell in Scottsdale. He's got an associate, too, but I didn't get his name. Auntie rushed us out of there. A little too quickly, if you ask me. But I guess I'll know more tomorrow when we see Dr. Farrell."

"Farrell, huh?"

"Yeah, why? Do you know him?"

"Not him. But I do know his partner. Farrell does all the cardiac caths in that office. His partner is a cardiologist, too, but does the non-invasive things like treadmills and stuff." She sipped some more iced tea, and I noticed her hand shook when she placed the glass back down on the table. She played with the condensation on the outside of her glass. "Char, there's something I have to tell you."

I looked at my friend and saw genuine pain. "Hannah, honey, whatever it is you can tell me."

"I'm not sure exactly how to start." She fiddled with her fork.

"Okay, now you're scaring me. We've never had secrets before. Just say it." I put my own fork down and looked into her face. "Is it Sean? Is everything okay?" Fear gripped me. "It's not his heart again, is it? Oh, my God, is it you? What's wrong?"

"No, no, everything's fine. Everyone's fine. It's not that at all."

"Okay, now I'm totally confused. What the hell is going on?"

"It's really about you...and Luke."

"Luke? What could he possibly have to do with anything? That's ancient history."

"Not so ancient, Char. He's here. In Arizona. Scottsdale, to be exact."

I felt my blood stop in its tracks. My hands

felt tingly, and the room started to spin. I stared at Hannah, unable to say one word.

Hannah eyes widened. "Charlotte, are you okay?" She reached across the table and grabbed my hand.

I snatched it way from her. "What are you saying? I don't understand."

"Luke lives here. He moved to Arizona many years ago."

My thoughts were racing, and I was having trouble making sense of what Hannah was saying to me. "You must be wrong. This can't be right. What do you mean he's here? How do you know this? Have you seen him?"

Hannah took a deep breath. "Luke is Dr. Farrell's partner. He was Sean's cardiologist. That's how I found him."

Suddenly, Hannah's hesitance weeks ago to talk about Sean's doctor made sense. Anger bubbled up as realization finally dawned. "You knew about this all this time? You've seen and talked to Luke and you never told me? How could you do this to me?"

"Charlotte, it's not like that."

I threw my napkin on the table and stormed off to the ladies' room. The restroom was two rooms, an anteroom with a vanity counter and sofa and just beyond that the room with the stalls. Thankfully, both rooms were empty. I gripped the edge of the marble vanity and stared into the mirror. Red blotches had erupted on my neck. The room was cool but sweat was trickling down my ribs. My knees shook and I wasn't sure I was going to be able to stand much longer. I plopped onto the sofa and placed my head between my knees. After a moment, my head cleared a bit and I sat up. A woman I recognized from the restaurant table next to ours walked in and smiled. I smiled back weakly and watched her as she entered one of the stalls. I contemplated going back out to my table but the thought of seeing Hannah just made me upset all over again.

Hannah was my best friend. How could she have kept this information from me? She knew how devastated I was when Luke left me. I tried to imagine how it might have been when she first saw Luke. What did she feel - shock, anger, curiosity? Did they talk about me? Oh, God, did he know my marriage was falling apart? I didn't want him to know that. I wanted him to think I was happy, better off without him. I wanted him to suffer, knowing what he'd lost.

A happy picture of Luke's pained expression was forming in my mind when Hannah burst into the restroom. She had both of our purses with her and the shopping bag containing my shoes.

"Are you okay?"

"What do you think?"

Hannah sat next to me on the chaise lounge. "Charlotte, I never meant to hurt you. I didn't want to keep this from you, but I just couldn't figure out how to tell you without upsetting you. I was absolutely floored when Sean's doctor recommended Luke to us. I had no idea he was in town. But I was glad, too, that Luke would be taking care of Sean. I was so scared then. You remember."

"Yeah, I remember." Hannah had been frantic when Sean was having his chest pains. She was convinced something bad was going to happen to him.

"Luke was so good to us. I felt safe with him

and I knew he was going to take good care of Sean for me. After the dust settled, I planned on telling you all about it but by then Peter was making life so hard for you with the divorce that I just didn't think it was the right time. Then, when you said you were coming out here, I figured we'd handle it when you got here."

"Well, I don't want to handle it. I can't. Can we just not talk about it anymore? I want to go home. I have to talk to Auntie about this. I'm not so sure I want to go to the doctor with her tomorrow, after all. I don't know if I can be in the same office with Luke."

"Sure, honey. I understand. The bill's been paid. I'll drive you home."

Auntie was napping when I got home. I threw my purse and shopping bag into my room. I needed some space and time to think. Grabbing a glass of water, I headed out to the back deck. Sam followed me. He placed his head in my lap and I absently stroked his head while I swung on the deck swing.

Luke is here kept running through my mind like a mantra. Not an elusive dream figure but living, breathing, able to destroy my heart all over again. Emotions I had long buried bubbled up from the bottom of my heart and hurt all over again. I thought about the last happy night with Luke and wondered again just what could have gone wrong. What didn't I see? What did I do to make Luke leave? We had been so good together.

I drifted back to the first day I had met Doctor Luke Andrews.

Or rather rammed into him.

Chapter Five

⚬

It was the end of summer. I was living in New York City. Young, independent, and renting an apartment in a small building on East 81st Street, I was convinced life was sweet even though I had just broken up with Jake, a fellow nurse I had been dating for over a year.

I had allowed myself to get serious about Jake, even though we had been having problems. When he had broken yet another date with claims that he had an upset stomach, I decided that I was going to be damned if I would spend another Friday night alone. Hannah and I met for dinner at a restaurant near Bloomingdale's. Dinner and shopping, the perfect combination.

The waitress had just escorted us to our table when who should I spy at a corner table holding hands with an attractive young blonde? The supposedly ill Jake.

I immediately walked over to their table and

introduced myself to the young woman.

"Hi, I'm Charlotte." I offered her my hand. "And you are?"

Instead of taking the hand I offered, she just looked at me. Then she looked at Jake. He shrugged as if he had no idea what was going on. She looked back at me. "I'm Faye," she said. "Do I know you?"

"No, you don't. But Jake does," I turned to him. "Don't you, Jake, dear?" I looked at the food spread out in front him – hamburger with chili, cole slaw, fries. "Enjoying dinner? I guess you're feeling better."

"Charlotte, please, don't make a scene. I can explain. I'll call you later, okay?"

"No need, Jake. Enjoy your meal. Here, have some tea. You look thirsty."

I gave Jake his freedom and a tall glass of iced tea in his lap.

Despite the blow to my social life, I was feeling good about things that September. The air was crisp, New York was looking especially pretty, and I was happy with my job. I was staff nurse on a cardiac floor at a teaching hospital on New York's East Side.

That fateful day I was coming out of a patient's room and, as usual, was thinking about the twelve things I had to do in the next hour. I had my head down as I read my little "cheat sheet" that I always carried with me. Before I knew it, I ran smack into what felt like the proverbial stone wall. Two strong arms grabbed my arms and kept me from falling over.

"Whoa, it's best to keep your head up when running around corners like that."

I looked up and into chocolate-brown-colored eyes so intense, I was immediately speechless.

"Um."

"You're welcome."

"I – thank you. I'm sorry. I ..."

"It's okay." The arms released me, but their owner did not attempt to move out of my way. Instead, he extended his hand. "I'm Luke Andrews. Second year. I just started my rotation here."

It was a Saturday and he wore a white lab coat over jeans and a yellow polo shirt. His brown hair was slightly long so that it curled over his forehead and shirt collar. His smile crinkled the edges of his mouth and I caught myself staring at his lips just a second too long, imagining how they would feel if I kissed them.

"I'm Charlotte Winston. I work the day shift here." I shook his hand. His grasp was firm. He placed his other hand over mine and I was immediately struck by how intimate that felt. He was crumpling my cheat sheet, but I didn't care.

Luke released my hand. "Glad to meet you, Charlotte. I'm sure we'll be seeing a lot of each other."

"I – I guess so. I mean, sure. Thank you." I scurried off before I made a fool of myself, more than I had already.

Over the next few days, we ran into each other frequently, in the figurative sense. No more crashing into Dr. Andrews. He would wave or smile if he saw me across a room. We had short conversations as we crossed paths in the hall or in the nursing station. I definitely felt an attraction to him. Soon, I found myself looking for him first thing when I arrived on the floor in the mornings.

The following week, a Thursday, I was in the medication room getting a pain pill for one of my patients when he walked in.

He leaned against the counter and stared while I locked the medication cart.

"Do you have a minute?"

"Not really. Mr. Gaines needs this."

"Sorry, I just wanted to know if you would have dinner with me tomorrow night."

I stopped in my tracks. "Dinner?"

"Yeah, you know, that meal at the end of the day."

I smiled. "I know what dinner is. I was just – I ..."

"Are you always this articulate?"

"Yes. I. Will. Have. Dinner. With. You. How's that?"

"That's better. Seven o'clock, okay? I get off about six. That should give me enough time to freshen up."

"Seven is fine. Where?"

"There's a new little Italian place over on First that I've been wanting to try. Luigi's. Why don't we meet there? That way if you hate my company..."

"Luigi's? I know that place. It's around the corner from my apartment."

"You're kidding. Where do you live?"

"81st between First and York."

He extended his hand. "Hi, neighbor. 82nd and Third."

I took his hand and felt a thrill at his touch. "Small world."

Luke smiled that killer smile again. "And getting smaller and better all the time."

I called Hannah as soon as I got home that night. "You know that hunky doc I ran into last week?"

Hannah was thrilled with my news. She had never cared for Jake and was glad when I dumped him. "What are you wearing?"

I looked at my bed covered with outfits I had tried on and discarded as not good enough. "I haven't a clue. I think I need to buy something."

"Give me ten minutes and I'll meet you. This calls for a master plan."

The next day, I walked from my apartment to the restaurant feeling good in my new outfit. Hannah had talked me into a complete makeover - skirt, sweater, and shoes. It had cost a good chunk of a week's salary, but the effect was worth it. I wanted to make a good impression on Luke. I got there a few minutes before seven, expecting to be able to catch my breath and relax before Luke arrived. All day, my stomach kept doing little flips every time I thought about sitting across a table from him. I was more attracted to Luke than I realized – or wanted to let myself admit. I was afraid I was going to make a fool of myself as soon as I was in his presence.

The restaurant was dark, and it took a few minutes for my eyes to adjust. I approached the young girl standing behind a small hostess console and gave her my name. She checked her sheet.

"Yes," she said. "Dr. Andrews is already at your table. Let me take you." So much for arriving before Luke and having time to relax.

I followed the hostess through the maze of tables, being careful not to bump into other patrons as we made our way to the back of the restaurant. Luke was seated at a corner table. He wore a dark suit and a light-colored shirt, and I was struck again by how handsome he was. I noticed that a bottle of red wine sat on our table, two wine glasses, ready for us. Nice touch.

He smiled when he saw me approach. He rose and pulled out my chair.

"Have you been waiting long?" I asked.

"No, I was here early. A little anxious to start our date. I hope you don't mind - I ordered some wine."

"No, that's fine." I took my seat and watched while Luke sat and then poured us each a glass.

He raised his glass to me. "To a wonderful evening."

"Yes, to a wonderful evening." I clinked glasses with him. "It certainly seems to be starting out that way."

I picked up a menu that had been placed next to my place setting. "I've heard the stuffed shells are really good here." I looked up and found Luke staring at me. "What?"

"I just can't believe we're sitting here. I've been consumed with thoughts about you ever since you threw yourself at me in the hallway."

"I did not throw myself at you." Then, I saw Luke smiling again and realized he had been teasing me.

"Seriously, I've been looking forward to this ever since you said yes."

"Me, too."

Luke was either an expert at empty compliments or he was the nicest man I had met in quite a while. Such a nice change from Jake.

Dinner was over all too quickly and Luke offered to walk me home after he paid the dinner bill. We strolled the short distance back to my building. It was only ten o'clock and yet the streets were still bustling with people. We stood in front of my building, under the streetlight, hands clasped. Luke placed his hand under my chin and tilted my face towards his. "I had a wonderful time tonight, Charlotte. I'd like to do this again. Would that be okay with you?"

I had trouble finding my voice. His touch was electric and driving all rational thought away. "Mm-hmm" was all I could muster.

He kissed me softly on the lips, his lips barely grazing mine. I was aware of nothing else but Luke's mouth and his arms holding me tenderly. His kiss lasted only a couple of seconds, but the world changed in that short span of time. Luke Andrews planted his flag on my heart and set up residence.

"I – I'd better go in now."

Luke still held onto me. I didn't want the moment to end but unfortunately, the weather gods intervened. A soft rain started. We stood there a few moments more and I watched as drops of rain fell and landed in Luke's hair, sparkling like small diamonds.

"I'd better let you go in. We're going to get pretty wet out here in a minute."

I wasn't prepared for what might happen if I asked him up to my apartment. I didn't trust myself alone with him. But I couldn't leave him out there to get wet, could I?

"Would you like to come up – at least until the rain stops?"

"I'm very tempted, Charlotte. More than you know. But I don't think that's a good idea. Not yet. I'd better go before this rain picks up."

Oh, God, beautiful and a gentleman. This couldn't be happening.

He kissed me softly again and then turned

me and propelled me in the direction of my building.

"Go."

I felt drops hit me harder and I ran to the door of my building. I fumbled with my key and opened the outer security door. I turned around and waved. Luke waved back and then, flipping his suit jacket collar up, he ran off in a quick jog, back in the direction of his own apartment.

I rode the elevator up to my floor, all the while imagining I still felt Luke's lips on mine. I ran to my window as soon as I entered and peered out hoping to catch a glimpse of Luke, but he was already gone.

The next morning, I awoke to the sound of the apartment buzzer, loud and insistent. Thinking it was my alarm clock, I blindly swatted at it. But the buzzing didn't stop. It rang once, twice, a third time. I threw the covers off and glanced at the clock on my nightstand. It sat there mutely telling me that it was only 7:30 in the morning. It was then I realized that the buzzing I had heard was coming from the lobby. Someone wanted to come in.

Wondering who would have the nerve to ring the buzzer this early on a Saturday morning, and planning dire consequences for whoever it was, I ran to the intercom, and pressed the wall button.

"Who is it?"

"Hey, gorgeous. Rise and shine. Feel like breakfast?"

It was Luke!

I looked down at the scruffy oversized T-shirt I had worn to bed. Instinctively I put a hand to my hair and knew I was a mess.

"Luke – what are you doing here?"

"Is that any way to greet a man bearing

bagels and cream cheese? Can I come up?"

"I wasn't expecting you. I- I just got up."

"I figured. I'm sorry. I just couldn't wait to see you again. Charlotte, please let me up. I'll make coffee while you freshen up."

"Okay."

I pressed the buzzer. I hoped I'd have a few seconds at least before the elevator made it to my floor. If I exceeded the speed of light, I might have enough time to throw on some jeans and a shirt, brush my teeth and drag a brush through my hair.

I only had time to brush my hair and gargle some mouthwash. I wasn't sure I had improved myself much, but I let Luke in a few minutes later. I felt like something found in a dumpster, but Luke looked like he had just stepped off a page of GQ. He was wearing khaki slacks and a freshly pressed open neck shirt under a leather bomber jacket. His curly brown hair was perfectly coifed, and he smelled wonderful. He was carrying two bags and he held them up as he entered my apartment.

"Bagels and cream cheese, as advertised," he announced. He leaned over and planted a casual kiss on my cheek.

"You don't look so bad."

"You're either blind or a saint. I look like hell and we both know it."

Luke cocked his head to one side. "Well, your hair has looked better. Why don't you take a shower and I'll make us some coffee? Just point me in the right direction."

I looked around the room that was part kitchen, part dinette, part living room. My apartment had never seemed so small to me as it did just then.

"The kitchen's not hard to find. It's kinda

right here."

"Hmm. I see that. Well, I'll make myself at home. You go do whatever it is you need to do. Pretend I'm not here."

Fat chance, I thought. Luke's presence in my cramped quarters was all I could think about. I left him to rummage in my cabinets while I grabbed some clean clothes from my bedroom. Twenty minutes and a shower later, I felt human enough to rejoin him. He had found a tablecloth, cups, and plates and made a nice setting on the small table and chairs in the eating corner of my multi-purpose room.

"Voila," he said spreading his arms. "Breakfast is served." He poured me a cup of coffee as soon as I sat down.

"Everything looks great."

"Thank you. Here, try this cream cheese. It's got salmon bits in it. I think you'll like it."

He handed me a tub of the cheese and watched me while I spread it on the bagel he had already cut for me and placed on my plate.

"Do you do this for all your dates? Show up with breakfast, I mean. It's a strange custom. I've never run into it before."

"No, I've never done this before. I just couldn't wait to see you. I apologize for being so brazen, but it was all I could do to keep from running back here last night. I couldn't wait for the sun to come up and then when it did, I just found myself here again. Charlotte, you've turned my world upside down. I've never felt this way before."

"You're serious."

"Never been more serious in my life." He took my hand and kissed the inside of my palm.

My insides were mushier than the cheese on

my bagel. This man had gotten to me in ways I never thought possible. He could have asked anything of me at that moment and I would have agreed. It was all I could do to swallow the bagel in my mouth. Words were impossible.

Luke released my hand. "Eat your bagel. Then, let's plan our day. Unless you want me to go."

My voice suddenly returned. "No," I said, probably a little too forcefully. "I mean, no, I don't have any plans and I'd love to spend the day with you."

"Good, then that's what we'll do."

And we did. We shopped, we ate, we walked. By the afternoon, we were tired but energized all at the same time. It was 5:30 and we were back at my apartment building again under the same streetlight as the night before. This time there was no rain and Luke held me in his arms.

"I don't want to let you go," he said.

I looked into his eyes. "I don't want you to."

"Can I come upstairs with you?"

I knew what he was asking, and we both knew if he set foot in my apartment, we would be making love within minutes. In answer, I took his hand and led him through the security door. As we stood waiting for the elevator, he caressed my hair and I felt shivers go all through my body.

I turned and we started to kiss just as the elevator door opened. It was Mrs. Kirkland, the old lady from across the hall. She cleared her throat.

"Good evening, Charlotte." Her frown told me she did not approve of people kissing in the lobby.

"Hello, Mrs. Kirkland. Nice day, isn't it?"

"Hmmph." She brushed past me and hurried

out the front door.

For some reason, Luke and I found that to be the funniest thing we had ever seen, and we giggled like little kids all the way up to my floor.

By the time we reached my apartment door, I felt the moment from under the streetlight had passed and we would be able to contain ourselves.

I flipped the light on and threw my sweater over a dinette chair. "Want some wine?"

I had misjudged Luke.

"No, I want you. Come here." He pulled me into his arms again and caressed my hair. "I've been wanting to do this all day." He kissed me, his tongue darting into my mouth. Shivers started at my feet and worked their way all up my body. I felt warmth in places that hadn't felt that way in a long time. Luke pressed himself against my body and I could tell he was aroused.

"Let's go in the other room," I said. I took his hand and he followed me into the bedroom. His other hand made trails along my back.

As soon as were inside the bedroom, I turned to face him.

"Are you sure?" he asked.

"Never surer." I put my hands to his face and drew him to me. I kissed him on the mouth as he had done to me moments before. "I want to make love to you," I said.

Luke scooped me up into his arms and placed me on the bed. "Charlotte," was all he said.

My four-poster bed became our world for the next hour. Luke's hands and mouth were all I wanted. When we merged, it felt like the most natural thing in the universe, and it was all I wanted. I couldn't get enough of him. I explored and stroked and caressed every inch of his body until I felt I knew it as well as I did my own.

We must have dozed off because the room was dark when I woke up. I looked over at Luke. He was on his back, arm flung across his pillow, hair tousled in a way that made me want to touch him all over again. I gave in and stroked his cheek. His eyes fluttered.

"Is that you, Mom?"

I punched him in the ribs.

"Ouch, I'm weak. Don't pick on me. You've used me all up and now you beat on me, too?"

"I'm hungry."

"I'll bet you are. I think we burned up a few calories."

I leaned across Luke to look at my alarm clock on the nightstand next to him.

"Hey, you do that anymore and we're never going to get out of this room. Pick one. Me or dinner."

My stomach growled then. "I think I have to vote for dinner. If I don't, I won't have enough energy for any more love-making."

"Well, we can't have that." He sat up. "Let's go back to Luigi's."

The rest of the weekend was a blur of Luke, food, Luke, sleep, Luke, long talks, and more Luke. By the time I met Hannah for dinner on Monday evening, I wasn't sure I'd ever walk normally again. I also couldn't get the silly grin off my face.

"Okay, what gives?"

"What?"

"Don't be coy with me. You know damn well what. Why are you looking like that?"

"Like what?"

"Charlotte, spill it. This is about that date on Friday, isn't it? That doctor from work? I gather it went well."

We were sitting at an outside table at a restaurant near my apartment. I could see the Luigi's awning across the street, and I caught myself looking over at it often.

Hannah waved her hand in front of me. "Hey, over here. Remember me? Boy, you've got it bad. That must have been some dinner."

"Dinner, breakfast, lunch, dinner, breakfast…"

"Whoa, wait a minute. Back up. Breakfast? Breakfast!"

"He brought breakfast to me on Saturday morning."

"You said breakfast twice."

"Well, yeah, he spent the night on Saturday."

"Wow, Charlotte, I don't know what to say. Are you sure about this?"

"More than I have ever been about anyone."

"Well, spill, girl. I want details."

The following week, I talked Luke into setting Hannah up with one of the other residents and we double-dated. The date was a disaster and Hannah begged off on any more fix-ups.

"He may be good in bed," she said. "But his friends stink."

Luke had planned to take me to meet his mother and stepfather at their home in Scranton, Pennsylvania for Christmas but they surprised him by telling him they had decided to vacation in Bermuda instead. I knew he was disappointed, so I suggested we visit my Aunt Camille in Arizona. Luke was thrilled and I talked Hannah into joining us, too.

Luke charmed Auntie as soon as he met her.

Every time she got me alone, she asked me when we were going to get married.

"Auntie, stop it. We hardly know each other.

"Sure, and I was born yesterday. I'm no prude, you know."

"I didn't mean that way. I meant we need to learn more about each other. I haven't even met his folks yet."

"So, you think that's going to matter? It's clear you two are in love. What are you waiting for?"

I just shook my head and kissed her.

"You're a hopeless romantic, Auntie."

Hannah met some guy while shopping at the grocery store our second day there and brought him home for dinner. His name was Sean, and he was an attorney. Coincidence of coincidences, he lived in New York and was visiting his own parents in Phoenix.

It was obvious all during dinner that Sean was smitten. Hannah was just as enamored. By dinner's end, they were making plans to meet up when everyone was back in New York.

Hannah took a walk with Sean after dinner and Auntie retired to bed early. Luke and I were alone, curled up together on the sofa in the living room. The tree was lit, and a fire was blazing in the hearth. Luke put his arm around me and pulled me to him. His kiss was warm and slow.

"Would you like to live here someday?"

"With Auntie? I don't know how she'd feel about that."

Luke laughed. "No, goofball. I mean here in Arizona."

"I don't know. I never thought about it. I always assumed I'd stay somewhere back east. Like

New York or Philly. Are you saying you want to move out here?"

"I don't know. I know I don't want to stay in the city." I knew Luke was planning to specialize in cardiovascular surgery and was looking into a fellowship in Philadelphia. I just assumed he wanted a big city practice. "The hospitals out here will need me just as much as New York or Philly. Maybe more. It's something to think about. I just like the lifestyle out here so much more."

"How can you say that after one visit?"

"Haven't you ever been somewhere, and it just felt right?"

"Yes." I cuddled closer to him.

"I don't mean us." He hugged me. "Although, I feel that way about you, too." He kissed my nose. "But I meant here, out West, in Arizona, maybe even in this very town. I just feel I'm meant to live out here."

"I never thought about it."

"Well, think about it, baby."

I fell asleep that night warmed by the thought that Luke had pretty much told me he thought we would be married someday.

The next couple of months were busy both with work and personally. Hannah and Sean fell madly in love and spent every minute, it seemed, together. At the end of March, Hannah announced she was getting married.

"I know it seems sudden, but we just don't want to wait," Hannah said when I asked her why so soon. "It just feels right." Typical Hannah – going head on full tilt into life. "Please just be happy for me. Be my Maid of Honor."

Somehow, she managed to pull off the perfect wedding in a matter of weeks. The ceremony was on the last Saturday in April. The reception was at her parents' home on Long Island. Sean asked Luke to be an usher. He looked so handsome in his tuxedo. I admit it definitely started me fantasizing about my own wedding to Luke. We took pictures in the backyard that had been decked out with a huge white tent complete with flowers and bows. It was a fairy-tale wedding and Hannah had never looked happier.

"So, when are you and Luke going to do this?"

We were in her parents' master bedroom suite. Hannah had just changed into her suit to go off on her honeymoon. Her wedding gown was strewn across her parents' bed. I sat next to it, stroking the fabric absently. I slipped off my shoes. "Wow, that's a relief. I think I may go barefoot the rest of the afternoon."

"Don't change the subject. When are you and Luke getting married?"

"I don't know. Maybe never."

"What?" Hannah turned to me. "You're not kidding. What's going on?"

"I want to get married and Luke keeps putting me off."

"Why?"

"I don't know. Something about this isn't the right time."

Hannah tilted her head. "That doesn't sound like him."

"Well, apparently it has to do with his surgical fellowship." Luke had an interview with a prestigious hospital in Philadelphia. It was scheduled for the Monday morning after Hannah's wedding. I hadn't decided if I was going to go with him to the interview or not. "He's afraid the fellowship is going to take up all of his time and he won't be able to be a perfect husband."

"That's bullshit."

"Thank you. That's exactly what I told him. But he won't listen. He wants me to go to Philly to live with him and get married after he finishes and is ready to start his practice. You know that will be years from now."

"And he won't be too busy setting up a practice to be a husband? Sounds like he's stalling to me. Maybe he just doesn't want to get married."

"That's what I'm afraid of, too. I don't know how I could have misread him, but that's what it looks like to me."

"Well, you two are practically living together now. Would it be so bad if you made it official and lived with him in Philly? Just see where it goes."

"I thought of that, but I just can't do it. I'm afraid if I give in now, he'll never want to marry me."

"Well, only you can decide that, but I'd move to Philly, if it were me."

Ironically, I caught Hannah's bouquet after that. I teased Luke about it, but he brushed me off.

That night, when we were in bed, I snuggled up to Luke thinking we were going to make love, but he kissed me on the forehead and rolled over on his side.

I cuddled up closer to him and walked my fingers up his side.

"Charlotte, stop it. I'm tired."

I was instantly angry. "Sorry, didn't mean to bother you."

He rolled over to face me.

"Don't be like that. I'm just not in the mood,

okay. Let's just go to sleep and see what happens in the morning."

"Since when are you not in the mood? You'd have to be dead to not be in the mood. What's going on?"

"Nothing."

"Don't tell me nothing. I know you better, Luke Andrews. What gives?"

"Don't say I didn't warn you." Luke sighed and sat up. "I'm feeling pressured. By you."

"Me? About what?"

"You know damn well about what. You want to get married. You don't think I was getting those digs today? The bouquet?" He pointed to Hannah's bouquet that I had placed on my dresser. "What's that supposed to be? Some damn reminder to me while I lie here?"

I got out of bed and threw the bouquet across the room.

"There. Does that make you feel better? They're just flowers, for God's sake!"

Luke got out of bed and started to put his pants back on.

"Where are you going?"

"This is going to be another fight and I don't have the energy. I have to get ready to leave for Philly anyway. I may as well go back to my place so I can start packing in the morning. My train leaves first thing on Monday."

"I thought you wanted me to go with you."

"Well, I don't think that's a good idea right now. In fact, I think we both need a break. I'll call you after I get back."

Luke didn't call me for over a week. I left messages but they were never returned. I was beginning to think the break was going to be permanent.

But Thursday of the second week he called me and asked me to dinner for the following night. We wound up spending the entire weekend together and everything felt like it had before the fight. We talked about moving to Philadelphia and I finally agreed to try it Luke's way. He had found an apartment while he was in Philly, and I agreed to move in with him. He would go down at the end of June, and I would move in after my lease was up in July. I felt that everything was going to be all right. But it wasn't.

Just before he was scheduled to move to Philadelphia, we had another fight. It was on a Saturday afternoon. Days before, Luke and I had made plans for a picnic in Central Park. But when I showed up at his apartment, he was dazed and seemed to have forgotten all about our date. When I questioned him about his mood, he snapped at me, and we fought. The fight quickly escalated, and I left, thinking it would blow over in a couple of hours.

It didn't.

This time Luke was out of my life for good and no matter how much I called and asked to talk he was adamant. It wasn't going to work, and it was best that we move on with our lives. Luke moved to Philadelphia as he had planned, and I never heard from him again.

Chapter Six

ɔʒ

At first, I was numb. I just could not believe Luke was out of my life. I think part of me still hoped he would wake up one day, realize the colossal mistake he had made, and come knocking on my door. Maybe even bring bagels and cream cheese again. But as the days turned into weeks and the weeks turned into months, I had to accept that Luke was gone for good.

Hannah tried to be there for me, but she was a newlywed now and Sean wanted her at home with him, not holding the hand of some hysterical female. They tried to include me in things, invited me to their home, but their wedded bliss just reminded me of what I no longer had. I went a couple of times but then I just refused their invitations. To avoid Hannah's questions, I pretended to be doing exciting things. Instead, I was usually home watching TV or listening to sad songs and devouring chocolate mint ice cream.

Then, a few months later, on a cold November afternoon, I met Peter.

I was walking home from an afternoon of Christmas shopping. It was the first afternoon I had spent out of the apartment alone that I actually was enjoying myself. Congratulating myself on being over Luke once and for all and feeling very smug, I decided to stop and watch the skaters at Rockefeller Center, something Luke and I used to do, just to see if I could do it without crying. Morbid, I know. But there I was, hanging over the balcony, watching people skate, fall, and laugh, when I saw a little girl who looked to be about four years old dragging a man I assumed to be her father around on the ice.

I don't know why but I couldn't keep my eyes off them. The little girl was laughing, her blond curls bouncing under a blue knit cap. I was amazed at her coordination for one so young. Her father was handsome, or at least I assumed he was from a distance. He was tall and thin, and smiled at the little girl while he held her hand. While I certainly couldn't hear what he was saying to her from my vantage point, I had the distinct impression he was trying to talk her into coming off the ice and she would have none of it. I watched them for a few more minutes and when I couldn't stand the cold myself anymore, I decided to duck into the ringside café for a snack.

I followed the hostess to my table and as we approached the glass wall that overlooked the rink, I had the urge to ask her for another table. Luke and I used to always request a ringside table. It was our custom. But I was in the mood to test myself, so I smiled, thanked her, and took my seat. As I sank into the cushioned armchair, I congratulated myself on my newfound bravery. That, and the glass of wine I ordered, would get me safely through the next hour.

Halfway through my white wine, my Cobb salad arrived. It was as good as I remembered, and I scolded myself for allowing Luke to rob me of the things I loved about the city. I vowed to get out more and enjoy my city again. Just then, I looked up and saw the man and little girl I had watched earlier walk in. They followed the hostess to their table and, as luck would have it, they were seated directly across from me.

The little girl looked over and shyly smiled at me. I smiled back and she giggled. She was dressed in jeans and a little pink turtleneck. Her blond curls formed a cap around her head. She had pulled off her knit cap and some of her hair stood straight up from the static electricity it had made. Her father reached over and tried to smooth it with little luck. I tried not to stare but he was probably one of the handsomest men I had ever seen. He had dark curly hair which accounted for his daughter's curls. The blond probably came from her mother. He was thin but muscular if the bulges in his cable-knit sweater meant anything. He too wore jeans and if truth be known I had admired how they fit him as he had sat down. I took a sip of my wine to cover up the fact that I was trying to sneak more looks at this attractive man. It was then that his daughter announced in a stage whisper that she had to "go potty".

"Now? I thought you went before we left home."

"But I have to go *now*, Daddy." She was starting to squirm in her seat and her father was looking around anxiously. "Take me, Daddy."

"I can't sweetheart. Daddy's can't go into the Ladies Room. Let me see if I can find the waitress."

"Can I help?" The words were out of my mouth before I thought about it. "I know you don't know me, but I promise I'm not a kidnapper." I stood and walked the short distance to their table. I extended my hand to him. "My name is Charlotte Winston and I'm a nurse. I'd like to help you, if I can. I can take your daughter to the Ladies Room. You can stand right outside within shouting distance. Here," I leaned back and grabbed my wallet out of my purse which had been hanging on the back of my chair. "Hang onto this if you need reassurance."

The man looked at me and the wallet I still offered.

"Daddy, I have to go," the little girl said again and grabbed my hand, pulling me in the direction of the rest room.

I dropped my wallet on the table next to his water glass. "Be back in a flash," I said as the little girl propelled me in the direction of the bathroom.

She headed for one of the stalls as soon as we were through the inner door.

"Do you need me to go in with you?" I asked. I had no idea what she was capable of and was quickly thinking I may have volunteered too hastily. And what did that say about her father who allowed me to go off with his daughter so readily? Not that she had given him much of a choice. What was her mother going to think? Where was she anyway?

"I'm okay," she said. "I can do it myself.

I'm almost four." I saw her little feet dangling off the ground under the stall, her jeans around her ankles.

"Let me know if you need me. I'm right here," I called to her. I heard sounds that told me we had gotten there not a moment too soon. After a couple of minutes, she ran out of the stall and stood on tiptoes in front of the sink trying to reach the faucet.

"Here, let me help you." I twisted the knobs and got the water to flow for her. I squeezed soap into my hand and helped her wash. "You certainly are a big girl. You didn't need me at all."

"I know. Daddy worries but I can take care of myself."

"I can see that. Did your Mom teach you to be so independent?" I couldn't believe she was so well-spoken but then again, I knew very little about children her age.

"I don't have a Mommy. She left us."

Well, that wasn't something I expected to hear. "I'm sorry. I didn't mean to upset you."

"I'm not upset." I handed her a paper towel, and she dried her hands. "She's been gone forever. Would you like to eat with me and Daddy?"

"I don't think that's a good idea. I don't even know you guys." She handed me her paper towel and I threw it away. "Let's get back to your Dad before he starts to worry." And I have to answer any more questions.

We no sooner reached her father than she piped up with "Can she sit with us, Daddy?"

Her father handed my wallet back to me. "Thank you. I hope she didn't talk your ear off. She tends to do that."

"Thanks. No, she was fine." I was turning my wallet over in my hand, looking for a way out of this without any more awkwardness. "Well, I think I'll get back to my lunch. Glad to be able to help." I turned to go back to my seat when the little girl grabbed my hand.

"Don't sit by yourself. Miss Frances says we should make new friends every day."

I looked at her father.

"That's her daycare teacher. And Miss Frances is right. Sit with us. It's the least I can do to thank you. That is, if you want to."

What the heck? I thought. If Miss Frances thought it was a good idea, who was I to contradict her?

So, I grabbed my wine and food and coat and purse and sat across from this gorgeous man who extended his hand to me. "My name is Peter Hobson and this is my daughter Beth."

I shook his hand. It was warm and the grip was strong, and I thought he lingered just a fraction of a second longer than was necessary. I wondered if his daughter was a babe magnet for him, much like puppies in Central Park in the Spring.

Over the next hour, Peter and I exchanged the usual bland information while his daughter babbled. In spite of my inner warning signals, I found myself becoming attracted to this stranger with the precocious daughter. I learned he was indeed divorced as Beth had told me although the reason remained a mystery. Peter conveniently failed to divulge that fact and I was too polite to pursue it. I also learned he was an investment attorney and based on the designer clothes on both him and Beth, I assumed he did quite well for himself.

Before I knew it, lunch was over, and Beth was once again squirming in her seat. This time she was complaining that she needed to see her friend Carly.

"We have a play date scheduled for this afternoon," Peter explained. Was it me or did he look disappointed?

"Well, I won't keep you." By now the waitress had brought both our checks. I grabbed for mine, but Peter snatched it out of my hand.

"My treat, I insist. I owe you." He smiled and I knew I was in trouble. I was enjoying his attention far too much.

"Thank you. Well, I hate to eat and run but I need to get home as well." *And out of here.* I stood and gathered my things. "I really enjoyed meeting you guys and," I turned to Beth, "I hope you have a great time with your friend."

As I turned to leave, Peter took my hand. "Can I have your number?" he whispered. "I'd like to do this again. Without," he flicked his eyes toward his daughter. "A grown-up lunch – or dinner. That is, if you want to."

"Yes, I'd like that." He gave me two of his cards. "Write your phone number on one of those and keep the other for yourself."

I stashed his card in my purse and handed the other back to him with my name and phone number written on its back. He looked at it and placed it in his wallet. "I'll call you tonight after Beth is in bed."

He squeezed my hand, and I felt a tingle I hadn't expected. But I had heard smooth lines before. Peter Hobson certainly seemed too good to be true. I assumed I had seen the last of him. I just smiled back and left.

I was wrong.

Peter called me that night as he had promised. I had just settled down in my bed with a book and a glass of wine. I held no delusions and was sure Peter had just been acting as so many men did and had said something that he didn't mean. So, I was pleasantly surprised when I answered the phone and heard his voice at the other end.

"Hi, Charlotte. I'll bet you never expected to actually hear from me," Peter said in his deep baritone.

I took a sip of wine for courage. Feelings were stirring. Familiar feelings. Dangerous feelings.

"The thought crossed my mind."

"Well, you're going to learn that I mean what I say." If only he had kept to that philosophy. But I'm getting ahead of myself. Suffice it to say that we had a thoroughly pleasant conversation and I agreed to go out with him the following night.

Peter picked me up as he promised, on time, and a bouquet of pink roses in hand. Major points, indeed. We dined at a posh restaurant on the Upper East Side, where they obviously knew him and hovered over us, attending to our every need. I was duly impressed as I'm sure Peter intended. While my internal warning system kept telling me to be wary, my need for attention, and my ego that had suffered terribly at the hands of Luke, sopped up every morsel of attention. After dinner we walked and window shopped while we learned about each other. Peter took my hand and it felt good. Just when I was wondering if I should invite him back to my apartment, he told me he had to be back home to relieve his babysitter. A devoted and responsible father – more points.

Over the next few weeks, Peter and I saw as much of each other as our respective jobs and his responsibility to Beth allowed. But he never let our physical contact go past kisses and caresses caught in the back of a cab or on our after-dinner strolls.

Just when I was wondering if Peter's sexual appetite was non-existent, he asked me to go away with him.

"I've made arrangements for my sister to babysit Beth for a couple of days – and nights. I want to spend some quality time with you, Charlotte."

"What we've done so far wasn't quality?"

"Of course, but I want to be alone with you." He kissed the back of my hand. We were back at the restaurant we had gone to on our first date. I shivered and it wasn't from the cold. "Christmas is coming up, and I need to be home for Beth but I want this weekend for us. What do you say? It will be our Christmas."

Peter had been careful not to flaunt me in front of Beth, saying that he didn't want to confuse her. I felt uncomfortable about that but told myself he was right. I had assumed (wrongly, obviously) that I would get to spend Christmas with him and Beth, that it would be a natural progression. But Peter's offer to spend the weekend together before Christmas so he could be "home for Beth" made it painfully clear to me how wrong I had been.

Still, the thought of going away for the weekend with a man who wanted me was food for my ego.

"Okay." The word fell out of my mouth and

the die was cast.

"Great. I'm really looking forward to it. I have a cabin in the Poconos. You're going to love it."

He was right. The weekend was everything I wanted it to be and more. The "cabin" was really a beautiful seven room house, complete with a fireplace in the bedroom. The first night we went to a wonderful restaurant, rustic, and cozy. We walked afterwards under the stars, snow crunching under our feet. When we got back to the cabin, Peter started a fire in bedroom fireplace and we made love finally, while the fire made sensual shadows on the wall. Afterwards, he held me in his arms and kissed my hair, my eyes, and then lingered on my neck, until I couldn't stand it any longer. I turned to him, hungry for more. It had been too long since I had been with Luke and this man who was here, now, wanting me was a powerful aphrodisiac.

He smiled. "You're insatiable, aren't you?"

"You've awakened something in me that I thought had died."

"That's a sad thing for someone so young to be saying."

"Maybe. But that's all in the past now."

"I hope so, Charlotte. I want to spend the rest of my life making you happy." And just like that, I was engaged to Peter Hobson.

But he still didn't ask me to spend Christmas with him and Beth. I thought it was strange. I should have seen it as alarming. I found out, years later, that Peter was able to put many parts of his life into compartments, keeping things separate, away from each other.

Like his wife and his mistress.

But I didn't see it then. Instead, I consoled myself by telling myself he had his reasons and as long as he loved me, it didn't matter. Things would work out eventually.

Hannah wasn't so sure.

"How much do you know about this guy?"

We were in her living room, after dinner. Sean was in the kitchen, topping off our pecan pie dessert with ice cream. Hannah took the opportunity to grill me without him present.

"His name is Peter and I know enough."

"Really?"

"Yes, his name is really Peter."

Hannah gave me her look that told me she wasn't amused. "You know what I meant. You're on the rebound. You're in a vulnerable place. You need to be careful."

"It's been months since Luke and I broke up. I hardly call this a rebound. I'm not vulnerable. I know what I'm doing."

"Do you love him?"

There it was, the $60,000 question.

I hesitated, just a fraction of a second and Hannah pounced. "See? You don't, do you? You're just doing this because of Luke. You're making a mistake, Charlotte. You're going to regret this."

"I'm a big girl. I can take care of myself. I don't need a mother."

"Here we are." Sean walked into the room, holding a little precariously three plates full of pie and towers of ice cream. Hannah jumped up before one of her new plates hit the floor and all talk of Peter was dropped.

I spent the next week with Auntie in Arizona and rather than listen to her pick up where Hannah had left off, I avoided all talk of Peter and my future. I returned to New York the day after New Year's and I wasn't in my apartment a few minutes when Peter called.

"I missed you."

"I missed you, too."

"I want to see you. Now."

"Peter, I just got home. I haven't unpacked, I'm tired, and I have to go to work in the morning." I felt a stab of – I wasn't sure what. If this had been Luke, I knew nothing would have prevented me from saying "yes".

"You're right, I'm sorry. That was selfish. How about dinner tomorrow night, instead? You come here. We'll have a nice quiet family meal."

"There? What about Beth?"

"What about her? She'll be here, too. I told her all about you while you were gone, and she's thrilled. I think it's time we started wedding plans, don't you?"

Take that, Hannah Rafferty.

Peter and I were married in late June. Despite her misgivings that she had no trouble hiding, Hannah agreed to be my Maid of Honor. Auntie flew in from Arizona. Sean even gave me away. It was a glorious day, marred only by the news that Sean and Hannah had decided to move away. To Arizona of all places. Sean's parents were getting older and his father's health was failing. He wanted to be there for them and also he had an opportunity to join a very nice law firm in Phoenix. Hannah left a week after I returned from my honeymoon. I was sad to see her go but glad she would be in Arizona to keep an eye on Auntie for me.

100

Hannah and I had lunch one last time the day before she left.

We were seated in a quiet little restaurant on Second Avenue in New York City, a few blocks from the apartment that she and Sean were vacating. I had spent the morning shopping for camp clothes for Beth.

"You're really enjoying this whole mother thing, aren't you?" she asked.

"It's not bad and not nearly as hard as I thought it would be."

"Sure, when you have camp and nannies and babysitters."

"The camp is only a day camp and I'm thinking of dropping the nanny. She only works during the day anyway when I'm at work."

"Don't be so defensive. If Peter can afford it, so what. It's his kid. Let him take care of her."

"What's with you? You're awfully irritable today."

"Sorry, just moving jitters. I apologize. That was out of line."

I placed my hand over Hannah's. "You're shaking. Are you all right?"

"I'm fine. Let's drop it, okay?"

She withdrew her hand and took a sip of her wine. Then she just stared at me.

"What?"

"Are you happy? I mean really happy?"

"You *are* in a mood. Yes, I'm happy. Really happy. Peter and I are talking about buying a house. Out on the island somewhere. We want to get settled before Beth starts school next year."

"Luke is definitely in the past?"

"Luke? What brings him up? That's ancient

history. Yes, he's in the past. Why are you asking me about Luke?"

"Nothing. No reason. Just wondering."

"You know, Hannah, sometimes I wonder if you're more upset about him dumping me than I was."

Hannah gave me a look that told me I was so wrong. "Please, don't tell me you don't remember the hysterics you went through after he left.'"

"Okay, you got me there. Yes, I remember, but I'm over it now." I wiggled my left hand in front of her. "Married. Remember? You were there."

"So, if Luke walked through that door," she indicated the front door of the restaurant, "you wouldn't jump his bones?'

I turned to look at the door she had indicated and immediately knew I had made a mistake.

"See, you looked. I knew it. You're not over him. You married Peter on the rebound."

"Hannah, stop. This is silly. Read my lips. I love Peter. I no longer love or care about Luke Andrews. Now quit worrying. Tell me about the house you and Sean are buying in Arizona and how you're going to take care of Auntie for me."

Hannah didn't mention Luke again – ever. Not until this trip. As for me, I put him safely in the basement of my heart with all my other memories and he stayed there until my marriage fell apart. Then he started creeping back into my dreams and now – now, he was about to creep back into my life. If I was honest with myself, I knew my heart could still ache if I gave it half the chance. Luke would always be my one true love. He would always occupy a place in my heart unrivaled by anyone else. But I also knew if I didn't guard myself, I would hurt. Still, I refused to even contemplate that anything could come of this. I had resigned myself to believing that Luke would never ever be in my future. That part of my life was sealed over - until Hannah's announcement at lunch.

As I swung on the swing and absently patted Sam's head, I thought of all the possible scenarios that could play out if I went with Auntie to her appointment.

Luke would walk into the waiting room and see me sitting next to Auntie. Our eyes would meet and his heart would melt. He'd sweep me into his arms and decry all the wasted years. We'd kiss and the world would be right again.

Charlotte, you read too many romance novels.

More than likely, he'd walk in, our eyes would meet, and I'd throw the nearest heavy object at him.

Chapter Seven

ↂ

"There you are." Auntie interrupted my revenge fantasy. "I figured if I found Sam, I'd find you." Auntie sat next to me. Sam shifted and placed his head in her lap.

Auntie stared at me for a second. "What's wrong? You don't look so good."

"Hannah told me some disturbing news over lunch."

Oddly, no response.

"You don't want to know what it was?"

"I think I already do."

I looked at her and suddenly everything made sense - dangling money for the house, the ploy to get me out here, all the talk about her ill health.

"You knew about this?"

Auntie lifted her chin in defiance. "It was for your own good."

I stood up and walked away from her. I couldn't believe that this was happening. After a few cleansing breaths, I turned to face her again.

"What were you thinking? Did you think I would just fall in his arms and everything would be okay?" I put my hand up to stop her before she could answer. "Don't tell me. I know you. Well, guess what? It's not going to happen. Besides, I'm sure he has his own life now. A wife, a family. He definitely hasn't been pining away for me."

"It can't hurt to at least talk to him. Find out what happened. See if maybe something is still there."

"Did you not hear me? We've both moved on."

"You don't know that."

"Is there something you're still not telling me?"

"Just meet him. Talk to him. Hear him out."

"Does he know I'm here?" I was getting angry all over again. Did everyone know about this but me?

"Just come with me to the doctor's tomorrow. See what happens. That's all I ask."

"Have you been faking this heart stuff all along?" Dr. Kramer had sounded sincere, but I didn't put it past Auntie to make up a few symptoms for effect. "I swear, Auntie, if you have, I'm going home right now. Forget the deal. Forget my house. I'll be fine all by myself."

Auntie stood next to me and put her arm around my waist.

"I didn't lie. I have been feeling bad and I do want you to go with me to the doctor tomorrow. That much is true. I just thought it was God's way of getting you out here to maybe put everything right. My offer was genuine. And it still stands. If after everything, you still want to go back east to live, I'll help you. But, please, see Luke first."

I looked at Auntie and could see the desperation in her eyes.

"All right. If it means that much to you, I'll talk to Luke. But that's all. I'll talk. Period. I'm not promising any more than that."

Auntie hugged me. "That's all I ask."

"I can't believe I'm agreeing to this lunacy."

I called Hannah later that day and cancelled dinner with her and her family.

"I just need some time alone to let this all sink in."

"I understand," she said. "Maybe tomorrow night."

"Maybe. I'll call you."

The next morning, I sat in the waiting room of Scottsdale Cardiology Associates next to Auntie and felt like a calf being led to slaughter. Just in case, I had made sure I was the best dressed calf I could be.

It had been decades since Luke and I had seen each other. I had no idea what I would say, how I would say it. Breakfast had been a lost cause. I spent more time in the bathroom trying to control my jittery stomach.

So, I concentrated on my appearance. It was important to me that I still looked attractive. We might be walking away from each other for the final time after today, but I wanted his last look to be one that burned his retinas. I had spent the last couple of hours in front of the mirror making sure my hair, clothes, and make-up were perfect. I decided on a simple blue sundress that showed off my legs (what I – and Luke in days gone by - considered my best asset) and a pair of the new sandals that I had bought while shopping with Hannah the day before. I had even practiced facial expressions in front of the mirror, hoping to find one that hid the wrinkles that were creeping around my eyes and mouth.

Still, as I sat there next to Auntie, I couldn't help feeling how the whole situation was surreal. I kept vacillating between anxiety and nausea. The first jolt was seeing Luke's name on the door as we entered the small waiting area. Then, when I signed Auntie in at the front desk, Luke's name was printed in large letters across the top of the page along with Dr. Farrell's. There were places to check which doctor the patient was seeing and I checked Farrell all the while looking to see if anyone was scheduled to see Luke that morning. There had been several, but all were crossed off save one. I assumed she was the woman sitting on the settee reading a magazine.

Auntie and I sat in adjoining armchairs, and I attempted to read a magazine while I stole looks at the door to the offices every time it opened. Despite my nervousness, I was curious to see if I would catch a glimpse of Luke.

Auntie filled out the pre-printed questionnaire the nurse had given her. Occasionally, she patted my knee. She knew what I was feeling even though she had orchestrated the whole thing.

So many thoughts were running through my head. Did anyone alert Luke to my arrival? Did he know I was at that very moment sitting in his waiting room?

I hadn't spoken to Hannah about Luke since my blowup yesterday afternoon. I had no idea what her relationship was with Luke now and wondered if she had called him last night to let him know what was happening.

The door to the suite of offices opened again and a nurse entered. She looked down at her clipboard and then scanned the room. "Diane?"

The woman reading the magazine stood up.

"Dr. Andrews will see you now." My heart lurched at the sound of Luke's name.

Diane grabbed her purse and followed the nurse through the door. I craned my neck to try to look past the door down the corridor but again saw no one. Maybe Luke was avoiding me, too.

Get a grip, Charlotte. He probably doesn't even know you're here.

Or care.

A tall thin young man with close-cropped blonde hair opened the door. "Mrs. Monti?"

Auntie stood. "That's me."

He smiled and offered his right hand to Auntie. "Hi, my name is Vince Ashford. I'm Dr. Farrell's physician assistant. I'm going to take you back to the exam room and get you ready before the doctor sees you."

Auntie pointed to me, still sitting. "I want my niece to come with me."

"Certainly. This way."

He led us down the hall, past a few closed doors. There were two office doors that were open. One was sparsely furnished, the other decorated more to my own taste. I assumed one of the offices was Luke's, but we walked past them too quickly for me to read nameplates. I did notice that one of the desks had on it photographs of a mother and baby.

Vince opened another door and ushered us into a small exam room.

"Here we are, Mrs. Monti." He handed Auntie a patient gown. "Please remove your blouse and put this gown on, tied in the back. I'll be back in a few minutes."

Auntie changed into the gown and sat back on the exam table, her legs dangling like a child.

A few minutes later, Vince knocked on the exam room door. "Okay to come in?"

Auntie said "Yes," and Vince got down to business. "I'm going to take your vital signs and get some basic information."

He took Auntie's blood pressure and pulse and spent the next few minutes asking her the same mundane questions always asked to get the basic information for every new admission. I had done the same thing myself so many times and I found myself tuning out.

"Do you have any questions?"

Vince had been talking to me.

"What? I'm sorry. I was distracted. What was that?"

"I asked if you had any questions."

"No, but I'm sure I will after we see Dr. Farrell."

"I think you'll like him. He's very thorough."

He smiled again and then quickly left. A few minutes later, a man I assumed was Dr. Farrell barreled into the room. He was younger than I expected, tall, although not as tall as Vince, with short dark hair and dark-rimmed glasses.

He shook Aunt Camille's hand. He smiled but his smile never reached his eyes, and I took an immediate dislike to him. "I'm Dr. Farrell. Nice to meet you, Mrs. Monti."

Auntie nodded.

Dr. Farrell looked at me. "And you are?"

"I'm her niece. Charlotte Hobson. I'm a nurse, if that helps."

"It usually doesn't. I find that medical people usually are the worst when it comes to their own family's medical conditions."

I felt my face flush. Dr. Farrell was getting under my skin quickly. I tried to imagine Luke picking him for a partner and failed. But I had dealt with doctors like him before. I tried a different approach.

"Ordinarily, I'd agree with you, Dr. Farrell, but I happen to work on a cardiology floor myself back in New York. I probably know more than the average nurse when it comes to this sort of thing."

Dr. Farrell didn't even respond that time. Instead, he took his stethoscope off from around his neck and motioned for Auntie to turn around. I had obviously been dismissed. After listening to her lungs, he spent a few seconds listening to her heart.

He moved his stethoscope up to her neck and listened to both sides and frowned. Then, he sighed loudly.

"Mrs. Monti, I usually don't run my cases this way but I'm doing this one as a favor to Dr. Kramer. I want my staff to get an EKG on you and then we'll talk some more."

Then he blew out of the office as quickly as he had blown in.

Auntie and I stared at each other.

"I guess he skipped Bedside Manner 101," she said to me.

"He's a jerk. Are you sure you want him to take care of you?"

"He's supposed to be one of the best."

"I can't believe Luke is in practice with him."

The exam room door opened again and a nurse I had not seen before rolled an EKG machine into the room.

"Mrs. Monti, Dr. Farrell wants an EKG done. Let's get you set up. If you'll just lie down on this table for me."

It took a couple of minutes for her to rearrange Auntie's clothes and get the leads set up. I patted Auntie's hand and tried to reassure her. I could sense her anxiety level rising.

I tried to sneak a peek at the EKG as it spit out of the machine, but the technician folded it up as soon as it came through and stashed it in the drawer below the machine. She removed the leads from Auntie and told her to get dressed.

"If you and your niece will go across the hall to Room 4, Dr. Farrell will meet with you and go over everything."

Auntie and I easily found Room 4. It was one of the offices we had passed on the way to the examining room. I realized as soon as we walked in that it was the sparsely decorated one, the one *without* the pictures of the mother and baby. I felt the room spin a little as the reality of what that meant sunk in.

Luke was married. He had a child. Of course, he did. What did I expect?

Somehow, I had to get through the next few

minutes, get out of this building, get in the car, get on a plane, and get as far away as I could from Arizona and Luke Andrews, forever and ever.

I was still planning my escape route when Dr. Farrell strode in. He had a way of taking command of a room that I didn't like. I decided he reminded me of Peter. He sat behind his large desk and opened a manila folder, unfolded Auntie's EKG and spread it out in front of him. Auntie and I were seated in functional Swedish style chairs facing him across his desk. The chairs were a little low forcing us to look up at him. I wondered if he had done that on purpose. I kept trying to sneak peeks at Auntie's EKG but Dr. Farrell held it away from me. I couldn't decide if it was on purpose or not. We had clearly drawn our lines in the sand.

"Okay, here's the deal." He looked straight at Auntie. I wondered if he was making a point of ignoring me. "As I said before, normally, I don't do these kinds of cases in reverse but I'm doing this because Dr. Kramer made it sound like she needed this done as a special favor to her. My usual procedure is to have Dr. Andrews work the case up with a full blood work panel and a treadmill stress test. We don't have the luxury of those results in your case."

He looked down at the EKG in front of him and sighed. "Nevertheless, I see some things here that worry me. Even without the tests that I just mentioned, I think you should consider scheduling yourself for a cardiac catheterization. And soon. We can do the blood work here in the office before you leave today and then get you on the schedule for the cath. Probably in a day or so. I understand you have some time constraints that you're working under. In any case, I don't want to wait, based on what I'm seeing."

"Whoa, wait a minute. Isn't that a little drastic? What could you possibly have seen on an EKG that makes you want to jump to that conclusion?"

Dr. Farrell looked at me over the rim of his glasses. "I'm sorry, where did you say you went to medical school?"

"Look, we seem to have gotten off on the wrong foot and -"

"I don't care what your feelings are, Miss -"

"Mrs. Hobson."

"Whatever. You brought your aunt here for my medical opinion. Now you have it. The next step is yours. If you don't want to go along with my opinion, that's your right. Contact my office when you've made your decision. Just keep in mind that any delay could be injurious to your aunt's health."

He folded the EKG and slipped it back inside the manila folder. He stood and extended his hand to Auntie, saying "It was nice to meet you, Mrs. Monti."

Then, still clutching the manila folder, he turned and left the room without so much as a backward glance.

Dr. Farrell had only been in the room a couple of minutes but in that short time he had declared that Auntie needed a cardiac catheterization or she could die, and that, if I didn't agree, her death would be on my head. Great. The last few minutes had turned my world completely upside down.

And just like that, that plane out of Arizona was leaving without me.

113

Chapter Eight

Cߐ

Neither of us said anything for a few seconds. I could hear the low hum of Dr. Farrell's computer, the ticking of his desk clock.

Auntie sighed loudly. "Well, if that don't beat all."

I looked at her. "Are you all right?"

"In a word? No. Why don't we get out of here? I think we need to go home and digest this before we make any decisions."

As we made our way down the hallway, we passed Luke's open office doorway again. I peered in and tried to get a better look at the pictures of the mother and baby, but another patient and nurse were walking by in the opposite direction, and I didn't want to be obvious.

We hurried out to the front desk.

"Auntie, I thought you wanted me to stay and meet with Luke. Maybe we can talk to him about all this."

Auntie stopped just as we reached the receptionist's desk where we had signed in earlier.

"That's a good point. That doctor got me so rattled, I can't think straight." She turned to the young woman behind the sliding glass partition. "Is Doctor Andrews available? I was supposed to meet with him. I'm a friend of his. Tell him Camille Monti is here."

The young woman turned and addressed another woman further back in the room. "Francie, is Doctor Luke back there? Someone is asking for him up front."

"He stepped out to his car for a minute."

The receptionist turned back to Auntie. "Sorry, he's not here right now. Do you want to leave a message?"

"No, that's all right. I'll just call him later."

I was beginning to wonder exactly how much Auntie and Luke had talked about me before I had come to Arizona. I was surprised at the sudden depth of disappointment I felt when I heard he wasn't in the office.

Auntie was unusually quiet as we walked back to her sedan. Despite her penchant for hypochondria, I suspected even in her own wild dreams, she never suspected anyone would have handed her an offer for a cardiac catheterization.

I clicked the key fob at the door on the driver's side of Auntie's car, unlocking it. I was looking at Auntie's permed gray hair over the hood of the car and thinking how small and frail she was and how much I wanted to protect her and how much I hated Dr. Farrell at that moment when –

"Charlotte!"

I knew that voice. No matter how many

years it had been, my heart would always know that voice.

Luke!

"Charlotte, wait!"

The blood stopped flowing in my arms and they immediately began to shake. I turned in the direction of the voice and saw a man in a lab coat running toward us. He was still several yards away and from that distance, Luke looked the same as he did the last time I had seen him. Tall, slim, the curly dark hair that I loved to run my hands through. His lab coat flapped open as he ran and he still looked trim. Time had treated Luke Andrews well.

Within minutes, he had caught up to our car and stopped to catch his breath. He stood facing me, panting a little. Now that he was closer, I noticed a few strands of gray hair at his temples, and I thought it made him look even more attractive. He smiled awkwardly and his eyes crinkled a bit at the edges. I found myself staring into them but then I remembered the picture of the mother and baby on his desk.

We both said "Hi" at the same time and then just stood there, awkwardly looking at each other.

Auntie broke the silence. "I left you a message yesterday, Luke. Did you get it?"

"Yes, I did, Camille, thanks. I was hoping to catch you guys before you left this morning, but I had to get something I needed from my car." Luke turned back to me. "How did the exam go?" How could a simple question seem so sexy?

"Not well. Dr. Farrell wants Auntie to have a cardiac cath."

"Well, that's not the end of the world. Those things are fairly routine now. They can do a world of good."

"I guess. It just wasn't what we expected to hear. Kind of a shock, you know?"

"Yeah, I guess."

We stood there again, suddenly out of things to say. The man who I used to share my most intimate thoughts with was a stranger to me now.

"Look, Luke, I should get Auntie home."

"Sure."

Now that Luke was standing in front of me, I wondered what I had expected. This all seemed so pointless. It had been a mistake to even agree to come here. Auntie was my only concern now. Luke had to stay in the past – with that woman and her baby.

I turned toward the car and grabbed the door handle. Suddenly, Luke placed his hand on mine and his touch sent fire through me.

"Charlotte, I really need to talk to you."

I tried to twist my hand away but he held fast. "Ever since I heard you were coming back to Arizona, I haven't been able to think of anything else. I owe you an explanation."

"Forget it. You don't owe me anything."

"You're wrong. I owe you a lot. Please. Can we talk? At least let me explain what happened." He let go of my arm and I actually felt disappointment. Boy, was I messed up.

"And how will that change anything?" I was having trouble thinking.

"Charlotte, please. Just hear me out. Can you at least meet me for coffee?"

I looked over at Auntie. She was nodding at me and trying to give me signals with her eyes.

"Okay, coffee. But that's it." The picture of

the mother and baby kept hovering over Luke's head, and I was not going down that road. "Let me take Auntie home first."

Luke looked at his watch. "It's just a little after Noon. How about lunch instead?" He smiled that infectious Luke smile. "You have to eat anyway."

"Fine. Where should I meet you?"

"My office hours are over for the day. I don't have to make hospital rounds for a while. There's a nice little place right in Fountain Hills where I can meet you. It's right near Camille's house. *Casey's.*"

"I know where that is," Auntie said. "It's right on the lake, by the fountain." She looked over at Luke. "Very nice."

I shot Auntie what I hoped was my most scathing look and then turned back to Luke. "I'll meet you there in about forty-five minutes."

We had one of those "I don't know if I should kiss you on the cheek or not" moments (we didn't) and then Luke left.

Auntie patted my knee as we pulled out of the parking lot. "It's going to be okay. This is why we came here, remember?"

"It's one thing to say that. It's quite another to see him standing there in the flesh."

"And mighty nice flesh, too, if you ask me."

"What is wrong with you today?"

"Nothing. Just lighten up, will you? Why don't you drop me off at Hannah's instead of at home? *Casey's* is closer to her house anyway."

"How do you even know she's home and wants you there?" I looked at Auntie and knew my answer before she even opened her mouth. "This

118

was all arranged, wasn't it?"

"Not down to all the details but we did talk about it. Let me just call her to confirm." Auntie pulled out her cell phone and dialed while I drove and shook my head. I just had to resign myself to this. Auntie was determined to get me back in front of Luke. I guessed there were worse things. I really wanted to see him again, truth be told. Despite my misgivings and my dread at finding out whatever it was he felt compelled to tell me, my heart was looking forward to being in his presence again. It wasn't a wise choice, by any means.

Auntie ended her call. "There's no need for you to come in, you know. I don't want you to be late. Just drop me off in front."

"I'll do no such thing. I want to say Hi to Hannah."

"There's plenty of time for that afterwards."

"Why all the rush?"

Auntie just sighed. "Just don't be late, that's all."

"Auntie, relax, please. This is just lunch, remember. Just me and Luke talking. Nothing more."

We arrived at Hannah's house within twenty minutes. Despite having not driven there in a few years, I was able to find my way to Hannah's without much difficulty. I pulled into her driveway and parked next to her SUV and noticed Auntie bounded out of the car with more energy than I had seen in a while, certainly not like someone who was recently told she needed a cardiac catheterization. I made a mental note of that and decided it was one of the things I planned to discuss with Luke over lunch.

I rang Hannah's doorbell and Willie, her border collie, barked in response. The door was yanked open and two identical twelve-year-old girls stood there bouncing up and down.

"Aunt Charlotte!"

"Hey, guys, so good to see you again." I knelt down and hugged both of them. They were little Hannah clones right down to their curly red hair. "How come you're not in school?"

"Teacher's conference," they said in unison.

"We're going horseback riding."

"Wanna come?"

"Now girls, Aunt Charlotte, has other things to do, maybe some other time." Hannah came out from around the corner, a dishcloth in her hand. "Welcome to Activity Central. It's hard to keep up around here." Hannah shot Auntie a look I couldn't quite decipher, and Auntie just shrugged.

"I tried to tell her she was going to be late, but she wouldn't listen to me."

I waved my arm in the air. "Hello, I'm still in the room."

Hannah hugged me. "It's okay. We're just anxious for you, that's all. Camille, you're just in time to help me make some trays for a job I have to deliver this afternoon." She turned to the twins. "You'd better go change into your riding clothes. Darcy is going to be here any minute."

The two girls ran off screaming to their room.

"How do you handle the noise level?"

Hannah stuck a finger in her ear. "Huh? What was that? Did you say something?"

"Never mind, smartass. I'm dropping off my matchmaker. She's all yours. I'm assuming you two will have lots to discuss while I'm gone. If you don't mind, I'm going to use your bathroom to freshen up and then I'll be out of your hair for about an hour."

Auntie patted my arm. "You take all the time you need."

"Quit it. We're going to talk and that's going to be the end of it. Frankly, I intend to talk to him about your heart more than anything else. I want to know about this Dr. Farrell and whether we should trust him and his ideas. I'll be right back."

I spent the next few minutes staring at my reflection, deep breathing and wondering just what I was letting myself in for. Seeing Luke again was probably the biggest mistake I was making but the die was cast now.

I found Auntie and Hannah in Hannah's kitchen when I came out. Auntie was sampling some canapés. The twins were staring out the front living room window in anticipation. I assumed they were waiting for their friend.

"Hannah, I'm going to need directions to this restaurant."

"Sure thing." She grabbed a small notepad from the granite kitchen countertop and wrote a few directions down while she said them aloud to me. "You shouldn't have any trouble, Charlotte. It's barely a mile from here. The place is right on the lake. It's real easy to find."

"Thanks. I'm sure I'll find it okay."

"Darcy's here, Mom," one of the twins yelled from the living room.

"I'll be right there," Hannah called. She looked at the kitchen wall clock and frowned. "She's early."

"Is that a problem?" I asked. "The girls seem ready to go."

"Huh? No. No, it's not a problem." She looked at Auntie. "Camille, can you walk the girls out to the car?"

"Hannah, it's all right. You don't have to stay here on my account. Go walk your kids out to their friend. I'm ready to go anyway. We can all walk out together."

"Sure. That's fine."

"Are you all right?"

"I'm fine. Stop asking me that, okay?"

Hannah grabbed the girls' riding helmets off the sofa and rushed them out the front door. "Come on, kids. Let's not keep Darcy waiting." But the twins were already out the front door ahead of her and were squealing with their friend outside.

I followed Hannah and the twins. As I exited the house, I saw a dark-haired young woman standing in the driveway. A dark blue SUV I hadn't seen before was parked at the curb. I assumed it belonged to the aforementioned Darcy.

Darcy was hugging first one twin and then the other. She raised her head when she heard the front door open again. I was struck by her good looks. She had deep brown eyes and a smile that had me staring at her, wondering why she looked so familiar.

Gloria ran back to me, grabbed my hand, and dragged me over to her friend. "Aunt Charlotte, this is my friend Darcy. She teaches horseback riding. English," she added in a way that was meant to imply that it was something special.

"Hi, Darcy."

We shook hands. Her handshake was warm

and firm. I immediately liked her.

"Darcy has lots of horses," Gloria continued. "She's the best rider in Arizona."

Darcy hugged Gloria to her again. "Well, I don't know about that. Where's your helmet? Are you all ready?"

Gloria ran to Hannah who held her riding helmet out to her. "Enough chatter, girls. Let's go. Don't keep Darcy waiting. You're going to be late for your lesson. See you all later." She kissed the girls and they all climbed into the SUV.

Hannah walked to Darcy's car and leaned into the open passenger side window. "I'll pick the girls up at a little after three, Darcy."

"That's fine. We should be done by then."

I watched the car turn the corner and then turned to Hannah. "She seems very nice."

"She is."

I was caught off guard by Hannah's terse reply but shook it off. "Well, I guess I'd better be going, too, or I'll be late."

Hannah hugged me. "Are you nervous?"

I took a deep breath. "Yes."

Auntie had followed us out to the driveway by now. She patted my back. "It's going to be okay. This is the way it's supposed to be. Trust me."

"Trusting you is what's gotten me into this mess in the first place. You're a conniving old bat, you know that, don't you?"

"Yes, I do, it's part of my charm. Now get out of here."

As I drove to the restaurant, I tried to imagine all the ways I would greet Luke. None of them felt comfortable. How do I greet the man I had slept with and planned to marry? A man I had planned to spend the rest of my life with? A man I had shared the most intimate parts of my soul with?

A man who had ripped the heart right out of me.

Chapter Nine

ဗ

I found the restaurant without any problem just as Hannah had promised. It was located at the edge of the park that surrounded the lake in the center of town. The fountain in the middle of the lake was erupting as I pulled into the restaurant's parking lot. There was a slight breeze and the water's spray was carried a bit making a faint rainbow in its wake. I sat and admired it, hoping it was a good omen. For a brief moment, I toyed with the idea of turning the car around and forgetting this whole insane idea. But I was more afraid of disappointing Auntie than I was of being alone with Luke. I shut off the engine, sighed deeply and exited the car.

Casey's took full advantage of its location with a sweeping balcony on one side that overlooked the lake. Tables with large green market umbrellas dotted the balcony. As I approached the side entrance, I could see Luke seated at a far table, with a pitcher of iced tea already on it. He was holding a menu open in front of him but kept scanning the parking lot. As soon as he saw me, he waved. I waved back and put a finger up, signaling that I would be there in just a minute, and instantly realized it was something I used to do when we dated.

I entered the restaurant and approached the hostess.

"I'm meeting someone here for lunch."

"Name?"

"I see him outside on the patio already. Dr. Andrews."

She looked down on her sheet. "Certainly. You must be Charlotte." She grabbed a menu. "Follow me, please."

Luke started to rise as I approached his table, but I motioned with my index finger again for him to stay seated. I was struck by how easily I was falling back into old habits with him. I eased into my seat opposite Luke and took my menu from the hostess.

"Coffee, miss?'

"No, thanks. I'll have some of this iced tea."

"Very good. George is your waiter. I'll have him bring you a glass with ice." She hurried off and I finally took a hard long look at Luke.

"How are you?" we both said at once.

"You first," Luke said.

"Okay. I'm good. But there's a lot going on right now."

"Uh oh. Sounds ominous."

"Quit teasing. I'm serious." Luke was flirting with me, and I was flirting back. I knew I was in trouble. Luckily, our waiter appeared with my glass of ice and set it in front of me.

"Are you ready to order?"

"Sorry, I haven't even looked at the menu."

"They have a wonderful Monte Christo sandwich here," Luke said.

"You're kidding. That's my favorite."

"I know." Luke smiled and I saw his dimple reappear. I had missed that dimple. It also sent a nagging feeling to the back of my mind.

I handed my menu to the waiter. "I'll have the Monte Christo."

As soon as the waiter was gone, Luke said, "So tell me about your appointment with Mark."

"Who?"

"I'm sorry. Dr. Farrell."

"Oh, you mean Dr. Personality? How did you wind up in practice with him anyway? You and he are polar opposites."

"Yeah, Mark's personality is a lot different from mine but he's a good doctor. He knows his stuff. Although he seems to have been having a run of bad luck with some patients lately. I'm not sure what that's about." Luke took a sip of his tea. "I guess that just comes with the territory, though. Most of our patients, especially his, are in pretty bad shape by the time they get to us. But to answer your question, I needed someone to share call with me. After my wife died, I wanted to be home more for my daughter – what?"

My face must have registered so much hearing Luke say *wife* and *daughter* and then the word *died*. I thought of the mother and baby photograph on his desk.

"It's startling to hear you say all this. I guess there's a lot I don't know. Maybe we should fill each other in on the last twenty years or so. Although I get the feeling you know more about me than I know about you."

"Yeah, I guess we should. This isn't going to be easy, though. I'm not really sure where I should start. It's easier to talk about other things instead of the elephant in the room, you know?"

Luke reached across the table and took both my hands in his. "Charlotte, I know I hurt you so much when I left. I can't tell you how sorry I am about that. It was the hardest decision I have ever made."

"Then why did you do it, Luke?"

Luke rubbed the back of my hand with his thumb, a gesture from the past. I felt a shift in the air, a sense of peace. I felt he was about to open up to me finally. Then the waiter arrived with our lunch and we both quickly withdrew from each other.

I took a bite of my sandwich. "Wow, this really is good. You weren't kidding." I decided to give Luke a reprieve and try to get information from him from a different angle. "Why don't you tell me how you and Hannah found each other."

"That was the strangest thing. It was an ordinary Monday morning at work. I was looking over the appointments for the day. Nothing jumped out at me. I saw I had a new patient Sean Rafferty. The named rang a familiar bell but I didn't pay much attention to it. I knew that was the name of the guy that Hannah had married but I didn't think in a million years it was the same one. Then they walked into my office two hours later. I wasn't sure if Hannah wanted to hug me or kill me. She's very protective of you, you know."

I smiled remembering the evenings filled with tears and hugs from Hannah after Luke had left me. "I know."

"Anyway, after we were sure that Sean was going to be all right, we got to talking about you and what was going on and here you are."

"That's an awfully simplistic version. Makes you sound really innocent."

"I am."

"No, you're not."

Luke sighed. "I guess we're back to your question from before then, aren't we?"

"Yes, we are." I put my sandwich down and looked straight at Luke. "What happened? Why did you leave me?"

"Charlotte, I made a horrible stupid mistake and I had to pay for it. I had to somehow make it right. I had to do the right thing."

I stared at Luke and shook my head. He was making no sense.

Luke looked down at his plate and sighed. He looked up and just started talking really fast. "Okay, remember that weekend after Hannah's wedding when we had that big fight and I went to that interview on my own?"

"Yes." I felt a knot forming in my stomach. Somewhere in my heart, I knew what was coming.

"Well, I met up with someone from med school while I was in town that night. Someone I used to date. Someone I was close to." Luke's expression was full of remorse. "Charlotte, I cheated on you."

My worst fears were confirmed. I had had a feeling all along that someone else had been involved. A woman just knows these things. But that was old news now. I certainly couldn't be angry with Luke for a transgression that happened so many years ago. I ached to make him feel better. Besides, the story still didn't sound right. I knew there had to be more.

"You broke up with me because of a one-night stand? But we had gotten back together after you came back. I thought things were better. Don't you remember? This isn't making sense."

Luke took a deep breath and sighed. "There just is no way to say this except to say it. You're right. We did get back together. I felt awful about what happened between me and Cathy." I winced when I heard her name, but Luke didn't notice or pretended not to and continued.

"I wasn't in love with her. I was in love with you. But I was angry. Upset. Hurt. And, yes, I was scared. I knew where we were headed, and I was afraid. That doesn't make anything I did right. It's no excuse. But I came back to you and I intended to make everything better between us. I even planned on proposing to you."

He smiled at me and I smiled back. Then, when the import of his words hit me, I realized the full extent of what we had lost. I opened my mouth to say something, but Luke put his hand up.

"Let me finish. A few weeks later, Cathy called me." Luke stopped again. He took a sip of tea. Obviously, what he was about to tell me was very hard for him and I was beginning to feel that I didn't want to hear it. What could it matter now anyway after all these years? How could a one-night stand from over twenty years ago mean anything now? What was I missing? Luke was widowed. I was getting a divorce. Maybe Aunt Camille's crazy plan was going to work. Maybe Luke and I could actually pick up where we had left off. Maybe...

Luke looked down at his plate and I wondered if he was even going to continue.

"Cathy called and said what? She wanted you back? What?"

Luke looked into my eyes and I saw such sadness in him that my heart broke. "She said she was pregnant."

Suddenly, I remembered the Saturday when I had gone to Luke's apartment just before we had broken up for good. His anger. How none of it made sense. How he refused to talk about what was wrong. Now, all the pieces were falling into place.

And falling apart.

Again.

I stared at Luke. The picture of the smiling mother and baby on Luke's desk reappeared in my mind. "She was pregnant? You got her pregnant?"

"It was stupid, I know. I thought we had been careful but obviously, it didn't work. I had to do the right thing."

"The right thing being dumping me and marrying her."

"Charlotte, she was having my baby."

"Yeah, you mentioned that."

"Charlotte, please, the baby was innocent in all this. What was I supposed to do? Abandon her? Cathy offered to abort but I wouldn't hear of it. You know how I feel about that." Luke touched the top of my hand. He looked at me and I saw such pain in his eyes. "I had to make a choice. I knew what I *had* to do but my heart didn't want to. I knew if I saw you, I wouldn't be able to go through with it. So, I just left. Please forgive me."

I looked down at my sandwich and stared at the now congealing cheese. The very qualities that I admired in Luke had conspired to destroy the life I had wanted with him.

Luke took my silence as permission to go on. "And Darcy has been the light of my life. Especially since Cathy's death -"

My head snapped up. "Darcy? Your daughter's name is Darcy? She doesn't happen to like horseback riding, does she?"

"She loves it. She teaches it, in fact. Hannah's twins are students of hers. Why?"

That smile that had haunted me now made sense. Luke's kid. I had met Luke's baby. I felt ill.

The waiter reappeared then. "Can I get anyone anything?"

"No, I'm done here." I threw my napkin on the table and stood up with such force that my chair tipped over.

Chapter Ten

ᚲᚱ

I was hardly aware of leaving the restaurant. I dimly heard Luke calling my name as I raced past the hostess' desk, out the front door, and headed for my car. My heart beat wildly, tears blurred my vision.

I had often wondered if someone had taken my place with Luke. I knew he didn't become celibate after we broke up and certainly when I saw that picture on his desk, it made sense that he would have settled down and started a family. But never in all my dreams had I never expected the bomb he had dropped on my lunch plate. Never in a million years did I think he had cheated and conceived a child with someone else and then left me over it.

For some reason I couldn't name, it hurt even more having been in the company of that child, the soul who had taken my love from me. Logically, I knew she was innocent. In my heart, however, I hated her. No wonder that smile had looked so familiar. It was the same smile that haunted my dreams. The smile that had won my heart - and broken it.

Despite my shaking fingers, I managed to start the car. I knew I had a few minutes before Luke could follow me. He still had to pay the lunch bill. If I were lucky, I'd be halfway back to Hannah's house before he made it out to the parking lot.

I was wrong. Just as I was backing up out of my parking space, Luke was banging on my window, calling my name. I stopped the car, afraid I would run over him. He tapped the window, wanting me to roll it down. I shook my head. I had no intention of talking about this anymore.

Luke flattened his hand on my window. "Charlotte. Please. Can we talk about this?"

I rolled my window down just enough so that Luke could hear me. "What is there to talk about? What's done is done."

"What happens now?"

"There is no now, Luke. Good-bye." I rolled my window back up and Luke took that as a signal to back away.

I drove off and before I even realized it, I was back at Hannah's house.

I turned the car off and rested my head on the steering wheel. I couldn't think. I had no idea what I was going to say to Auntie and Hannah or how I was even going to face them. It was obvious that they knew all along what the true story had been and were just waiting for Luke to tell me himself. Obviously, they thought I was going to be okay with it. Or at least accept it.

But I wasn't okay with it, and I never would

be. I was angry with Hannah more than Auntie. She should have known how this would have affected me. She was my best friend. The one I trusted the most. How could she have let me walk into that, knowing full well what Luke was going to tell me?

Then, I remembered how nervous she had been just before Darcy's arrival just a little while ago. Everything made sense now.

I blew my nose and checked my face in my rear-view mirror. There was nothing to do now except go in and get this over with. The front door was open, and the security screen door was unlocked. I went in.

"Hannah? Auntie?"

"We're on the deck, Charlotte," Hannah answered.

I walked through the house to the back. Hannah and Auntie were stretched out on two identical lounge chairs on the deck by the pool. Both were wearing large sun hats and sunglasses. They sat up as I approached.

"Well, if it isn't Lucy and Ethel," I said. "Cooked up any more hare-brained schemes while I was gone?"

They looked at each other. Hannah pointed to her hair. "Dibs on Lucy." Then she looked at me and all signs of joking left. "You don't look happy."

"Did you honestly think I would be?"

"I'm guessing things didn't work out between you two."

"Work out? What the hell were you expecting? I was going to fall into his arms and all would be forgiven and forgotten? It's worse now that I know the reason. And Darcy? Hannah, how could you?"

"Ok, in my defense, I wasn't expecting you two to show up today. I didn't want you to see Darcy until you had a chance to talk to Luke first." She looked over at Auntie and pointed. "That was Ethel's fault."

I ignored her attempt at humor. I was way beyond that. "Fine. I talked to Luke. I'm done."

"That's it?" Auntie finally spoke.

"Yes, that's it. Auntie, I'd like to go home, if you don't mind."

She got up and gave her sun hat to Hannah. "Sure."

Hannah walked us out to the car. The sun was high overhead and the glare made it hard to see. I squinted.

"Why don't you let the car cool off a little before you get in?" she suggested.

"We're only going home. It's barely ten minutes from here." Then I realized Hannah wanted to talk. "Okay, let me turn the AC on."

We both started talking at the same time.

"Look, Hannah. Let's just forget this, okay? You meant well. Everyone seems to think that Luke and I are supposed to be together but that ship has sailed. It's ancient history. We're both in different places now." I took her hand. "I'll be okay, really. Maybe it's a good thing that I saw him today and heard him out. I can now put all that to rest. Now I know the whole story. It's finally over." I could see that wasn't what she wanted to hear but she knew me well enough to let it go.

Hannah hugged me. "I'm so sorry. I never meant to hurt you."

"I know."

"I don't want this to come between us."

"It won't. Nothing could do that."

"Will you still come to dinner tonight? You promised me you would."

"Okay. But no surprises. I don't want to see any sudden dinner guests." Hannah gave me an "I have no idea what you mean" look. "I'm serious. First whiff of Luke and I'm gone."

She raised her hand. "Promise."

"Ok, then. See you tonight."

"Be here at six."

Auntie was unusually subdued on the way back to her house. "I'm really sorry about this. I really didn't think it would turn out so bad."

"Well, it did. Let's just let it go, okay? I don't want to talk about it."

Another few seconds went by.

"I got a phone call from Dr. Farrell's office while you were with – while you were at lunch."

"What did they want?"

"They wanted to know if I had decided about the cath. They want to schedule my blood work and stuff to get me ready for it. They can schedule me for Friday if I have the blood work tomorrow."

I heard the nervousness in Auntie's voice.

"What do you want to do?"

"I was kind of hoping to have Luke to guide me in this."

"Look, just because I don't want to have anything to do with him doesn't mean you can't. Obviously, he and Hannah have a relationship and her kids have one with his daughter. The world isn't going to stop dealing with Luke Andrews just because I want to forget he exists. If you want to talk to him, talk to him."

By this time, we were back in Auntie's driveway. I turned the car off and faced her.

"Auntie, I said I would be here for you and I meant it. Call Luke, go to his office, meet with him. Do whatever you feel you need to do to get through this. Let me know what you want from me and I'll do it. My feelings for Luke have nothing to do with my feelings for you. If helping you means I have to deal with Luke on occasion, I can handle it. I'm here for you, regardless. Please remember that."

"They want me to go in tomorrow morning to their lab and get my workup done. I thought I would call Luke later today and talk to him. But I have a feeling I know what he's going to say. Maybe I should just do it. Will you go with me tomorrow?" She knew that meant probably running into Luke again.

I grabbed Auntie's scrawny little hand and squeezed it. It felt cold despite the summer heat. For all her bravado, Auntie was scared. "Sure. You can count on me."

Luke be damned. He had turned my world upside down once. I was not going to let him do it again. I had come out here to take care of Auntie and that was what I was going to do. If Luke was there, so be it. I could rise above this.

I just hoped my heart was going to cooperate with my brain.

Chapter Eleven

ᴄ꙼ᴢ

Auntie and I returned to Hannah's home that night for dinner as promised. As I drove up to the house, I was afraid the specter of Luke would hang over the evening. Two seconds after I walked in, I realized nothing could be further from the truth.

My senses were bombarded. The twins ran to me, screaming my name. The television blared in the background. Willie barked. I smelled fresh-baked apple pie coming from the kitchen.

Sean hugged me and handed me a glass of wine at the same time. "Welcome to our home. Here, you're going to need this." I looked at him, a question in my eye. "Trust me."

"Is it like this every day?"

"Like what?" He smiled. A tall man, Sean had been downright skinny when he first started to date Hannah. All of her good cooking had added a few pounds, but they only served to fill him out in the right places. He wore his dark curly hair a little long and it corkscrewed around his head now from the heat. He was dressed in shorts and a Hawaiian shirt.

"I'm barbecuing hamburgers on the deck. Come on out. It's a little less hectic out there." He turned to the twins. "Is homework done?"

"Yes," they said in unison.

"Books put away?"

"Yes."

"Is Willie fed?"

"Yes."

"Fine, then turn the TV off and go wash up. Dinner's almost ready." They ran off. He turned to Auntie and me and pointed to the open sliding glass doors that led to the deck. "Make your escape while you can."

We preceded him out to the deck. Willie followed us and immediately stood sentry by the barbecue grill.

"Where's Hannah?" I asked after we had settled into our deck chairs.

"She had to drop off some trays for a party. She'll be back soon."

"Her business really has taken off, hasn't it?"

"Yeah, and she loves it, too. It gets her out of the house a lot. Sometimes, too much but I help when I can. If things get much busier, she's thinking of hiring some permanent people. As it is now, she just hires on occasionally as the need arises."

Sean turned a couple of burgers over. "I'm going to feed the twins first so we can eat in peace after Hannah gets back." As if on cue, both girls appeared on the deck.

"You're not burning those burgers, are you, Dad?" Gloria asked.

Sean put a hand to his heart. "Me?"

"Daddy, you know you do."

"They're done just the way you like them. Grab your plates." The girls obeyed and Sean placed two burgers on buns that were warming on an upper level on the grill and then placed a burger on each outstretched plate. "Go sit at the table and I'll bring you some potato salad." They did as they were told. He grabbed the bowl of potato salad and placed a large scoop on each plate. The next few minutes were blissfully quiet while the girls ate.

Sean grabbed his wine off the picnic table and sat in a deck chair next to Auntie and me.

"Camille, Hannah tells me that you had less than good news at the doctor's today."

"No one can accuse you of skirting the truth."

"Hey, I'm a lawyer. I like to get to the heart of the matter. No pun intended."

"Yeah, well, apparently, my heart has seen better days."

"Don't jump to conclusions. I've been there, you know. I was sure I was buying bypass surgery and it turned out to be just stress."

"But your EKG was probably normal," I chimed in. "According to Dr. Farrell, Auntie's EKG doesn't look so good. He wants to go right to cardiac catheterization. I'm afraid of what we're looking at after that. Do you know him at all?"

Sean shook his head. "No, I saw Lu –." He stopped short.

"It's okay, Sean. You can say his name. I'm not going to fall apart. I don't want everyone walking on eggshells around me. You saw Luke," I finished for him. "I know that. I was just wondering if you had any visits with Dr. Farrell."

"No, I didn't. Luke was my only doc. He did a stress test and some lab work. Everything came back normal. I followed his instructions regarding stress and diet. My trial ended and I haven't had the need to go back. Thankfully, that was the end of it."

"Well, Dr. Farrell and I didn't hit it off. He's arrogant and very impressed with himself and, frankly, he seems a little knife happy to me. I can't picture him with Luke."

"Lots of people wind up in practice together who wouldn't normally be friends. It's a business relationship, not a marriage. But if you don't like Farrell maybe you should get a second opinion."

"No, Luke likes him, that's enough for me," Auntie said.

I looked over, surprised at the amount of resolve I heard in her voice, but Auntie didn't meet my gaze. Instead, she was staring into her wineglass. Then she turned to me.

"As long as we're being honest, I'm sure you know I'm friends with Luke. And, yes, we talked about you, not me. But I respect and trust his medical judgment, just the same. If he thinks I should follow Dr. Farrell's advice, I'm going to."

I looked over at Sean and he just shrugged. I was dying to know what Luke and Auntie had talked about, but I just squeezed Auntie's hand. I'd find the rest out when I was ready. And I wasn't ready now. "Okay, then, I guess that's settled. Dr. Farrell, it is."

"Hello? Where is everybody?" It was Hannah back from her catering drop off.

"Back here, hon." Sean set his wineglass on the picnic table and greeted his wife with a kiss. The twins abandoned their burgers and hugged Hannah while Willie jumped up and down and barked. I wondered how Hannah managed to have any hearing left at all living in this house of non-stop noise. I found myself longing for Auntie's house where I rarely heard anything except the hallway Grandfather clock.

Hannah looked over the heads of her twins at me and smiled. "Sorry I'm late, guys, but Mommy made lots of money tonight." She turned to Sean. "And I got a referral for a big job for this weekend, too."

Sean kissed her again. "My kind of wife. Mommy gets special treats tonight."

Hannah slapped Sean on the behind. "Pig." She hugged the twins again. "Go finish your dinner, sweets. Mommy will be back out soon." Then she looked in my direction and mouthed "Follow me" and walked back into the house.

I excused myself from Auntie and found Hannah in her kitchen pouring herself a glass of white wine and looking very pleased with herself.

"What's up?"

"You're not going to believe the evening I've had. Sit." She motioned to one of the bar stools at her breakfast bar.

"You know I had to drop off some trays for a party tonight, right?"

"Yeah, that's what Sean said."

"Well, when I got there some of the guests were already there. I got to talking with some of them. One thing led to another and I got hired to do another party." She looked straight at me for dramatic effect. "At Dr. Farrell's house!"

"What?"

"Yeah, can you believe that?"

"Was he there?"

"No, some chick he's dating. Not very serious, I don't think. From what Camille has told me about him, I don't think he gets serious with anyone. Can you picture it?"

"Please."

"Anyway, I guess he's entertaining some bigwig business types. They had a caterer all lined up but something happened at the last minute and it fell through. I didn't get the details on that. Apparently, she's under a time crunch. The party is this weekend. Saturday afternoon, in fact. He told his girlfriend to handle it and I happened to be at the right place at the right time."

"Wow."

"Yeah, but that's not all. When she left the room, I heard some more." Hannah stared into her wine glass, obviously waiting for me to ask for more details. She was enjoying stringing me along and dragging out her news.

"Hannah, if you don't stop playing games with me, I swear, I'm going to strangle you right here and now with one of your own dish cloths."

"Okay." She took a sip. "It seems our dear Dr. Farrell is going to be sued by one of the pillars of the community."

"What?"

She raised her right hand in the air. "I swear it's true. I guess some guy who had a cath and a stent placed last year now thinks that he didn't really need it. He had some complications afterwards and since he feels he didn't need the procedure in the first place, he's planning on suing the good doc."

"How do you know this?"

"The guy's wife was there and told us herself. She shouldn't have said anything. Her lawyer is going to be pissed at her, believe me. But I guess she had had a couple of glasses of wine before I got there and it loosened her tongue."

"Wow."

"Yeah, wow is right. Can you believe that? It's probably nothing. People try to sue doctors all the time from what I hear. Most of them go nowhere. Just because someone thinks something didn't turn out the way it should have, doesn't mean something was done wrong, you know what I mean?"

"True, but I bet this puts Farrell's shorts in a knot. He doesn't strike me like the kind of guy to take this lying down."

"I never met the man. All I know is what I've heard from you and Camille...and someone who shall remain nameless."

My expression must have changed as soon as I realized she was referring to Luke. Hannah immediately looked uncomfortable.

"It's okay, Hannah. You can say his name. I know you and Luke are friends."

Her face softened. "I just don't know how to handle this. You and I have never *not* talked about something. Especially something this big. I don't want to hurt you. But ..."

I put my hand up. "There is no 'but'. I know you and Auntie meant well. I was angry with you guys at first but I'm over that now. You're not responsible for Luke's actions."

Hannah put her hand over mine and squeezed it. "I'm so sorry you're hurting. I would do anything to make this better for you."

"I know that, Hannah. I really do." I squeezed her hand back and then took another sip of my wine. "Your hearts were in the right place. I just wish I could say the same for Luke."

"Charlotte, I know you don't want to hear me defending him but I kind of understand where Luke was coming from. You know how he is. He feels responsible for everyone. It's part of what makes him a good doctor."

"Maybe that makes him a good doctor, but it certainly didn't make him someone I could trust. Look, what happened between me and Luke is old news. The past. Nothing can change that. He made his decisions and now we all have to live with them."

"I know you don't mean that. I saw you two together, remember? I know what you meant to each other. I know how much you loved him. Maybe even still do. Things have changed."

"Not for me, they haven't."

"Why? You're both free now. Are you saying you don't still have feelings for him? I know better."

"Sometimes that's not enough. There's another person involved now." I saw Hannah's questioning look. "Darcy, remember? The kid that caused this whole thing?"

"Surely, you don't resent her."

"No, resent is the wrong word. But I see her and I see the woman that he left me for. I know it's not rational but it's how I feel. I don't see that changing."

Hannah turned away and busied herself wiping off the countertop. "If you say so."

Something told me not to trust that statement but I pretended to believe her. If I knew Hannah, I hadn't heard the last of this. She would just find another way to champion Luke's cause. She was a lot like Auntie in that way.

A few uncomfortable seconds ticked by. I swirled my wine in its glass and decided to change the subject.

"Hannah, I wonder if I should say anything to Auntie about this thing with Farrell. Maybe she shouldn't have anything done to her by him right now."

"Why? Because of the lawsuit? Charlotte, these things can go on for years. Besides, it might not even go anywhere. Don't say anything to her. I probably shouldn't have told you, either. Forget I mentioned it, okay? Sean will say I was speaking out of turn. He hates it when I talk about legal stuff." She took another sip of her wine. "But that's not the reason I asked you in here."

"There's more?" I couldn't imagine what else Hannah had up her sleeve.

"Yeah, there is." Hannah took another sip. I knew her. She was stalling.

"Hannah, what?"

"Will you help me work that party at Farrell's house?"

My mouth dropped open. "You're kidding."

"No, I'm not. Look, it's going to be pretty big, bigger than I'm used to." Hannah's words were coming in a torrent now. She was obviously afraid to stop for fear I would say no. "From what I understand, he's hiring some wait staff but I'm still going to need help in the kitchen and with getting food set up and put out. The kinds of things his friend ordered need to be timed just right so I have to stay for most of the party. It's a big break for me. Please? It's Saturday afternoon. Auntie won't mind if you leave her for a few hours."

"But she might have her cath on Friday."

"And she'll be fine, probably home by that night."

"I don't know. I don't know anything about catering."

"You don't have to know anything. The food will already be prepared. It's mostly just warming and setting up. And I'll be there. You'll be helping me. It will only be for a few hours. You'll be home by supper time. Besides, it will be fun to work together. What do you say? Come on." She poured me some more wine.

"Plying me with alcohol isn't going to help."

"Sure, it will."

"You're devious and conniving. You know that, right?" I was softening and Hannah smelled a victim.

"Yes, that's why you love me. Is that a yes?"

I took another sip and nodded. "I just know I'm going to regret this but, yes. I'll help you."

Hannah whooped and raised the wine bottle in the air.

"Ladies and gentlemen, we have a winner."

A few minutes later, arm in arm, we joined the others on the deck. I spent the rest of the evening laughing and sharing a meal with old friends, all thoughts of Luke and Doctor Farrell and heart surgery on hold.

Auntie and I stayed longer than I thought we would. After the kids went to bed, we retired to the living room and Sean put on a CD of some old tunes. One of them reminded me of the days when he and Hannah had first started dating, back when everything was still hopeful for Luke and me, too. Between the wine and the music, I felt my earlier resolve about Luke slipping. I found myself daydreaming about Luke and wondering if I had been too harsh with him at lunch. Maybe Hannah was right. Maybe I should rethink my position. Had it only been earlier that day when he dropped his news on me? It felt like an eternity.

"Charlotte?" Auntie said.

"What? I'm sorry, I was distracted."

"So, I noticed. I said I think we should head out. I'm having trouble keeping my eyes open."

Hannah walked us out to the car.

"It's going to be okay," she whispered when she hugged me good night. Something told me she wasn't referring to the catering job.

Auntie was very quiet on the way home. I assumed she was thinking about her upcoming surgery and I thought I would just let her be for a while. It wasn't until we were back in her driveway that she spoke.

"I'm sorry, Charlotte," she said. "I'm a meddlesome old woman and I should have told you about Luke a long time ago. I didn't mean to hurt you. I honestly thought it would work out between you two."

I looked at Auntie and my heart melted. There was no way I could stay upset with her and I needed to make her feel better. I didn't want her to go into this procedure with any doubts about my feelings for her.

"Auntie, it's okay. I'm not angry. Now that I have had a chance to get over the shock, I know you meant well. This will work out. Luke and I aren't starry-eyed kids anymore. He did what he felt he had to do and that's that. All I care about now is you. If Luke can help us help you, all the better."

By now, I had pulled the car into the garage and I could hear Sam barking his greeting in the house. I turned the car's ignition off. I reached over in my seat and hugged Auntie. I could feel her trembling and my eyes watered. There was no way I was going to allow her to be hurt by all this.

"Let's get some sleep. We have a big day ahead of us tomorrow."

Chapter Twelve

For all my brave words, my stomach was in knots as I sat in Luke's waiting room with Auntie the next morning. This was not going to be as easy as I had thought. I was keenly aware that Luke could walk through the waiting room at any moment. Granted, it was more likely that he was already back in his office or one of the exam rooms with a patient, but it still sent my mind whirling that at that very moment he was literally just feet from me.

Every time, a nurse opened the door to the waiting area and called for a patient, my entire nervous system was given a jolt. I needed to get a grip if I was going to survive the morning here.

"Camille Monti."

"That's me." Auntie stood.

"This way, please."

I stood to follow Auntie.

"It's okay, Charlotte. I can go back by

myself."

"I know you can, Auntie. I want to go with you."

Auntie's expression told me how grateful she was, and we followed the technician back to the lab. On the way, we passed Luke's office, but the door was closed. I wondered if he was with a patient or had shut it on the chance that I would pass it and he didn't want to run into me. I decided I was being foolish and making more of this than I needed to.

Auntie sat on the chair the technician indicated and I stood in the doorway.

"Mrs. Monti, my name is Lisa and I understand we're going to be drawing some blood today to get you ready for a cardiac catheterization. Is that correct?"

"Yes."

"Okay, can you verify your birth date for me?" Auntie told her and Lisa then started to gather the tubes she needed.

"I'm sure you've had this done before," she said as she tightened the tourniquet around Auntie's left arm. Auntie nodded.

I turned away as the needle was pushed into Auntie's vein. Even though I had done the very act that Lisa was now doing many times, it upset me to watch Auntie's blood being siphoned off. When I turned away, I saw the door to Luke's office open. I watched as a young woman exited and then my throat caught as I saw Luke walk out behind her. He didn't see me; he was still talking to his patient. He put his hand on her shoulder and she shook her head. He said something else to her and she nodded. They shook hands and she walked off in the direction of the check-out desk.

As Luke turned to go back inside his office, he looked up and our eyes met. I saw his expression change as he realized it was me. He took a half-step toward me and then immediately changed his mind. Without another word, he turned, went inside his office, and closed the door.

I was amazed at the depth of sadness and disappointment I felt. It made no sense. I had told myself it was over between us and here I was upset that he agreed.

"There we are. All done." Lisa removed the tourniquet and placed a small bandage on Auntie's arm.

"Thanks." Auntie stood to leave and then fell back in the chair. She put her hand to her head. "I think I feel funny," she said.

I immediately went to Auntie's side. "Are you okay?"

Lisa grabbed a blood pressure cuff and wrapped it around Auntie's skinny arm. She grabbed a stethoscope, pumped up the cuff and listened. "Her blood pressure's a little low. You fasted for your blood work this morning, right?"

Auntie nodded.

"Her blood sugar is probably low. Let me get her something." Lisa left and within seconds came back with a small glass of orange juice. "Here, drink this, Mrs. Monti. It should help." She turned to me. "You should probably get her some breakfast as soon as you leave here."

"Thanks, I will."

Auntie leaned on my arm as I walked her back out to the reception area and helped her to a seat in the waiting room.

"I feel so foolish," she said as she lowered herself into one of the chairs.

"Don't be silly," I said. "You just need some food. Sit here a minute while I square the bill."

I verified Auntie's insurance at the front desk and grabbed the receipt. I turned to walk back to where Auntie was sitting and stopped in my tracks. There was Luke, kneeling in front of Auntie. He had his hand on her knee and was speaking softly to her. It was obvious the two had a relationship and I wondered again how much Auntie had been keeping from me.

While I fought with my emotions and tried to decide what to do, I saw Luke extend his hand to Auntie and help her up. At that point, Auntie caught me staring at them. Luke sensed her tense and turned in my direction.

"I was telling Camille that I wanted to bring her back to my office for a minute and look her over," Luke said to me. "I don't like that she almost fainted."

"Sure, okay, fine," I stammered.

I stood there while Auntie and Luke walked past me. Luke turned, "Come with us, Charlotte. I didn't mean for you to stay here."

"Oh, I – it's all right."

Auntie grabbed my hand and dragged me along with them. "For a smart girl, she's awfully dumb sometimes."

When we reached Luke's office, he motioned for us to take the two chairs opposite his desk. He grabbed his stethoscope and listened to Auntie's chest. I tried to avert my eyes but no matter where I looked, I was overwhelmed with Luke - Luke's desk, Luke's pictures on Luke's desk, Luke's books on Luke's bookshelf, Luke's jacket hanging on a hook behind Luke's door. I was finding it hard to breathe and was afraid I was going to be the one to faint next.

Mercifully, Luke stood and started to speak to Auntie.

"I think everything's okay, Camille. I don't hear anything concerning."

"I'm sure it's just because I haven't eaten anything yet. Charlotte and I were going to go get some breakfast."

"That's probably a good idea."

"I think I'm just nervous about the cath coming up. I wasn't really expecting it. I was expecting some prescription, not surgery."

"Well, a cath isn't really surgery per se but I know what you mean."

There were a few seconds of uncomfortable silence and then all three of us started to talk at once. Auntie put up her hand.

"Look, I'm old and I have nothing to lose. So, listen up, both of you. This whole thing is ridiculous. Instead of burying the hatchet in each other, I think you should both sit down like two rational human beings and talk." She turned to Luke. "Charlotte is stubborn, you know that. She gets her feelings hurt and she gets nutso."

I opened my mouth to speak but Auntie shot me a look that made me close it again. She turned back to Luke. "And Luke, you're no better. You get ideas in your head and you don't listen to anyone. Now, I'm wrong for not telling Charlotte about you before she came out here but what's done is done. She's going to be here for at least another week and a half. Make the most of it. I'll be in the waiting room."

And she left.

Luke and I stared at each other for a second and then both of us laughed nervously.

"I guess we've been told," he said.

"Well, Auntie has never been one to hide what she felt. That's what I love about her."

"So."

"So." I stared at the carpet.

"Look, Charlotte, I know what you're feeling. I really do."

I started to answer but Luke put his hand up. "Let me finish. I know this is a lot to absorb. I'm sorry. So sorry. I never wanted to hurt you. I bungled this whole thing. Then and now. If I could undo all of it, I would." He looked over at his desk and I saw that the picture of the woman and baby had been removed. A more recent picture of Darcy on horseback sat in its place. "Well, maybe not all of it. Darcy is an amazing woman."

"Look, Luke, I didn't come out here to mess up your life. I had no idea you were even here."

"I know that."

"What I mean is, I'm only going to be here for a little while, just until I know Auntie is all right. We can tolerate each other until then. Maybe even fake it a little, for Auntie's sake."

Luke took a step toward me. "Charlotte, I'm not faking how I feel about you. Now that I've seen you again… I know I still have strong feelings for you. I – I still love you."

I took a step back. "Please, don't. I don't need this complication now."

"Loving me is a complication?"

He kept walking toward me. I could feel my

resolve melting. I knew if he touched me, I wouldn't be responsible for my actions.

"Luke, I mean it. I don't want to start things again."

"I know. I understand. It's over between us." He was standing right in front of me and I could smell his cologne, feel the heat from his body.

"Right, it's over. We're over."

Luke pulled me into his arms. "All over," he said.

Was he referring to us or my ability to resist him? I put my hands on his chest to push him away. I could feel his heart beating beneath his shirt. His arms encircled me. Instinctively, my arms went around him, too. Then his mouth – his sweet mouth - met mine and the years just melted away. He kissed me, tentatively at first and when I didn't pull back, he kissed me again. His tongue brushed my lips and then softly reached further.

I kissed him back with an intensity that took me by surprise. Those dreams were happening in real life now. I moaned as his hands caressed and touched places that remembered. Remembered love, passion, hope.

"Charlotte," Luke said, his voice gruff with emotion. "I want you."

There was a sharp knock on the door and I hastily pushed Luke away when I heard his office door click open.

"Doctor Luke?" said a male voice.

Chapter Thirteen

ଔ

Luke turned to the visitor and I quickly pretended to look at something on his desk. I took this opportunity to grab the picture frame containing Darcy's picture. I turned it over and gazed into eyes that left no doubt whose child she was.

"Yes, what is it?" Luke said. I sensed irritation in his voice.

"The lab work just came back on Mrs. Henshaw. Marjorie said you wanted to see it."

"Sorry, yes, I did ask for that, didn't I? Thanks." I heard paper rustle and took this as my chance to check out who had interrupted the most important moment in my life. I sat in the chair that Aunt Camille had previously occupied and casually turned to watch Luke and the intruder. I shyly smiled at him while Luke looked over the slip of paper that he had handed him. I immediately recognized him as Vince, Dr. Farrell's assistant. He had been the one who had taken care of Auntie just yesterday. Vince smiled back at me, but I couldn't tell if he recognized me or not. I decided not to say anything and silently wished for him to leave as soon as possible.

"Has Mark seen these?" Luke asked him.

"No, he's at the hospital making rounds," Vince said.

"Okay, this can wait until he comes back. Thanks."

Vince left. Luke turned to me and smiled. "Now, where were we?"

"You were about to complicate my life," I said.

Luke sat in the chair next to me and took my hand.

"Charlotte, give me a chance. Please. Give us a chance."

"What does that mean?"

"I honestly don't know. Why don't we just spend some time together and see what happens? Go out with me. Let's talk, really talk and see how we feel. Then, if you honestly think we don't have a future, I'll let you go."

"You're going to leave this all up to me?"

"Of course. You can trust me."

"Famous last words." Luke was softly rubbing my hand and I was finding it impossible to think. "Okay, let's say for a minute that I go along with this idea, what then?"

"For starters, have dinner with me."

"When?"

"How about this weekend?" That was in two days! Then, I remembered the party I had promised to help Hannah with.

"I can't," I said. "I promised Hannah I'd

help her with a party she's catering on Saturday afternoon. I don't know when I'll be finished with that. And Auntie's cath is tomorrow. I want to be with her."

"How about Saturday night after Hannah's party? I don't care what time. You call me when you're back home."

Damn! Instead of putting things off, Luke was going full speed ahead. He was probably afraid I'd change my mind. I didn't answer and Luke pounced on my silence.

"What do you say?"

"I don't know, Luke. I hate leaving Auntie alone like that."

I looked at the carpet. I knew if I met Luke's eyes I would lose my resolve.

"She'll be okay. We won't be far away. She'll be all right. Don't tell me you don't want to. I can feel that you do." His fingers were making their way up my arm and I was having serious trouble thinking.

"I'm afraid, Luke."

"Of what?"

"This. Of us. The future. This makes no sense. Yesterday I was ready to throw something hard at you and now I find myself wanting to start things up again. I don't know if I can do this."

"Charlotte, I know how I feel about you. You can't imagine all the thoughts that have been going through my mind ever since Camille told me you were coming back."

"See? That's just it. I'm not coming back. That's Auntie's fantasy. I came out here because she needed me and because she promised to help me with my divorce. I have a life, Luke. A life I'm not willing to throw away on a whim."

"Am I a whim?" Luke had my hand in his and was drawing lazy circles up my arm. I could feel goose bumps forming and it was becoming increasingly harder to think. I pulled my hand back.

"I should get back to Auntie."

"What about Saturday night?"

"Let me think about it."

"Well, you didn't say No. That's a start." We both stood and Luke pulled me toward him. We kissed, more fervently than before. I felt my resolve melting and pushed him away.

"I really need to get back to Auntie."

Luke sighed. "Okay, let me walk you out."

Luke hugged me again. He tilted my chin toward him and looked at me with an intensity I had missed so much.

"I can't believe you're back in my life," he said.

We found Auntie sitting in the waiting room reading a magazine. She looked fine now. I wondered if this had all been a ploy to get Luke and me together. Was she that devious? I dismissed the thought and decided to blame the orange juice for her improvement. Not even Auntie was that warped.

Luke touched my elbow and whispered, "I'll call you tonight." Then he turned and went back to his office.

Auntie smiled at me when I approached her. She put the magazine down on the little table next to her chair and stood up. There was no hint of unsteadiness.

"Everything better?" she said.

"Let's just go eat before I kill you."

Chapter Fourteen

℃3

Over breakfast, Auntie drilled me about what had happened with Luke after she left. I tried side-stepping her questions, but she wouldn't let it drop.

"Are you going to see him?"

"I don't know."

"Did he ask?

"Yes."

"Well?"

"Well, what?"

"What did you say?"

"I said I'd think about it."

"Good. So, what are you going to wear?"

"I don't know, Auntie. Aren't you listening? I said I'd think about it."

"What is there to think about? You still love him, right?"

"It's more complicated than that."

"It's not complicated. You're making it

complicated. You love Luke. He loves you. Neither of you is married now. End of story."

I looked at her. "Are you serious? Where have you been these last twenty odd years? You know how hurt I was when Luke left me. Things have happened in between. I can't just sweep that all away as if it never happened."

Auntie put her fork down and laid her hand over mine. "Charlotte, I'm not trying to make light of this. I'm really not. I just want you to be happy. I worry about you. I love you and I know you and Luke are good together. I also know how stubborn you can be especially when you're faced with backing down. You hung in with Peter long after you should have kicked his butt to the curb. You let your pride get the better of you sometimes. You can be your own worst enemy."

I sighed. When Auntie was right, she was right. I had known it was over with Peter long before I admitted it. Was she right about Luke, too? Was I just being stubborn and throwing away a chance for real happiness with a man I still loved?

Auntie took my sigh for agreement. She patted my hand and grabbed her fork again. "See? You know I'm right."

I didn't answer her that time and decided to let it go.

What did it matter anyway? Luke and I had taken steps to consider the possibility that we might get back together. To say I was willing to hope was putting it mildly. Auntie, for her part, was happy and seemed to think it was just a matter of time before all was well again.

After breakfast, Auntie said she felt like she needed a nap. I drove her home and she immediately went to her room, followed by her dog and cat.

I, on the other hand, felt like my emotions were spinning. Despite my reluctance to believe that Luke and I had a ghost of a chance, thoughts of him and our kisses in his office wouldn't give me any peace. I needed Hannah to help me sort it all out. I called her on my cell.

"Hey, Charlotte. What's up?"

"Hannah, can I come over? I need to talk to you about something that happened this morning."

"Is Camille okay?"

"She's fine. Probably going to outlive both of us if I don't strangle her first."

"Uh-oh. What happened?"

"You don't know the half of it. I don't want to go into it on the phone. It's really kind of good, actually. I think. I don't know. Hannah, I really need to talk to you."

"Okay, now, I'm curious. Get your butt over here. Besides, I could use an extra hand anyway. You can help me get all this stuff together for Farrell's party while we talk."

On the drive over to Hannah's, my cell phone rang. It was Luke.

"I'm distracted," he said. "I can't stop thinking about you. Have lunch with me."

"Luke, I can't. I'm on my way over to Hannah's right now. And how did you get this number?"

"I just called Camille's hoping to catch you there. She gave me the number."

"I'm surprised it took her this long."

"She just loves you and wants what's best for you. That would be me, by the way. Charlotte, please meet me. We really need to talk."

"I can't just ditch Hannah." By this time, I was pulling into Hannah's driveway. I heard voices in the background on Luke's end and heard him sigh.

"I'll be right there," Luke said to someone in his office. "Okay, Charlotte, looks like I've got to go anyway. I'll call you later. Have fun with Hannah. Tell her Hi for me."

"I will. Bye."

"Bye, baby." And he was gone.

But "baby" lingered in the air. I hadn't heard Luke call me that in years.

I walked into Hannah's kitchen with the world's cheesiest grin on my face.

"Okay, I remember that smile. Spill it. No, wait. Something tells me I need to sit down for this."

Hannah poured two cups of coffee. She placed one in front of me and grabbed the other for herself. Then she sat down at the breakfast bar opposite me.

"Okay, tell me every blessed detail."

Over the next few minutes, I told Hannah everything that had happened that morning up to the phone call just minutes before. When I finished, she just stared at me for a few seconds.

"Wow," she said finally. "I can't believe this. It's like a TV movie. What are you feeling?"

"That's just it. I don't know. On the one hand, I'm as skeptical as hell. I mean, it's been years with no word. I had gotten used to the idea that Luke was out of my life forever. I came out here with every intention of going back to New York with enough money to buy my house and start over – alone. Now - I don't know. I keep having these memories of what it was like before. I was so in love with Luke." My voice caught in my throat and I took a sip of coffee to forestall tears that I was afraid would start. "What do you think?"

"I think you know what I think. I think you should give Luke a chance. I know he still loves you. The first words out of his mouth when he saw me were 'How's Charlotte?'."

I sighed. "This is so hard."

"Why does it have to be? You don't have to make any decisions right now. You're over-thinking this."

"Am I? What about Darcy? I can't get past looking at her and seeing his dead wife, the woman he left me for. What was her name?"

"Cathy."

"Yes, Cathy, the woman who couldn't master birth control." Hannah winced. "What's the matter? I can't speak ill of the dead? That woman ruined my life. I was supposed to marry Luke, remember? Not her."

"I know, Charlotte, I know. But what's done is done now. And Darcy is a really nice person."

"I'm sure she is but I'm not too anxious to have a relationship with another woman's child again. I've done that and look where it got me."

Hannah reached across the counter and took my hand. "I wish I could make this all better for you. All I can say is that Luke is a terrific father and I really think you should give Darcy a chance. And this is entirely different. It's not like you have to raise her. She's already grown and will probably be out on her own soon."

"I don't know. Sometimes, you just can't go

home again. Maybe it's time for Luke and I to just
realize that too much has happened and move on."

"Is that what you really want?"

"Honestly? No."

Hannah got up and put her half-drunk cup of
coffee in the sink.

"I think you should just go out with him and
see what happens. You're putting too much pressure
on yourself. What happened between you and Peter
has nothing to do with you and Luke. Peter was a
shithead from the beginning."

Hannah had never liked Peter and made no
pretense of hiding it, then or now.

"Maybe you're right. One date couldn't hurt,
right? Maybe I'll find that I don't even care for
Luke anymore."

Hannah frowned. "You're not serious."

"No, but let's just pretend for now, okay? It
makes my life easier."

"Okay, how about some real help then? We
need to make some trays of little quiches."

"You're kidding, right? I thought I would be
making bowls of dip and stuff."

Hannah put her hand to her chest and
feigned pain. "I'm crushed. 'Hannah's Heavenly
Treats' wouldn't be caught dead just serving dip
and stuff, as you so eloquently stated. We're more
sophisticated than that." She grabbed an apron from
a hook on the wall by the stove and tied it around
my waist. "Welcome to the world of culinary
delights."

I looked at my friend expecting her to break
into a laugh at any moment but the look on
Hannah's face told me she wasn't kidding. "You
take this cooking thing really seriously, don't you?"

"Stick with me, kiddo. I'll have you challenging Martha Stewart before the afternoon is over."

Hannah and I rolled dough and made filling for the next two hours. After I got the hang of what we were doing, I found myself getting into a rhythm and enjoying myself. I could see why Hannah liked her business so much and it was fun watching her shine in her element.

When the first batch came out of the oven, we took a couple of samples and some iced tea and sat out on the deck for a quick lunch.

"I don't know why you aren't as big as a house, eating like this all the time," I told her as I swallowed my second little quiche.

Hannah leaned back into her deck chair and put her feet up on another one. "The answer is simple. Twins. I challenge any woman to gain weight while rushing after those two." Hannah sipped her tea. "Do you miss not having any kids?"

I was startled by the sudden question and would have resented being asked that by anyone other than Hannah.

"Yes," I said. I thought about Beth and how much I missed her. "I always just assumed being a mother would be part of my life. I loved Beth but I really wanted a child of my own. The timing was just never right with Peter, though. First, he said it was too soon, he didn't want to upset Beth right after we were married. Then, he wanted to make more money. Then, I had miscarriages and a hysterectomy. Now, with the divorce, I guess I'm glad it didn't happen."

"I still don't know how you didn't kill Peter in his sleep when you found out. I can't picture you taking all this so calmly. I can't imagine how I would react if I found out Sean had some chippie somewhere."

"Oh, I was angry, believe me. I'm missing some lovely figurines that fell victim to that first night."

"I'm sorry I wasn't there for you, Charlotte." Hannah and Sean were going through his heart crisis right around the time that Peter moved out.

"That's all right, Hannah. I understood then and I understand now. Sean needed you. You couldn't possibly have left him alone then. And it's going to work out. Auntie's going to give me the money for the house and life will go on."

Hannah gave me that look again.

"Or not," she said.

I sighed. "Or not."

"Look at me, Charlotte. This is me, Hannah, you're talking to. You can fool a lot of people but I know you. I sat up nights with you when you cried your eyes out over Luke. I know what you felt, what I know in your heart you still feel. Don't kid yourself. If you go out with Luke, you're going to be right back where you were twenty years ago."

"Did you hear what you just said? Twenty years ago. That's a lifetime. I'm not the same person I was then. And neither is Luke."

"Some things never change."

"We'll see."

"Well, regardless of what happens or doesn't happen, I'm here for you."

"Thanks."

The phone rang and Hannah quickly looked at her watch. "Shit, I bet that's the twins."

She put her glass of iced tea on the deck table and rushed into the kitchen. I knew immediately from her tone of voice that it was indeed one of the twins. I picked up her glass and mine and followed her inside.

"Didn't I tell you about calling me and changing plans at the last minute, Frances? And why are you calling me from Gloria's phone?" Each of the twins apparently had their own cell phone. "Don't give me that. Did you think you could play that game with me? I'm your mother. I can tell you two apart from miles away. You'd better find your phone before you come home, young lady, or you're going to be very sorry."

Hannah listened to her daughter obviously giving an impassioned plea for something that Hannah was disapproving of.

"Let me talk to Darcy." A few seconds went by while Darcy was fetched.

"Hi, Darcy. I'm sorry to bother you. I guess the twins want to stay for dinner. I don't want them bothering you. I think they should come home tonight. It's a school night."

Darcy was now obviously pleading the twins' case.

"I see. Well, if you really think they won't be a bother. All right. I'll have Sean pick them up at seven-thirty. Thanks." She hung up.

"What was that about?" I tried to keep the curiosity out of my voice, knowing full well she had been speaking to Luke's daughter.

"The girls want to stay for dinner with Darcy. I guess they have some science project they're both working on and Darcy offered to help them with it."

"Did Frances lose her phone?"

"Yeah, Frances lost hers and called me on Gloria's phone and tried to pass herself off as Gloria. Even though those two are identical, they have different personalities. Frances is definitely the ringleader. She gets into more trouble than Gloria but she thinks she's so clever." She shook her head. "See what I meant before?"

I nodded. "She reminds me of you when you were her age."

Hannah smiled. "Maybe that's why she doesn't fool me."

"And why you're so proud of her, too?"

"Yup, that, too." Hannah placed our glasses of in the sink. "Okay, break's over. Back to work."

Auntie was awake and making dinner for Sam when I got home.

"Feeling better?" I asked.

"Much." She placed a bowl of kibble mixed with wet food on the floor and Sam buried his face in it. Auntie motioned for us to go into the living room.

We sat on the sofa and watched the birds at the feeder through the patio door. I glanced at Auntie, looking for signs of the weakness I had seen that morning and Auntie frowned when she realized what I was doing.

"Charlotte, stop watching me like I'm going to keel over. I have no idea what happened this morning. I've been up for hours and I haven't had a repeat of it."

"Amazing," I said. "One would think one was faking if one didn't know one better, wouldn't one?"

"Charlotte, let's get something straight. I

171

want you to get back with Luke. I'm not going to hide that. But I am not going to act like some old meddlesome lady and fake illness to do it."

I patted her hand. "I think the ship has sailed on the meddlesome thing, Auntie. But thanks, I appreciate you being honest with me."

"Farrell's office called. My blood work is okay, and they want me to come in tomorrow for the cath. It's all set up. I have to be there at six A.M."

"Are you okay with this? We can get another opinion if you want. I don't think this is something you should rush into."

"No, I want to get it over with. No point in putting it off. It'll be okay. Luke didn't seem to think it was a big deal."

I refrained from telling her about how I thought Luke was sometimes a poor judge of what was and was not a big deal.

Auntie took my silence as agreement. "I was thinking we'd go out to dinner here in town tonight, if you'd like."

"Sounds like fun. Let's do it."

And just like that, things were back to normal between Auntie and me. She didn't even bring Luke up over dinner.

We spent the rest of the day together and simply enjoyed being with each other. The visit finally turned into the one I had envisioned before Luke had made his appearance.

Chapter Fifteen

೦೩

After Auntie went to bed that night, I went out to the deck and sat in the two-seater swing and just breathed in the night air. The jasmine was in bloom and perfumed the air. The full moon had already risen and somewhere in the distance, two owls called back and forth to each other. A bat swooped down low over the pool and caught an evening meal.

Slowly, the thoughts of Luke that I had pushed aside all day, took root in my heart and I allowed myself to think about what it would be like to be with him again. Dare I go out with him? If I said yes, I could be in his arms again very soon. My heart ached to abandon all reason and say yes. But was I leaving myself open for heartache? A wound that had long ago healed should not be re-opened.

While I was busy mentally applauding myself for my clever rational mind, my cell phone, which was buried in my purse, rang. Realizing it was on the kitchen counter, I raced inside to answer it before it went to voice mail.

"Hello?"

"Hello, yourself." It was Luke.

I felt myself smiling like an idiot in the dark kitchen.

"Hi," I said again as I walked back out to the deck.

"So, have you made up your mind? Are you going to make us both happy?"

"You're not wasting any time, are you?"

"We've already wasted enough time. I want to be with you, Charlotte. You know that. It's all up to you."

I sighed. "I don't know. It's just..."

"Just what? You don't love me? You're afraid I don't love you? What?"

"Don't you think it's a bit premature to talk about love?"

"Charlotte, we're not kids. One thing I've learned in the past few years is that life is short. You have to grab what you can when you can."

"That sounds pretty cynical."

"It's not cynical. It's practical. We don't know what's ahead. Just what is. And what is is that I love you. I never stopped loving you. But if that's too much for you right now, okay. I like you. Is that better?"

I smiled again. This was the Luke I knew – and truth be known - I loved.

Had always loved.

Still loved.

Damn!

"Oh, all right. You win. Yes, I'll go out with

you." The words came tumbling out of my mouth before I could stop them.

"Great."

"Of course, that's assuming everything with Auntie is okay after the cath. She comes first."

"Agreed."

I heard something in the distance and Luke said, "Just a minute, sweetie."

"What's the matter? Your girlfriend calling you back to bed?" I felt a jealous pang at just the thought even though I knew it wasn't true.

"No, goofball. That was Darcy. Look, I gotta go. See you tomorrow after Camille's procedure, babe." He blew a kiss into the phone. "Good night."

"Good night." And then I heard the phone click and disconnect.

I sat there for several minutes, listening to the crickets and imagining what a date with Luke would feel like again.

A smile stole its way across my face despite my best intentions.

Chapter Sixteen

☙

The morning started off very early and before my mind and heart were fully aware Auntie and I were in the pre-op area awaiting her cardiac catheterization. I still couldn't shake the fear that this was an unneeded procedure and could have an unwanted outcome.

Auntie, for her part, was looking extremely dwarfed as she sat on the hospital gurney in her oh-so-flattering hospital gown. A nurse was starting an IV in her left arm and Auntie winced at the needle prick.

"The anesthesiologist will be in shortly," she told us both as she taped the intravenous catheter and tubing in place.

"Well," said Auntie after the nurse left. "I guess this is it."

"You can change your mind at any time," I told her.

"I know but we're here now. Might as well see it through."

I was about to object to that irrational line of reasoning when a doctor entered our curtained cubicle. Obviously, he was the aforementioned anesthesiologist.

He extended his hand to both of us. "Hi, I'm George Cagle, the anesthesiologist who'll be taking care of you during your cath." He looked down at the papers on his clipboard and then at Auntie. "Can you tell me your name and date of birth?"

Auntie obliged.

"Good. So, let me explain what's going to happen. In a few minutes, the nurse will come in and give you something in your IV to help you relax. Do you have any allergies?"

"No," Auntie answered.

"Great. Then, when it's time, we will take you back to the cath lab. We'll give you something else to help you doze off during the procedure. We don't do general anesthesia unless it's absolutely necessary. The doctor will numb the area where the catheter will go in and before you know it, you'll be waking up in Recovery. It's not a long procedure and very few patients have any problems at all. Any questions?"

"No", said Auntie. She looked at me and I shook my head. I looked straight at Dr. Cagle. "I'll be honest with you, Doctor. I'm not happy about Auntie having this. I'm not convinced it's necessary."

"Well, I can't answer to that. That's between you and Dr. Farrell." And Dr. Cagle beat a hasty retreat.

The nurse reappeared a few minutes later

with medication that she put into Auntie's IV. Within a few minutes, Auntie's eyes glazed over. She reached for my hand, and we held on to each other. I felt her squeeze my hand and for the gazillionth time that morning I fought back fear.

"I love you," she whispered.

"I love you too."

Then Dr. Farrell's assistant appeared.

"Are we ready?" he said as he pulled the curtain back noisily.

Auntie waved to him. Vince undid the locks on the gurney wheels and angled the gurney out of the cubicle.

Vince looked back at me. "The nurse will show you where you can wait," he said.

And then they were gone, and I was alone. A few minutes later, the nurse who had started Auntie's IV came back and offered to show me to the Surgical Waiting Room.

Once there, I helped myself to some coffee and a cookie. There were a few other people seated around the room including an older gentleman reading a newspaper, a young couple with a small child who was having trouble sitting still despite his parents' best efforts, and one middle-aged woman praying her Rosary.

I didn't want to run the risk of anyone trying to start a conversation so I sat as far away from everyone else as I could. I grabbed a magazine and pretended to read it. I knew it was useless to try but it least it gave me cover.

My thoughts were a jumbled mess. Fear about what could happen to Auntie, anger that she insisted on this, confusion about Luke, memories of my life with Auntie – and yes, with Luke, too. I had no idea how I was going to get through the next hour or so.

I decided I needed to concentrate on something pleasant and so I tried to remember every happy memory I had with Auntie and Uncle Bob. My first day of school, my Prom, my graduation from high school, my graduation from nursing school. Camille and Bob had always been so proud of me. They made me feel as if nothing else mattered to them except my well-being. And I know I took them for granted – as any child would. My life with them was good in spite of its sad start and I had no worries thanks to them. I always knew I was safe as long as I was with them. Truth be told, I had felt that way with Luke too until – until –

And just like that all the feelings that I had buried after Luke had left me came back. Now, I had context which made it even worse. My mind took me to places I didn't want to go – Luke making love to someone else, Luke marrying someone else, Luke having a baby with someone else.

And now he wanted me to just forget all that and pick up where we had left off?

And accept Darcy as if she wasn't a constant reminder of what had happened to us?

I threw the magazine on an end table a little too forcefully. Rosary Lady shot me a disgusted look. I mouthed "Sorry" and decided to go for a walk. It was still going to be a while before Auntie was in Recovery and I needed to clear my head.

I wandered down the hallway away from the waiting room and saw a sign that pointed to a garden. I found the garden easily and sat on a bench near a wall with some bushes beside it and just listened to the birds. I leaned my head against the wall, closed my eyes, and felt a measure of peace steal its way back into my heart. I decided to put all thoughts of Luke aside for now. All that mattered was Auntie. We just needed to get through today and then I could worry about everything else tomorrow.

Chapter Seventeen

 જી

I must have dozed off because I suddenly woke up with a start and for a second didn't even know where I was.

Then – Auntie! Was she all right? No one knew where I was if they needed me. I glanced at my watch and saw that only about twenty minutes had passed. I hurried back to the waiting room.

It was a little more crowded and a little noisier now, but my old seat was still available, so I took it. Rosary Lady was gone, and the little boy was now playing a game on a tablet of some kind.

I was able to read an article in a magazine and was so engrossed I didn't even see Vince walk up to me.

"Excuse me."

I looked up. He was still wearing his OR scrubs and cap.

"I just wanted to tell you that your aunt is in Recovery. We'll be transferring her to Telemetry when she's stable."

"Stable? What? Why? Why isn't she going to a regular floor? What's wrong?"

"Nothing's wrong. She's fine. She just had some cardiac arrhythmias during the procedure, and we want to monitor her. We placed two stents. She had some serious blockages and during the placement she experienced some short bursts of arrythmia. She's stable now and should do just fine. Telemetry is just a precaution. The volunteer" – he pointed to a woman at a desk at the head of the room – "can tell you where she will be transferred." And then he just turned away and left.

I couldn't believe what had just happened. Auntie had not come through this as easily as I had hoped. Now she had the "sticks" we had once joked about and had also suffered some kind of cardiac event. I didn't feel comfortable believing Vince's cavalier description. If this warranted Auntie being transferred to Telemetry for monitoring it was possibly bigger than he was letting on.

And where was the illustrious Dr. Farrell? Why hadn't he come out to talk to me?

I needed answers. My first instinct was to call Luke. I dialed his cell but got his voice mail. He was probably with a patient. I left a message for him to call me as soon as he could and then sought out the volunteer to find out Auntie's room number.

"She'll be going up to Room 326 but she won't be there for a little while yet. She's still in Recovery. Why don't you grab a bite to eat and come back? She might be in her room by then."

I didn't think food would sit very well but I did need a change of scenery before I crawled out of my own skin. I went to the cafeteria, grabbed a coffee, and then headed back to the garden I had found earlier while I waited for Luke to call me back.

Halfway through my coffee Luke called.

"Hey, gorgeous, what's up?"

"Luke, it's Auntie," I blurted out without even saying Hello.

"Charlotte, what's wrong? What's happened?"

"I don't know. She had the cath this morning and Vince just came out and told me that Auntie had an arrythmia and they're transferring her to Telemetry. And she needed two stents. Luke, I'm scared."

"Did you talk to Mark? What did he say?"

"No, the great Dr. Farrell didn't even bother to see me. He just sent his lapdog out."

"Charlotte, I know you don't like him but that doesn't sound like him. I'm sure he had a reason. Probably patient-related. He'll come by soon. But let me see what I can find out. I'm booked solid through the afternoon, but I'll get over there as soon as I can. Why don't you call Hannah? You shouldn't be alone."

"I'll call her but she's probably busy. She has a big event tomorrow, remember? I was supposed to help her with it, but I probably can't now."

"Yeah, I forgot. Look, I'm sure Camille is going to be all right. An arrythmia isn't the end of the world. You know that. Take a deep breath. You can even probably still help Hannah. I'm sorry, sweetie. I gotta go. I'll call later and I'll see you as soon as I can."

Luke was right. I was just panicking for

nothing. I should probably be grateful that Farrell was being so cautious and putting Auntie on Telemetry instead of sending her home as we had hoped.

I finished my coffee and went in search of Auntie's new room. I would just wait for her there.

Chapter Eighteen

ↂ

I must have dozed off in the visitor's chair next to Auntie's bed because I was awakened by the sound of a nurse and an orderly wheeling Auntie into her room.

"Here we are. Looks like you have company already, Camille," the nurse said.

Aunt Camille was sitting up on pillows on the gurney and waved to me. A portable cardiac monitor beeped at her feet. She looked tired but otherwise all right. I rose and went to her. She immediately reached for my hand.

"I told you I would be fine," she said.

"Watch your feet," the orderly said to me.

I stepped back and let them transfer Auntie into her bed.

The nurse unhooked Auntie from the portable cardiac monitor and hooked the leads up to the monitor at her bedside. The screen immediately gave a readout of Auntie's heart rhythm. I was relieved to see that all looked normal.

The nurse saw me looking at the monitor. "She's also being read out at the nursing station too."

"I know. I'm a nurse, too. It's hard to turn it off."

"I understand." She patted Auntie's hand. "You're in good hands."

The orderly adjusted the bedding and handed Auntie the call light button.

"I'm going to give your nurse report now," the nurse said. "It was a pleasure taking care of you. You take care of yourself now. I hope everything goes well." She smiled at me and then they both left, pushing the gurney out the door ahead of them.

I scooted my chair as close to Auntie's bed as I could and held her hand through the side rails.

"Well, now you've gone and done it. Just can't handle not being the center of attention, huh?" I tried smiling but I knew my face betrayed me.

"It's okay, Charlotte," Auntie said. "I'm fine. They're just being careful. I can probably go home this weekend."

"We should have waited. I should not have let you do this. I blame myself. I should know better."

"Stop it. What's done is done. I'm a grown person. This was my choice. And I'm going to be fine. Now, you go home and get some rest. Feed and walk the dog. I'm going to take a nap and I don't need you watching me sleep."

I stood and leaned over the rails to kiss Auntie on the forehead.

"Okay, you win. Get some rest and I

promise to do the same. I'll take care of the furbabies."

Auntie pulled me closer to her and kissed my cheek.

"Good. Come back at suppertime and bring me something good. Vodka would be nice."

I called Hannah as I walked out to the parking lot and my car.

"Hey, Charlotte. What's up? Everything okay?"

"Yes. No. I don't know. I think so."

"Pick one, Sweetie. What's wrong?"

"Auntie had a slight complication during the cath and they admitted her to Telemetry to monitor her."

"No! You're kidding. What happened!"

"She developed an arrhythmia of some kind. I don't have the details. Farrell didn't bother to even speak to me. He sent out his PA and he wasn't full of details."

"Have you called Luke? Maybe he can find out more information."

"I talked to him but he's busy at the office and won't be available for a while. I saw Auntie. She's in her room now and she looks okay and her heart seems to be okay. She's in sinus rhythm now."

"English, please."

"Her heart rate is fine. No signs of trouble. She said she wanted to rest so she sent me home. That's where I'm headed now."

"Okay. You're sure you're all right? You want to come over?"

"No, I'm fine. I know you're busy right now. I'm going to check on the dog and cat and maybe catch a nap myself. I didn't sleep too well last night."

"Want to come for dinner later?"

"No, I'm going to eat with Auntie. Hannah, I hate to have to say this but I'm not sure about tomorrow. Do you have someone else who can help you?"

"I do but it might not come to that. I'm sure Camille is going to be fine. Let's talk tonight after you get home and we'll see what we need to do."

"Okay." I had a feeling I was not going to change my mind, and I also felt bad about letting Hannah down. But Auntie came first, no matter what.

I let Sam out into the back yard and walked around while he sniffed, peed and pooped. My mind kept going in circles. What if Auntie developed a permanent cardiac problem? What could it mean? Would she be okay to live alone? Should I think about extending my stay? Maybe I should move here permanently. By the time Sam was ready to go back inside I had completely rearranged my life. And I knew in my heart I was making more of this than I should. Catastrophizing. I was good at that.

I put fresh kibble in the cat's bowl and decided a nap was the best thing. I was emotionally drained. Besides, I wanted to be at my best so that I could enjoy Auntie's company tonight and see for myself how she was.

I awoke with a start. Snippets of a dream involving Luke were rapidly fading. Buster was sleeping on my pillow, loudly snoring which only added to my momentary confusion. Then it all came back and I shot out of bed. Auntie! I needed to get back to her.

I washed my face to wake myself up and ran a brush through my hair. I remembered Luke had said he would try to stop by Auntie's room at the end of the day, so I reapplied make-up. A girl had to be ready.

On the way to the hospital, I drove through a drive through at Auntie's favorite fast-food place and ordered a cheeseburger and a vanilla shake for her and an iced tea for me. My stomach was in knots, and I just couldn't handle the idea of food.

I found a parking spot right away close to the hospital entrance and within minutes was inside, up the elevator and heading to Auntie's room. As I approached her doorway, I heard conversation and laughter coming from within. I knew Auntie was in a single room so it couldn't be a roommate. Must be her nurse, I thought. Leave it to Auntie to make friends everywhere she went.

"Here I am, Auntie, I brought –" the words caught in my throat.

There, sitting next to Auntie in the chair I had vacated just hours before, was Darcy.

Chapter Nineteen

C3

The look on Auntie's face was like someone who had been caught red-handed cheating on their spouse.

"Hey, Charlotte, look who came to visit," she finally said.

Darcy stood and extended her hand. "Hi, we met at Hannah's."

"Hi. Yes. I remember." I fumbled with the food bags while I shook her hand.

There was an awkward couple of seconds and then Darcy turned to Auntie. "Well, I guess, I should go. I promised Dad a full report. He said he would try to check in on you later this evening after rounds." She bent over the side rails and kissed Auntie on the forehead. "You take care of yourself and get home soon. I'll call you tomorrow. I'll try to stop by if you're still here. Otherwise, I'll see you at home if that's okay."

Darcy's apparent ease with Auntie took me by surprise. I felt resentment rising.

"Call before you come by the house, Darcy. Auntie needs her rest. It might not be a good time if you just pop by."

Darcy seemed surprised by my tone.

"Sure. Whatever you think is best. Good night, Aunt Camille."

"Good night, Sweetie. Thanks for coming by."

After Darcy had gone and I was sure was out of earshot, I gave Auntie my fiercest look. "*Sweetie? Aunt Camille?* You want to tell me what's going on here?"

Auntie tried to look defiant which was a hard look for her to pull off while dwarfed in her hospital bed. The monitor she was hooked up to was now showing an elevated heart rate and was starting to beep occasionally.

A nurse appeared in the doorway.

"Everything okay in here? Mrs. Monti, are you experiencing any symptoms?"

"I'm all right. I was just excited to see my niece. No symptoms."

"All right. I'll be back soon." And she was gone.

I sat in the chair Darcy had vacated. "I'm not trying to get you upset, Auntie, but you have to admit I obviously walked in on something. You seem to be pretty chummy with Luke's daughter."

"I'm not *chummy*, as you put it. You make it sound so sinister. I'm friends with her. I have been friends with her for a while. Ever since Luke and I..." then she stopped. It was obvious she had said more than she cared to.

191

"What? You and Luke what?"

My cell phone rang. I checked the caller ID and saw it was Luke. Uncanny timing.

"Hi, Luke."

"Hey, Char. How's Camille?"

"I'm with her now. She seems fine. Better than fine. Up to her old tricks actually. In fact, I just ran into Darcy. She was visiting when I arrived."

"Oh, good. I asked her to check on Camille for me. I got busy here and wasn't able to get over as soon as I had wanted."

"Yes, Darcy promised to give you a full report."

"Char, are you okay? You sound funny."

"No, I'm fine. Look, can we talk later? Auntie and I were kind of in the middle of something."

"Sure. Maybe you'll still be there when I stop by."

"Yeah, maybe. Talk later." And before he could answer, I ended the call.

"Okay, where were we? What aren't you telling me?"

"There's not a whole lot to tell. I just have known Luke and Darcy for a while, that's all."

"She calls you Aunt Camille. That sounds like more than just a little knowing and certainly more than just a little while."

"Okay, it's been more than a while. It's been a few years."

"A few years!"

"Lower your voice or that nurse will be back in here again."

"A few years?" I whispered as loudly as I could. "What does that mean?"

"It means I've known Luke for quite a while, okay? Since Darcy was little. Since before Cathy died. Almost as long as I've lived out here."

She said the last few sentences quickly, anxious to get the worst out as quickly as possible. Maybe hoping it wouldn't be so bad if she said it fast.

I felt chills run down my legs and was glad I was sitting. I couldn't believe it.

Aunt Camille had been concealing information from me for just about all the time I had been married to Peter. She had known about Luke and about what had happened and why he had left me and had never breathed a word of what she knew to me. The enormity of what she had just confessed was hitting me in waves as I slowly digested this new information.

I felt so betrayed. Auntie – the one person I thought I could trust above all else. The person who had raised me. The person I would give my life for had kept the biggest secret possible from me.

For years! Many years!

Silence passed between us for seconds that seemed like hours, pierced only by the sounds coming from her monitor. I noticed her heart rate was up a little but not as much as before. Good, I was in no mood for that nurse to return just now and risk the possibility of being asked to leave.

I opened my mouth to speak but no words came out. I didn't know what to say, where to begin.

Auntie, for her part, just sat there. She knew me well enough to know that anything she said right now would just make things worse.

I took a deep breath and tried again.

"Tell me everything. Start from the beginning and don't leave anything out."

Auntie looked down at her hands in her lap. She gripped the sheets and twisted them between her fingers. I knew this was hard for her, but I had to know everything. It hurt me to see the pain on her face, but I was hurting too much to let it stop me from making her tell me what she had to. My whole world had been turned upside down in a matter of a few minutes and I had to make some sense of all this. Knowing the truth was the only way.

"I first met Luke about a year or so after he moved out here. A woman that I am good friends with developed a heart problem around that time. Her doctor referred her to a cardiologist, and she asked me to go with her for support. I had no idea who the doctor was. I almost fell over when we walked in and I saw Luke's name. Even then, I told myself it must be another Luke. It couldn't be your Luke."

I winced when Auntie referred to Luke as mine.

"It's true, Charlotte. I always thought Luke belonged with you. I still do."

"Go on."

"Anyway, Hilda – my friend – insisted I go into the exam with her and that's when I saw Luke for the first time. We were both shocked to see each other but we couldn't say much because of Hilda. I could see by the way Luke kept looking at me though that I just knew what he wanted to ask. As we were leaving the office Luke came out to the waiting room and called me back. He asked me if we could talk, and I gave him my phone number. I was torn. I knew you would be upset with me, but I just had to know what had happened. Maybe give him a piece of my mind for you."

Auntie smiled, trying to win me over. I just stared at her. She was not going to get away with what she had done so easily. When I didn't respond, she continued.

"He called me that night and told me the whole story – about Cathy, the baby, how he was so ashamed he had cheated on you and how he felt he had to do what was right for the sake of the child. You know how Luke is always trying to be so responsible."

She stopped. "Aren't you going to say anything?"

"If you're trying to make excuses for Luke and yourself, it's not working. I still can't believe you kept this from me all these years."

"I didn't want to, Charlotte. I felt awful. But you were married to Peter by that time, and I thought you were happy. I didn't think there was any point in disrupting so many lives. What would be accomplished? I didn't want to hurt you all over again."

"Okay, so Luke bared his soul to you. That still doesn't explain Darcy. Why are you so chummy with her?"

"After that first conversation, Luke and I just became friends. He invited me over to his house and –"

"Are you kidding me?" I almost shouted again and caught myself. "Are you serious?" I asked, trying to keep my voice down.

"I know it sounds weird. But I always liked Luke. He and his wife were really nice to me, and we just fell into it. Darcy was little and she took a liking to me too. I became "Aunt" Camille without any of us meaning for it to happen. And, honestly, being close to Luke made me feel close to you. I know it's weird, but I always saw you two as a couple. I saw how he was with Cathy and it just wasn't the same. I think he loved her, but he wasn't *in love* with her. There's a difference. He never looked at her the way he always looked at you."

"That doesn't matter, Auntie. He made his choice. And it wasn't me."

"I know, Sweetie. I know he hurt you. But you also know how Luke is. He did what he did out of obligation. Even if it hurt himself."

"I'm afraid to ask – did Hannah know about Luke all the time she's been living out here? Has she been lying to me too?"

"No, she met Luke when she said she did – when Sean got sick last year. That's when she found out how long Luke and I knew each other. Luke didn't even know she was out here until Sean's episode. I felt it was easier if I just kept everyone in the dark about each other. Hannah and I talked about telling you then. We knew we needed to. But I didn't know how. And then I was able to talk you into visiting. You know the rest."

"Yeah, I sure do." I got up finally and paced around the room.

My mind was racing so fast. Feelings were falling all over themselves. I was angry with Auntie, but I could also understand why she did what she did.

I had no idea what to do with this new information. It was too much to digest all at once.

196

Chapter Twenty

☙

I stayed with Auntie for about an hour after our uncomfortable conversation. She enjoyed the food I had brought for her, but we were awkward with each other, and conversation was stilted.

Luckily, Luke never came by while I was there although I jumped every time someone came near the room. The last thing I wanted to handle was a conversation with him and Auntie. I caught Auntie looking at the doorway several times and I knew she didn't want to see Luke either. At least, not while I was there.

Soon, I excused myself, claiming feeling tired. I know we were both relieved to see me go.

My mind was a jumble of thoughts as I drove home to Auntie's house. I had no idea how I was going to get through an afternoon working with Hannah without saying something. Yet, the last thing I felt I could do right now was talk about what

I had just learned.

I still didn't feel like eating anything when I got home so instead, I poured myself a glass of wine. Probably not a good idea on an empty stomach so I grabbed a box of crackers and took Sam outside. He quickly did his business and then curled up at my feet on the deck while I swung back and forth on the swing, drank, and thought.

After half an hour I called Hannah. We needed to talk about her catering job for tomorrow.

"Hey, Charlotte. How are you?"

"I'm not sure, if you really want to know."

"Why? What's wrong? Is Camille all right?"

"Oh, she's fine. More than fine probably. But she's in a world of trouble." I told Hannah what I had learned just a short while ago.

Hannah was quiet on her end.

"So, you did know all along."

"Only after I met Luke as Sean's doctor. After that, I went right over to Camille's thinking I was telling her something new and then she confessed that she had known for years. I was as shocked as you are right now. I had no idea she was keeping that information from all of us. Frankly, I didn't think she was capable of that. I begged Camille to tell you, but she refused. She said you were too unhappy with everything that was going on with Peter and she didn't want to lay one more thing on you. She figured she would find a way to get you out here and then tell you face to face. When the issue of the house came up, she used that excuse."

I sighed.

"What are you thinking, Char?"

"I don't know what to think. I know Auntie

just wants me to be happy but the fact that she could be this sneaky really shakes me. I don't know how I can ever look at her and Luke again and not ever wonder what else they're hiding from me. Especially Luke."

"Don't do this, Charlotte. You have a chance right now that few people ever get. Don't blow it."

"I just can't help feeling that it's just too late. Too much has happened and now it's even tainted by lies and deception."

"You're being overly dramatic. It's tainted by love. People care about you and want you to be happy."

"Well, that's a story for another day. Right now, my concern is Auntie. I just want to get her home and make sure she's all right before I go back home."

"You're still leaving?"

"Yes. Maybe. I don't know. I'll think about it tomorrow. Right now, I'm tired and I've had too much wine. I need to go to bed. What should we do about tomorrow?"

"Well, if you can give me a few hours in the afternoon to get everything over there and set up, I have someone who can help us. She can stay and help me clean up my stuff afterwards if you want to leave early."

"Okay, what time should I be at your place?"

"How about Noon? The party starts at two and you can leave a little after four if that works for you."

"Okay, see you then. Good night."

We hung up and I laid my head back on the

swing and closed my eyes. I knew I should get up. If I sat there any longer, I was in danger of falling asleep in mid swing.

My phone interrupted my dozing.

It was Luke.

What was I going to say to him?

"Hello?"

"Hi, Charlotte. I'm sorry I missed you tonight. I was really looking forward to seeing you but by the time I got to Camille's bedside, you were long gone. And she was asleep, so I didn't wake her. I was very disappointed though."

"I was tired. I needed to get home."

"Charlotte, you okay? You don't seem like yourself."

"I'm not. Auntie and I had a very disturbing conversation."

"About what? Tell me what's wrong."

"I'm not sure I want to get into it tonight. I'm beat. Can we do this tomorrow? I'll call you when I get back from helping Hannah."

"Call me? I thought we had a date."

"I don't think that's a good idea."

"What do you mean? Charlotte, I don't like where this is going. What happened tonight? Why won't you talk to me?"

"Luke, don't make me do this now."

"Charlotte, talk to me or I'm coming over. Your choice."

"Oh, all right. Aunt Camille told me about you and her. About how she's known about you all these years. She told me everything. And frankly, I don't know if I want to see you right now. My feelings are all over the place."

"What does that even mean? Okay, so

Camille kept our friendship from you. How does that affect anything between us now? It doesn't change anything. I still love you and I know you feel the same about me."

"I don't know. I can't explain it. It just does. I just feel like there is nothing but deception surrounding everything about us. Even more than before. It just makes your life with Cathy and Darcy more real. Darcy was there when I first arrived at the hospital, and she called Auntie 'Aunt Camille'. It was obvious there was this long-standing relationship there. I felt like an intruder. An outsider. I think I'm always going to feel that way around her. And every time I see her, I see Cathy. It's not rational but I find it hard to be around her. I know she's your daughter and I am probably hurting you to even say this but that's how I feel. She's a constant reminder of what happened between us. How would you feel if things were reversed?"

"I would be hurt. Of course, I would be. But I'd get over it. I'd be able to see the big picture. I would see the second chance that we have, and I would understand."

"Well, then you're a better person than I am, I guess."

"Look, Charlotte, you're tired and it's been a long day. Don't make any decisions tonight. Go help Hannah tomorrow and let's have dinner tomorrow night and at least talk. Let's see if I can't change your mind. I can't give you up a second time. Please don't do this. Please."

I was truly touched by the desperation in Luke's voice. Part of me still cared – so much. I knew that.

Was he right? Was I being too impulsive? What had really changed between us? If I was honest, nothing. It was Auntie who had kept the secret. Her knowing Luke and his family all those years did make it more real for me, but they were real anyway.

I sighed.

"You're right. Okay, dinner tomorrow. I'll call you when I get back home tomorrow evening."

"Great. Good night, Charlotte. And whether you want to hear it or not, I love you."

"Good night." No matter how much I wanted to, I couldn't say the same words back to Luke. Not yet.

I hung up. Sam nudged my knee, and I took him back into the yard and watched while he sniffed rocks and then peed. Then both of us went inside to try to get some sleep.

Chapter Twenty-One

ଔ

After a restless few hours, I finally fell into a deeper sleep and awoke when Sam pushed his wet nose into my face.

"I'm up," I grumbled.

He immediately started wagging his tail when he saw me sit up.

"I know. You're hungry. And you probably have to go potty. Me first."

A half hour later, teeth brushed, dog and cat attended to, hair brushed, and full coffee mug in hand, I finally started to feel human again. I sat in my new favorite spot on the deck swing and just relaxed, listening to the birds and Sam chewing on a dog bone.

I went over the events of the last few hours of the day before, trying to make sense of it all. Hannah was right. Auntie did what she did with only the best intentions. And it didn't change a thing regarding Luke. Except it did make me more aware of all that had happened since the two of us had broken up. I wondered if our getting back together was a silly fantasy. Had too much happened? We weren't the same people anymore. Maybe it was pointless to think otherwise. Maybe I could get Luke to understand that when I saw him at dinner that night. Maybe I should just get Auntie home and better and then fly back home, money in hand as promised. My house would be mine, Peter would be a distant memory, and life would go on.

End of story.

So, why was I not convinced?

My reverie was broken by the sound of my cell phone ringing in my bathrobe pocket. It was Auntie.

"Hi, Auntie. How are you? Everything ok?"

"I'm fine. Everything's good. I was worried about you. We had a rough patch, you and I, yesterday. Are we good?"

"Yes, Auntie. I apologize. We're fine. I had no right to be that way with you. You have done nothing but put me first my whole life and I was being a spoiled brat yesterday. I'm sorry. Forgive me? Please?"

"Nothing to forgive. I'm sorry I kept my news about Luke from you like that. I shouldn't have. You're not a child even though sometimes I still think of you that way. Anyway, I called because I just saw Dr. Farrell's PA. They were going to let me go home today but I had some weakness when I got out of bed this morning, so they want me to stay at least another day. I know you have that thing with Hannah this afternoon so there's no rush for you to come here today at all. I'll be fine. You help Hannah and then go see Luke like you had planned. I'll see you tomorrow."

"Are you kidding? I'm not going to go a whole day without seeing you. I'll stop by on my way over to Hannah's. Are you sure you're all right?"

"I'm fine. Just a little weak. Probably from the medications and staying in bed too much. The nurse was with me when it happened. In fact, I'm up out of bed in the chair right now and I feel great."

"Okay, I'll be by in a couple of hours. Love you."

"Love you, too, Sweetie."

As promised, I visited Auntie on the way to Hannah's house and she was right. She was walking around her room just fine by the time I saw her and I didn't notice anything that made me worry. She was bright and alert and had her usual sparkle in her eye.

She extended her arms and twirled slowly when she saw me.

"See? Good as new."

"Okay, I see that but don't overdo. Sit down. Please."

We chatted for a while and then before I knew it, it was time to go.

I kissed Auntie on the cheek and hugged her.

"I appreciate you, Auntie. I hope you know that."

"I do, Charlotte. Now, run along and go cater the hell out of that party."

On the way out I stopped by the nurse's station and asked to speak with Auntie's nurse. A few minutes later, a young gentleman appeared whose name tag read John and he introduced himself as the nurse taking care of my aunt that day.

After exchanging pleasantries, I asked him about the light-headedness incident that Auntie had shared with me earlier that day. I knew Auntie was famous for downplaying things when it suited her.

"She's right. She did have an episode of weakness when I was getting her out of bed after breakfast. Her knees seemed to buckle. Nothing happened since I was right there to support her. I checked her vital signs, and they were okay. I also checked her heart monitor, and I didn't see anything concerning. She did have some PAC's right around that time but she's fine now. It's hard to know if that was the cause of her weakness. But that's why we're keeping her at least for another day."

I was definitely upset to hear about the change in Auntie's heart rhythm. PAC's – or premature beats – could be a problem and be a precursor to other more upsetting rhythms. Was it caused by the catheterization or was this a good reason for her to have had it? Without further information from the elusive Dr. Farrell there was no way to know. I resolved to find out.

By the time I got to Hannah's, she was already loading trays and coolers into the back of her SUV. Another woman I didn't know was helping her. She had on a uniform - black dress, black hose - that told me she was going to help with serving. I assumed an apron was probably in her car. I learned her name was Amy and she had worked parties like this with Hannah before. The three of us got everything loaded up and then headed out. Hannah led the caravan in her SUV and

Amy and I followed her in our own cars.

Hannah called me on my cell as we drove and gave me a rundown of what we would be serving and how the afternoon was going to go. Dr. Farrell had hired someone to take care of the bar and drinks and the set up – chairs, tables, plates and cutlery, etc. He also had hired a couple of waiters. All we were doing was providing food. In keeping with the catered atmosphere, Amy would do a little of the setting up of the food in the guest area. Hence, the uniform. Hannah was all business as she spoke, and I was both amazed and proud of this side of her.

We arrived at a house that was beyond breathtaking. I hadn't seen many homes in Arizona in all the times that I had visited but I knew there were some mega-homes around. Dr. Farrell's in Scottsdale was apparently one of them. It was two stories, with a circular driveway. Lots of immaculate desert landscaping. Several steps up to the large double front door. Carrying trays inside was going to be a challenge.

For a second, I found myself wondering what Luke's house might look like. I couldn't imagine him in a mansion like this one, but it was possible, I suppose. Dr. Farrell was his partner. They must be making similar salaries.

Hannah and I walked up the front steps while Amy stayed with the cars. Hannah rang the doorbell, and a woman answered the door. She was well-dressed in expensive-looking pants and blouse. Diamond earrings dangled under long blonde hair. Rings flashed on her fingers.

"Yes?"

"I'm the caterer," Hanna said.

"Oh, right. I was beginning to get worried."

I looked at Hannah. We were on time. What was her problem?

"Can you pull around to the side? I'll meet you there and show you into the kitchen."

I wasn't used to being treated like the hired help in such a way, but it didn't seem to faze Hannah. I guess it came with the territory. At least we wouldn't have to traipse up the stairs and through Farrell's mansion with all of our stuff.

Over the next hour or so we worked quickly but efficiently – warming some food, arranging cold items on trays, making some dips. Hannah had the entire process down to a science and I was very impressed seeing this new side of my friend.

Before we knew it, it was show time. Amy put on her apron and grabbed a tray of canapes. Hannah and I filled chafing dishes and arranged some of the mini quiches on trays to be placed on tables arranged in the large great room being used for the party.

Guests were arriving and the room started to buzz with conversation. It was a small gathering, appearing to be mostly people who were acquainted through business as opposed to being personal friends based on the snippets of conversation I overheard as I worked.

Over the next couple of hours, I busied myself in the kitchen. A couple of times I noticed Dr. Farrell through the kitchen doorway. I was sorely tempted to ask him about my aunt, but I knew this wasn't the time. Besides, Hannah would be mortified and this was her livelihood. I had no right to ruin it for her.

I also saw Vince who arrived about an hour

after everyone else. He seemed flushed and anxious, and he caught me staring at him. He smiled weakly and I nodded. I didn't know if he was just being polite or remembered me from the day before.

"Those seem to be going over well," I said to Hannah as she took another tray of little quiches out of the oven.

"Yes, but I do think things are going to slow down at this point. You can leave any time you want."

"Are you sure? I don't want to leave if you need me."

"No, we're fine. Amy and I will only be needed for another hour at most and then we'll gather our things. Dr. Farrell has people who will clean up."

"Okay, I do want to lie down a bit before I meet Luke."

"Charlotte, try to have a good time tonight. Keep an open mind. Life is too short to throw happiness away. Remember what I said. You're being given an opportunity many people wish they could have and never will. Don't waste it."

I thought about Hannah's words as I drove home to Auntie's house. She was probably right. I wished with all my heart that Luke hadn't thrown me over for a one-night stand even if it had resulted in a child. He should have trusted me more. We could have worked through that together. I would have supported him having a relationship with the child. But he made the decision unilaterally. He took away my choice. That's what I kept coming back to. No matter how much I might still love Luke now, that one thing still hung out there. And what about Darcy? She was a living breathing reminder of what had been taken from me. I looked at her and I saw Cathy – and Luke.

I showered as soon as I got home. I called Auntie who sounded tired but assured me she was all right. I wasn't convinced.

"Tell me about your day, Charlotte."

I told her about the time I spent with Hannah, telling Auntie as many details as I could remember about Dr. Farrell's party and his huge house.

Auntie seemed to be enjoying the story. Then...

"He sounds like a character. I'll have to meet him some day."

"Auntie – he's your doctor."

"Who? Luke? I know he's my doctor."

"No, Dr. Farrell. He's your doctor too. He did your heart catheterization. Remember?

"Oh, right. That's what I meant. It's late. I should be going to bed."

Now, I was worried.

"Auntie, get some sleep. I'll stop by on my way to seeing Luke."

As soon as I hung up, I called the nursing station and asked for Auntie's nurse. The young man who I had met in the morning had left for the day and a young female voice came on. I explained my concerns about Auntie's apparent confusion.

"I'm sure it's nothing. I was told she was up out of bed for most of the day. She's probably tired. But I will check on her for you and call you back in a few minutes."

She called me back fifteen minutes later.

"I just checked on Mrs. Monti and I also took her vital signs. Everything is fine. She did seem a little tired, but she was oriented and her vital signs are good. And she's in sinus rhythm. Everything checks out but I'll keep an eye on her and call you if I have any concerns."

"Thank you. Do you think I should come in? I don't want to tire her out. I'm meeting a friend for dinner, but I could stop by on my way out."

"No, I don't think that's necessary. She was already starting to doze when I left her. Go. Enjoy your evening. We'll take good care of her."

"Okay. I'll have my cell with me. Call me no matter what. Please."

"I will. Your aunt will be okay."

After I hung up, I decided to lie down and take a short nap before I got dressed to meet Luke. I still had no idea where we were going. I called Luke and left a message, telling him I was home and asking him to call me when he had the chance.

Chapter Twenty-Two

ଔ

I awoke to the sound of my phone buzzing on the pillow next to me. Panicking that something was wrong I grabbed the phone and almost dropped it.

"Hello? This is Charlotte."

"Charlotte, I know it's you. Is everything okay?"

"Sorry, I thought you were the hospital calling about Auntie."

"Is she all right?"

"I think so. She just had an episode of confusion this afternoon. At least, I think so. Or maybe she was just tired. I don't know. But her nurse promised to call me if there was anything to be concerned about and I thought that was her when you called."

"I'm sure she's fine but if you want, I'll call over there and talk to her nurse and see what I can find out before I pick you up."

"That would be great if you would do that. And I can just meet you wherever we're going."

"Don't be silly, Charlotte. I'm picking you up. We're going to do this right."

Luke and I planned for him to pick me up in an hour and a half. Plenty of time for me to get ready.

While applying makeup a while later I tried to formulate what I was going to say to Luke. I didn't want an argument, but I also wanted him to know about my misgivings. Yet, despite all that, I still had butterflies at the thought of being with Luke in a romantic situation again. I knew I still loved him. But was that enough?

I fed the dog, took him outside to go potty, made sure the cat had food, and water was out for both of Auntie's babies and then I paced while I waited for Luke. I looked out the window every time a car drove by.

Finally, it was Luke.

The evening went better than I expected. I set my misgivings aside as soon as I opened the door. Luke still had the power to get to me. I decided to at least enjoy the evening, talk about what I was feeling, and see where things went. I still worried if we had any kind of a future. I was by no means as optimistic as Luke was but that didn't mean I couldn't have fun tonight.

Dinner was very enjoyable, no doubt helped along by a nice pinot grigio. Luke wasn't drinking. He told me he was covering Farrell's patients as well as his own. Hospitalists did all the work when patients were in-patient but there still was the occasional trip to the Emergency Room for a consultation.

We chatted about everything and nothing in particular. I waited for an opening to talk about Auntie and the big deception, and it finally arrived with dessert.

Luke had put his hand over mine. "I told you we could be good again."

I put my spoon down. The crème brûlée was good and I hated to stop but time was running out.

"Luke, we need to talk. This thing with Auntie hiding her relationship with you all these years has really shaken me."

"I know. Please don't be upset with her. She only had the best intentions."

"I understand that. I'm not upset with her. I'm disappointed but I totally understand why she did what she did. But it brings up a bigger issue."

"What?"

"Us."

"I don't understand."

"You. Cathy. Why you left me. Trust. Luke, I can't get beyond the reason why you did what you did."

"You mean that I cheated on you."

"That but it's more than that. Yes, you cheated but we could have worked through that."

"But Cathy got pregnant."

"Exactly. Something that serious and you shut me out."

"I was ashamed – and afraid. And I knew I had to somehow make it right. Cathy needed me. The baby needed me."

I felt my anger rising.

"And I didn't? We were contemplating spending the rest of our lives together and you ran out on me. And that brings up something else. We fought before you left for Philly because you didn't want to commit to marriage. And then you marry someone like Cathy that you hardly had any relationship with? Except for one night – one stupid night."

Luke looked down, refusing to meet my gaze.

"You robbed me of my choice. You robbed us of making a choice together. You might have thought you were being noble or gallant or whatever else you thought you were doing but I can't get past you just leaving me – us – like that. Auntie knowing you and Cathy all those years and then seeing the relationship Darcy has with her just made it too real for me. I need trust more than anything right now. Especially after Peter."

Luke sighed. Seconds passed. I wondered if he was going to say anything at all. I could see his jaw twitching. I knew he was upset.

He sighed again.

"You're right. I agree with everything you said. But I know that if you just give us a chance, we can work this out. We ..."

My phone rang in my purse. I grabbed it and saw that it was the hospital.

"This is Charlotte."

"Hi, this is Paula, Mrs. Monti's nurse. We spoke earlier this evening."

"Yes?"

"I'm calling because you need to come in. We think Mrs. Monti has had a stroke."

Chapter Twenty-Three

Cଓ

"Oh, my God!" I grabbed Luke's arm. "What happened?"

Paula told me how Auntie had been very confused when she awoke from her nap and had trouble communicating. Then Paula noticed one-sided weakness and a facial droop. She immediately called the intensivist assigned to her unit and he was right now doing an examination.

"We need to do a CT scan. Do we have your permission?"

"Yes. Yes. Do whatever you need to do. I'm on my way. Will you be administering tPA? Do we still have time?" I knew time was precious if they were going to try to use the drug to dissolve the clot.

"I can't answer those questions, but we should be able to tell you more by the time you get here."

"I'm leaving now. If she can hear you, please tell her I love her."

I hung up and faced Luke. He was on his phone. In my distress, I never even heard it ring. From what I was hearing, they were telling him about Auntie.

"We have to go, Luke."

I stood up and grabbed my purse. Luke handed me the valet ticket.

"Go get the car and I'll take care of the bill and meet you outside."

Within minutes we were on our way to the hospital. I prayed all the way, wishing the car could fly. Auntie had to be all right. She had to be. I couldn't lose her. Not now. Again, I blamed myself for allowing her to go ahead with this stupid cath. If only…

Thank God for the swift action of her nurse.

Luke pulled up to the entrance of the hospital. "Go on up. I'll park and meet you there as soon as I can."

Auntie still wasn't back in her room by the time I got there so I went in search of her nurse. She was at the nurse's station getting medication for another one of her patients. She nodded to me as soon as she saw me. "I'll meet you in Mrs. Monti's room. She's on her way back from CT now."

Luke was already in the room when I got there, and Paula was right behind me. She had a clipboard with her.

"Dr. Manganello is the neurosurgeon covering tonight. He'll be here in a minute to go over what he can do." Then she saw Luke. "Oh, hi, Dr. Andrews. They told me you were covering for Dr. Farrell. You can probably explain all this better

217

than I can."

"You're doing fine. I'm covering but I'm here as family too. Charlotte and I were out to dinner when you called."

Paula opened her mouth to say something but we were all distracted by the sound of the gurney coming down the hall. It was Auntie returning from Radiology. Her small still body broke my heart. Most of her face was obscured by the oxygen mask over her mouth and nose. An IV hung from a pole on the gurney and the tubing snaked down under the sheets into her left arm. Her right hand was outside the covers and was so pale. I longed to hold it.

"Wait up before you move her," said a booming voice. Soon a very tall dark-haired man appeared in the doorway, and he peered inside the room.

He addressed me. "Are you Mrs. Monti's niece and power of attorney?"

"Yes, I'm Charlotte."

Then he saw Luke and his face softened.

"Hi, Luke."

"Hey, Chuck. I'm covering for Mark, but Camille is a friend, too."

"Okay."

Chuck Manganello squeezed his large frame past the gurney and stood in front of me. He angled his body so that he could speak to both me and Auntie. Auntie's eyes were wide. I knew she was scared. I noticed that Dr. Manganello patted Auntie's hand while he talked. I liked him immediately and felt relieved.

"So, we were able to visualize a small clot in Mrs. Monti's brain. And we think we are in that golden window where we can dissolve it with medication. So, I need your permission to go ahead. We can take her back to the cath lab as soon as you sign permission."

I tried to tell him with my eyes not to say anything in front of Auntie. I didn't want her any more frightened than she already was. He seemed to understand. I took the clipboard and signed where I needed to.

"Can I see Auntie for a minute before you take her back?"

"Certainly." He turned to Auntie and held her hand. "Everything is going to be all right, Mrs. Monti. I know you're scared. We're going to fix you up and this will just be a bad memory. I'll see you in a few minutes."

After he left, I moved next to Auntie and finally held that scrawny little hand. She gripped it back so hard. "It's okay, Auntie. We're here. Luke is with me, too. Don't try to talk."

Luke peered over my shoulder.

"You're going to be all right, Camille. Chuck is a great doctor. You're in good hands."

Auntie nodded. I released her hand and watched helplessly as the orderly wheeled her back to that lab where all this probably started.

Luke and I walked slowly over to the surgical waiting room to await the outcome.

About an hour later, Dr. Manganello approached us. He had a big smile on his face, and I took that to mean good news.

He sat in the chair next to me. "You can wipe that worried look off your face. Mrs. Monti came through just fine. The clot was small, and we were well within our window. I'm confident we were able to restore circulation to the affected brain tissue. Of course, we won't know for sure what her deficits might still be until she is fully awake and we can start evaluating her. But I'm very hopeful. I'm not going to lie to you. She still has recovery ahead of her and she might very well have some impairment, but I think with therapy and support, she'll do just fine. I'm transferring her to ICU now. We need to keep a close eye on her for at least the next twenty-four hours. Go home and get some rest. There's nothing else you can do here. I'll call you if there's any change."

He shook Luke's hand. "Nice seeing you again, Luke. Wish it was under better circumstances."

"We're just glad it was you on call, Chuck. Thanks."

"Sure thing."

Luke put his arm around me as we watched Chuck walk away.

"You're shaking. Let me take you home."

"I don't want to leave her."

"Charlotte, she's going to be out of it for quite some time. She's getting the best care. There's nothing you can do for her right now. The best thing is for you to get some rest. Tomorrow is going to need all your attention. Once Camille is out of the woods, they're going to do evaluations and set her up for therapy. She's going to need you and you can't help her if you're dragging."

"You're right."

We walked back to Luke's car in silence.

Chapter Twenty-Four

 CB

"Do you want to call Hannah and let her know what happened?" Luke asked as he steered his car out of the hospital parking lot.

"No, I don't want to talk to anyone right now. I just want to go home and crawl under the covers and forget this day ever happened."

I looked over at Luke and immediately regretted what I had said.

"Luke, I'm sorry. I didn't mean ..."

"It's okay. This night hasn't turned out as either one of us had hoped. Look, I'm under no delusions. I know we have to talk some more but now isn't the time. Are you going to be okay by yourself? Do you want to stay at my place?"

"No, I need familiar. Besides, I have to take care of Sam and Buster."

"Okay."

Neither one of us spoke for the rest of the

trip home.

Luke pulled into Auntie's driveway and waited while I dug the house key out of my purse.

"You're sure you're going to be all right?"

"Yes, Luke. Don't worry. Call me when you get home if it makes you feel better."

Luke reached across and kissed my cheek.

"I know you don't believe me, but I love you. And Camille is going to be all right. I promise. I'll call you in a little bit. Good night."

"Good night."

I let myself in the door and heard Luke's car start up and then drive away. Sam came over and whined. I knelt and hugged him. Suddenly, the sobs just erupted from me and surprised us both. Sam whined some more, visibly upset at my crying.

"It's okay, Sammy. Your Mommy is going to be okay. Let's go potty." Sam perked up at the word and bounded to the back door leading to the deck. Once outside the night seemed to soothe me. The jasmine, the stars, the night breeze – it was almost possible to believe the last couple of hours were a dream.

Except Auntie wasn't home. And I didn't know when she would be home again.

Once back in the house, I gave Sam a treat from the pantry and we both headed back to my bedroom. Buster was curled up in his bed in Auntie's room, but he woke up and followed us into the guest room. I put my cell in the charger on my nightstand and changed into a nightshirt and crawled under the covers. Sam jumped onto the bed and settled down at me feet, Buster next to him. I turned off the bedside light just as my phone chirped. It was Luke.

"Hey, how are you doing?"

"I'm okay. I'm in bed with Sam and Buster. We're keeping each other company."

"Wish I was there with you."

"Luke –"

"I know. I'm rushing things. But as soon as we know Camille is going to be okay, we have to finish our discussion."

"If you say so."

"Charlotte, I'm not giving up on us. I want you in my life. I love you and I'm going to win you back no matter what it takes. Whatever misgivings you have, we can work it out. I know we can. Please. Don't give up on us."

"You sound like Hannah."

"Why? What did she say?"

"She told me I was throwing away a once in a lifetime chance."

"Smart woman. She's right. But tonight isn't the time. Get some rest. I'll check in on you in the morning. Sleep tight, Sweetie."

"You, too."

I slept fitfully, my dreams a distortion of fear and reality. I dreamt about Luke as I had in the early days after Peter had moved out. In one dream, Luke was walking away from me, and I kept calling his name, but he never turned around.

I finally gave up trying to sleep at around six and got up to brush my teeth. After I let Sam out, he decided to sleep on his bed on the deck and I went inside to make myself some coffee. I had just taken my first sip when my phone rang. I had left it in the charger on the nightstand and ran for it. I was afraid it was the hospital calling about Auntie. The caller ID told me it was Luke.

"Hi, Sweetheart. How did you sleep?"

"Not well."

"Well, I have good news for you. I just called over to the hospital and spoke to Chuck. Camille is doing great and they are going to transfer her back to Telemetry this morning. He thinks she has some weakness but he's going to have Physical Therapy evaluate her today and get started with a plan. He said she seemed quiet and a little withdrawn, but he thinks cognitively she's going to be all right. Her speech is a little slow, but she should do well with some speech therapy. We were lucky. If it's okay with her – and you, of course – I'm going to have Mark transfer her to my care for cardiac follow-up."

"Please. That would be great. I don't want him anywhere near Auntie after this."

"Charlotte, I know you don't like him but he's a good doctor and this wasn't his fault. Camille probably developed a clot during her arrythmia episodes and it just broke loose."

"Whatever. We're done with him."

"Do you have time for coffee this morning before I go to the office?"

"Not really. I think I'll go back to bed now that Auntie is better and catch a nap before I head over to the hospital."

"Okay. I'll check back with you later. Have a good sleep." And he hung up.

My heart felt so much lighter knowing Auntie was going to be all right. Whatever it took to get her well was what we were going to do. As I drifted off to sleep, I started mentally making lists of what I needed to do. I was probably going to have to extend my stay in Arizona, so I needed to call my supervisor. I might even need a leave of absence.

And the house!

What was I going to do about the house? What about my deal with Auntie for the money? That might have to be something I gave up. If Auntie needs me, she needs me. She gave up her life for me when I was a child. If I must do the same for her now, so be it.

Chapter Twenty-Five

ඔ

I woke up a couple of hours later feeling rested. A shower and more coffee and I was soon on my way to the hospital.

I called Hannah as I drove. She had called earlier while I had napped but it had gone to voicemail. I never even heard it. I knew she was eager to hear how my date with Luke had gone. She had no idea what had happened to Auntie. I was sure she thought my lack of communication meant that things had gone well with Luke and he might have even stayed over.

"So, tell me everything," Hannah said as soon as we exchanged hello's.

"It's not what you think. The date ended abruptly."

"Oh, no. Don't tell me you had a fight."

"Well, we did start to have a discussion, but we were interrupted. It was Auntie. The hospital called me while we were having dinner and told me she had had a stroke. We spent the rest of the evening at the hospital while she had tests and then medication to dissolve the clot."

"Oh, my God, Charlotte! I'm so sorry. You should have called me. I would have come to be with you. Is she all right? How is she now?"

"It's okay. Luke stayed with me and then I just went home afterwards. I was bushed. I really didn't want to talk to anyone. I'm on my way back to the hospital now. Luke checked on her this morning and he said she did well overnight. She was in the ICU but she's on her way back to a telemetry bed now. I'll know more after I see her."

"Did you talk to Dr. Farrell or his PA?"

"No, and they are off her case. Luke is taking over as of today. I don't want either of them near her."

"Hmm..."

"What hmm? What's going on?"

"Nothing. I just overheard something yesterday when I was cleaning up."

"What?"

"When I was gathering up my trays toward the end of the party yesterday, I thought I overheard part of a conversation between Doctor Farrell and his assistant."

"And?" Sometimes Hannah could really be exasperating.

"Well, they were obviously concerned about a patient who had developed problems during a catheterization and Farrell seemed especially upset about it. No names were mentioned. All I heard was words to the effect of 'Are you sure the records are okay?' and his assistant said 'Stop worrying.' If they were talking about Camille, I guess it made sense they were worried about her. Maybe he was afraid she was going to have a complication."

"Why would he ask about her records, though?"

"Charlotte, I'm not even sure that's what I heard. It was just a snippet of conversation. And why wouldn't he be worried about his records? He's being sued, remember? He's probably gun-shy. Don't worry about it. We don't even know who he was talking about. It might have been an entirely different patient. I'm sorry I even mentioned it."

By this time, I was pulling into the hospital parking lot.

"You're probably right. I have better things to worry about than Farrell. I just got to the hospital. I'll call you after I see Auntie."

"Okay, please call as soon as you can and tell Camille we're thinking about her."

"I will."

After parking Auntie's car, I checked in at the visitor's desk and found out Auntie had already been transferred. Her room was closer to the nursing station this time and as I got off the elevator and closer to her room, I heard voices. I was instantly reminded of finding Darcy at Auntie's bedside the other night. But it wasn't Darcy. Auntie was sitting in a chair at her bedside and talking with a young woman dressed in scrubs who was crouching in front of her. The young woman looked up as soon as I entered the room.

Auntie smiled when she saw me, and I bent down to kiss her cheek.

"This is my niece Charlotte," Auntie said. I noticed Auntie's voice was weak and seemed a little slurred to me. But I didn't notice any obvious facial drooping and felt encouraged.

The young woman stood and extended her hand to me. "Hi, I'm Amelia. I'm the physical therapist helping Mrs. Monti today. I was just evaluating her. She was able to get out of bed to the chair fairly well for her first day." She looked at Auntie and I swore Auntie puffed out her chest in pride.

"We're going to start PT in her room and see how she does," Amelia said.

She put a hand on Auntie's knee. "You're going to do great. I'm going to go back to my office and write up your plan and then we'll get started. How does that sound?"

"Good," Auntie said. Auntie patted Amelia's hand with her right hand. I noticed that she wasn't moving her left side as much as she usually did, and my heart sank.

Amelia turned to me. "Why don't you walk me to the elevator? Mrs. Monti has told me a lot about you this morning. Maybe you can help me with something."

I was puzzled but told Auntie I would be right back and followed Amelia out into the hallway. We walked slowly to the elevator while she spoke softly to me so that Auntie wouldn't hear.

"Sorry for being so cryptic in there but I didn't want to upset Mrs. Monti. Overall, I think she's doing very well and I have every confidence she will have a lot of improvement with therapy. But right now, she is weak on her left side, arm and leg. She can pivot to the chair with assistance, but she will need to gain strength back. Her speech is good and I'm sure you noticed it's slow. But she has no trouble understanding and she only had a little trouble with word-finding. That too should improve. Can you tell me about her house? Does she have stairs we need to be concerned about?"

"No, it's a one story. But she does live alone."

"I know. She told me that, too. But you're staying with her right now, aren't you?"

"Yes. My original plan was to go back to New York next week. My home and my job are there. But that may change. I was thinking about taking a leave of absence until Auntie is back on her feet. And then go from there."

Amelia hesitated. "Living alone might not be an option for her after this. It depends on her level of recovery. Most patients with her type of injury usually do very well and can go back to a full life but it's unpredictable. Everybody is different. We'll have to see how she does. We'll work with you and Mrs. Monti as we go forward and talk about discharge planning. For now, I think a couple of days in-patient until she's cleared medically. Then I think a short stay at a rehab hospital would be the best thing for her as we get her ready to go home."

I felt my eyes start to tear up. This couldn't be happening. Auntie would be devastated if she couldn't stay in her home.

"I know this is a lot to absorb. And I don't mean to upset you. Mrs. Monti told me you're a nurse, so I know I don't have to spell everything out to you. She's very lucky. She's lucky the stroke was treated so quickly and she's lucky to have you."

By this time, we were at the elevator.

"I'm sure we'll be speaking again over the

next couple of days. Try not to worry."

We shook hands and she left. I stood there while the elevator doors closed and felt a chapter of my life closing with them.

I walked slowly back to Auntie's room. I stopped outside her doorway, threw my shoulders back and put on my biggest smile. Auntie needed me and I was going to do whatever it took to get her well again and home.

Chapter Twenty-Six

ဢ

The next two days were largely uneventful.

Auntie scored well with her therapy evaluations. In-room therapy was started, and it was decided that she would benefit from a short stay at a rehab hospital.

I was given a list of possible facilities and spent Monday afternoon looking them over. We decided on one closer to Fountain Hills. It was small and the staff was very involved and supportive. It was important to me that Auntie felt as comfortable as possible. I knew she was scared. She was also highly motivated, and we were assured that with physical and occupational therapy and speech therapy she could return home in a couple of weeks. Whether she would ever be able to live alone again was a story for another day. One neither of us wanted to talk about just yet.

By the time I arrived at the hospital Tuesday

morning, Auntie was sitting in a wheelchair in her room. The remains of her breakfast were on a tray at the foot of her bed. I noticed that she hadn't eaten very much. She was dressed in the clothes she had been wearing the morning of her catheterization. I immediately felt sad at the reminder of how simple things had been just a few days before.

But Auntie smiled as soon as she saw me.

"I'm sprung out of here. We're just waiting for tr -" she hesitated for a minute – "transportation to show up."

It was good to see Auntie looking happy. It was the most relaxed I had seen her since her stroke. We both ignored her word stumble.

"I'm going crazy in here."

Auntie's nurse came back carrying a small sheaf of papers. "I have Mrs. Monti's discharge papers and some instructions to go over."

I sat on the edge of the bed. "I'll take care of all that."

As soon as we were finished with the paperwork, a young woman wearing a uniform that said *Medi-Trans* on her breast pocket arrived.

"Hi, I'm Sally. Are you Mrs. Monti?" She reached for Auntie's hospital wristband and read it. "I'm here to take you to Scottsdale South Rehab."

"Let's go," said Auntie.

"I'll follow you in my car," I said to Sally. "I know where it is." I reached down and kissed Auntie on the forehead. "I'll see you over there."

By the time I got to the rehab facility, parked, and made my way to the front desk, Auntie was already in her room. It was a lovely room, large, private, and with a window that faced a greenbelt area. A large mesquite tree was right outside her window, and I heard birds chirping.

Auntie was sitting in another wheelchair, one that obviously belonged to Scottsdale Rehab. The transportation driver and the old wheelchair were gone.

"Go home, Charlotte. I'm all right." I noticed all of Auntie's statements were very short. Not like her usual speech pattern. I hoped this wasn't her new normal.

"No, I want to know what their plans are and what your schedule is going to be like."

Over the next hour, I sat in the visitor's chair and watched as Auntie was officially admitted to her new temporary home. The admitting nurse whose name badge said simply "Shelly" very cheerfully told us both what we could expect in the way of amenities – each room was private with its own bathroom, complete with assistance bars and shower chairs. I cringed thinking this might be Auntie's life now. My sweet independent Auntie leaning on grab bars, needing assistance to do the simple things in life.

Meals would be taken with all the other patients in the large dining room. She then wheeled Auntie around the facility, with me following like a puppy dog, as she showed Auntie where the different rooms were – the dining room, the doctors' offices, the nursing station, a main gathering room where patients visited with each other and family members, and finally the therapy rooms where the various modalities would take place – a large room filled with all kinds of equipment and populated with patients and staff – staff giving words of encouragement while patients with various afflictions worked the many pieces of gear. I noticed Auntie's lip quivered just a little. She was as scared and worried as I was. I wanted our old life back and I knew she did, too.

"So, there you have it in a nutshell, Mrs. Monti," Shelly said. We were back in Auntie's room. Shelly had wheeled the chair alongside Auntie's bed and reached down to lock the wheels.

She looked at her watch. "It's almost lunchtime. You can visit with your niece for a bit and I will have someone come fetch you in a little while and accompany you down to the dining room. This afternoon, I'll post your schedule on your board" – she pointed to a whiteboard on the far wall – "and then pretty soon you will be getting yourself to your assignments all by yourself. It might feel overwhelming right now, but you'll be a pro in no time."

She patted Auntie on the shoulder and left.

Auntie and I just looked at each other. I was afraid to say anything until I knew how Auntie felt.

"Let's go home," Auntie finally said. "I hate it here." A tear trickled down her left cheek.

I sat back in the only other chair in the room and scooted it over so I could be close to Auntie. I reached over and held her left hand. I knew it was her weaker hand. I wanted to see how much of a grip she had without her knowing I was checking. Auntie grabbed my hand, but it was definitely weaker than I wanted it to be. I hadn't seen her out of bed or out of her wheelchair. I hadn't even seen her transfer from bed to chair but I didn't want to make her feel worse by asking how it went.

"It's going to be all right, Auntie. I know this is scary. I'm scared too but this is the best place for you right now. They have every reason to believe you're going to regain your strength and dance out of here."

Auntie looked me square in the face. "Don't lie to me, Charlotte." She seemed to take longer than usual to say my name.

"Okay, I won't lie. I don't know what's going to happen, but I do know this. Your weakness is not severe. So, we are hopeful that you will have very little lasting damage. Therapy is what you need now, and this is a very good place. And I am going to stay here as long as you need me. So, don't worry about anything except getting better. I'll take care of the house and Sam and Buster. And I will be here as much as they let me."

I saw surprise cross over Auntie's face. "What about your job?"

"Don't worry about that. I'll take family leave."

I knew Auntie wanted to object but I also saw relief in her face.

"And before you ask – don't worry about my divorce either. I'll call my attorney this afternoon and see if we can have more time. Under the circumstances, I don't see a problem."

Before Auntie could say any more, we were interrupted by a very cheery "Lunch time!". The promised aide appeared in the doorway. She was a short older woman, and I was glad Auntie would have someone her own age to talk to.

Auntie was wheeled off to lunch. I said my good-byes and walked to my car.

Chapter Twenty-Seven

ᘓ

Once I was home, Sam started whining and doing a tap dance at the back door. I let him out and topped off Buster's food dish.

I dug my cell phone out of my purse and went out onto the deck. Sam had finished his business and was resting on his dog bed.

I sat on the swing and stared at my phone. I had two important calls to make, and I was hesitant to make them both. But waiting wasn't going to make it easier. I decided the call to my nursing supervisor was probably going to be the less stressful, so I dialed her number first. She answered on the first ring.

"Ten West, Marge Simmons. How can I help you?"

"Marge, it's Charlotte."

"Charlotte! How are you? How is it going in Arizona? How is your aunt?"

"Not good, Marge. That's why I'm calling. She had her cath on Friday, but she had a stroke right after it. She's in rehab now and we don't know how long her recovery is going to take. I can't come back to work just yet. I need to be here. Is there any way we can extend my vacation or maybe give me family leave time?"

"I'm sorry to hear that, Charlotte. I hope she's going to be all right. We miss you here and staffing is getting short with summer vacations and all. Extending your vacation probably isn't an option and I don't know about family leave. Tell you what. Let me contact Human Resources and see what they say."

I had been expecting a more enthusiastic response. A little more sympathy. Marge and I had been friends for years. But she did have to put the unit first. "Okay, I appreciate anything you can do. I really don't have a choice right now. Auntie's well-being comes first. I'm not leaving her. If I can't have family leave, I'll just have to turn in my resignation." Maybe playing hardball would get me what I needed.

"Let's not rush into anything. Let me see what I can do. I'll call you back as soon as I know anything."

"Thanks, Marge. Talk to you soon."

"Sure thing. Take care, Charlotte."

And that was that. A few minutes of a phone call and my professional life had changed.

Oh, well. Might as well screw things up completely. I dialed my attorney's office.

"Hey, Charlotte, how's Arizona?" Tom's voice boomed as soon as he came on the line.

"It's great, Tom. Beautiful, hot. Just as I

remembered it. Look, I'm calling because something's come up and I need your advice and help."

"Sure. What's up?"

"Well, I know my plan was to come up with the money to buy out Peter's interest in the house. My aunt offered to help me with that, and I was hoping to have what I needed by next week. But it's not going to happen as soon as I thought it would."

I heard Tom sigh at the other end. "Charlotte, we can't string your ex out on this indefinitely. They were clear about their timeline."

"I know. But my aunt has had a health emergency, She had a stroke a few days ago and I am going to be here in Arizona a while longer. I'm hoping it won't be more than a month or six weeks at the most, but I don't know right now. Can you reach out to Peter's attorney and see if they can give me some more time?"

"Wow. I'm so sorry, Charlotte. I'll ask. But I won't give you false hope. It's doubtful they'll agree."

"Just do what you can. Please, Tom. It's important."

"I know it is to you, Charlotte. But it's not important to Peter. He's going to see this as a sign that you're not going to be able to make good on your offer. It really isn't practical. We've gone over this."

"I know. Just try. That's all I ask. Call me as soon as you hear anything. I appreciate it."

"All right. And I'm sorry about your aunt. I hope she's going to be okay."

"Thanks, Tom."

We hung up. I sighed loudly and Sam raised

his head to look at me. I smiled at him and he went
back to dozing. I envied him. My world had just
done a complete one-eighty-degree turn. But it was
out of my hands now. Job, house – nothing mattered
at this moment but getting Auntie back on her feet,
such as they were. I refused to think about the fact
that she might not be whole again. I just couldn't go
there.

I went back to the rehab that evening and
had dinner in the dining room with Auntie. It was
painfully obvious that she had weakness in her left
hand. Luckily, she was right-handed, and the deficit
only showed when she needed to do something that
required two hands, like buttering her bread. I found
myself reaching out and trying to help. The room
was being monitored by a couple of female aides
and one of them swooped in when she saw me
trying to help.

She tapped me on the shoulder and indicated
with a flick of her head that she wanted to talk to
me out of earshot.

I excused myself, pretending to get a coffee
refill.

"Mrs. Monti is doing very well for her first
day," the aide told me while we lingered at the
coffee machine. "I know it's instinctive to want to
do for her, but we discourage family from that. In
fact, I really recommend that family not visit around
mealtime. We find that patients are more inclined to
try to be independent when family isn't around. It's
also good psychologically if the patients interact
with each other. We try to make this have as much
of a community feel as possible."

"I'm sorry. I didn't know."

"It's okay. I know you want to help. It's a

learning curve for family as much as it is for the patients. But it's really best for Mrs. Monti that she start to do as much as she can by herself. She's got a very strong drive. I think she's going to do very well."

I thanked the aide and went back to Auntie. After a few more sips of coffee, I started to gather my things.

"Auntie, I'm going to go home now. I think I'll stop by Hannah's on the way home. I haven't had a chance to spend time with her in a while and we need to catch up. You'll be okay if I go?"

Auntie looked disappointed but she put on a brave smile. "Sure. That sounds good. Tell Hannah I said Hello."

I kissed Auntie on the forehead and left, feeling as sad as I possibly could. This entire day had been horrible. I had no intention of going to Hannah's. All I wanted was a glass of wine and some mindless TV.

Chapter Twenty-Eight

☙

The rest of the week went by faster than I thought it would. I took care of the house. Cleaned, watched after Sam and Buster. They occasionally seemed to look for Auntie but were okay for the most part. I visited Auntie whenever I could. I learned what her rehab schedule was and worked my visits around her treatment sessions. Luke called me and our talks were pleasant, but he was obviously avoiding continuing the discussion we were having when we received the call about Auntie's stroke. Frankly, I was a little disappointed that he wasn't being more forceful. It was becoming hard to read him. Was he giving me space and biding his time or was he no longer interested? I found it hard to believe he had given up so easily.

I finally had had a phone conversation with Hannah and filled her in on Auntie's condition. She tried to get me to talk about Luke and our "situation", but I quickly shut her down and she let it drop. It seemed everyone was backing away from me.

Finally, it was Friday, a few days after I had called both Marge and Tom and still no word from either of them. I assumed it meant bad news.

Then, just before lunch – which I knew was afternoon back East – Marge called my cell.

"Charlotte, I wish I had better news, but you don't qualify for family medical leave. I know your aunt is like your mother to you but technically FMLA only applies to children, parents, and spouses. I can offer you a leave of absence, but it won't have the job guarantees of FMLA. What do you want to do? I don't want you to quit."

"Wow, Marge. I was really hoping for better news."

"I know. But my hands are tied. If it was up to me, I would hold your position for you, but I can't. You can take leave and see what happens when you're ready to come back. You might get lucky."

"Can I think about it?"

"Okay, but don't take too long. Technically you're due back to work on Monday. I'll give you a personal day for Monday but call me before the end of business that day and give me your answer."

I thanked her and hung up. I was sitting at Auntie's old roll top desk, paying her bills online and I just wanted to cry. I loved my job. If I chose to stay with Luke, leaving my job would be a given. But losing it this way felt so unfair. Peter, the divorce, the house, Auntie, and now my job. Maybe I was supposed to stay in Arizona. Maybe I was supposed to be here for Auntie, to pay her back for all she had done for me.

I paid a few more bills and then logged off and closed my laptop. It was almost time to visit Auntie. I knew she would be finishing her lunch in about an hour, and we would have another hour before therapy started again.

I was heating up some soup in the microwave when my cell rang again. I was surprised to see that it was Beth. I almost let it go to voice mail but decided to answer.

I hadn't heard from her at all since the month after Peter had moved out. I knew she was feeling the need to be loyal to her father and I understood. I had hoped for a continued relationship with her though. Maybe it was happening now.

I took a deep breath and clicked the phone to answer. I decided to say very little and just see what she had to say.

"Hi, Beth. This is a pleasant surprise."

"Hi, Charlotte. I hope it's all right that I called you." She definitely sounded uncomfortable and my heart went out to her.

"Of course, it is. Don't be silly. I've missed you. How are you? And the children?"

"We're all fine. Thanks. Listen, I'm not going to beat around the bush. I know what's going on between you and Dad regarding the house. In fact, Dad's here now and he wants to talk to you."

I was totally surprised by this. This was the last thing I expected. I heard muffled talk in the background. I pictured Beth with her hand over the phone scolding her father. I heard a very distinct "Talk to her" and then a few seconds of silence.

Finally, a very soft, "Hi, Charlotte. It's Peter."

"So I gathered." I refused to say anything more and make things any easier for Peter. This was on him.

"I – I'm sorry to hear about your aunt. My attorney told me what happened. I hope she's going to be all right."

"Thank you."

"Okay, so he also told me what you wanted."

"Yes."

"And I want to make a counteroffer."

"I'm listening."

"I don't want the house anymore."

For a second, I didn't know what to say. This was a total shock. Finally, I found my voice. "Why?" was all I could say.

"Well, uh –" I heard the muffled talking in the background again. Beth was obviously getting frustrated with her father. I did make out the words "Tell her" and Peter whispering, "I'm trying."

He came back to me. "Here's the thing. Bianca and I decided we want to get a place of our own. And I know that was a sticking point for you – us living in the house. Would you be open to just selling it to a neutral third party?"

I smiled. So, Bianca didn't want to live in the house that Peter and I had shared. I tried to imagine their fights. The evil part of me was happy.

"I don't know, Peter. I hadn't really considered that. I don't like the idea of showings and going through all that. Especially right now. I'm in Arizona. I can't handle a sale right now. And I don't know when exactly I'll be back there."

"I know. That's what I'm calling about. A friend of mine approached me about the house. He had seen it before at one of our parties. He's willing to offer us a good price plus you don't have to move out right away. You could come back when it's convenient in a few weeks and pack up and our attorneys can handle the sale. You'll walk away with a nice chunk to start over with."

I hesitated and Peter took that to mean I was agreeing. "It's a really good offer, Charlotte. It would be best for both of us."

"Why are you being so reasonable all of a sudden?"

"I'm tired, Charlotte. This hasn't been easy on me either. We both need to move on." I knew Peter well enough to know there was more to this than him just having an epiphany. I wasn't expecting the next few words though. "Bianca's pregnant and she wants a place of our own."

I was suddenly at a loss for words. I wasn't expecting that at all. I didn't want Peter back. That wasn't it but the finality of them having a child was too much. This one stung.

"Are you there? Did you hear me?"

"Yes, I heard you, Peter. What did you expect me to say? Congratulations?"

"No, of course not but you asked me why and that's why. What do you say?"

"Let me think about it. I'll call my attorney on Monday and give him my answer. Say good-bye to Beth for me. And Peter…"

"Yes?"

"Don't ever call me again." And I hung up before he could answer.

I sat on the bar stool at the kitchen counter before I fell. My legs suddenly felt like rubber.

Bianca pregnant! I thought about Peter's

early reluctance to have children of our own and all the trouble when we did try.

And now he was going to be a father again. I felt as if I had been punched in the gut.

And Beth - how did she feel about it? Bad enough her stepmother-to-be was just about her age. Now she was pregnant with her half-brother or sister. This was worse than any soap opera.

But Peter's offer – it was tempting. Especially now. My reason for keeping the house was fast fading now that Auntie needed me. If Peter and Bianca weren't in my house, it was easier to let it go. The money would sure come in handy.

And then there was Luke. I knew what he would say if he knew about this. Maybe the Universe was giving me direction after all.

I had to think. I picked up my phone and dialed Hannah.

Chapter Twenty-Nine

ↂ

Talking things over with Hannah had helped and I replayed our conversation in my head as I drove to visit Auntie.

If I would be able to control the sale of the house on my timetable, it was probably a good thing. The money I would be paid as my share of the equity in the house would be substantial. Certainly enough for me to buy a small house out here in Arizona if that needed to happen.

In any case, the money would give me options I didn't have before Peter's offer. Auntie was going to improve. She had to be. She was going to be as she was before her stroke. Or at least enough that she could still be independent. Or independent enough to feel good about herself. I hated the defeated look I saw in her eyes now.

I kept playing different scenarios over in my head. By the time I had myself thoroughly confused and stressed I was in the parking lot of the rehab facility.

I didn't stay long. Auntie was visibly tired and I encouraged her to nap before her afternoon sessions.

I shopped for groceries on the way home and as I was putting the last of them away, my cell phone rang. It was Luke.

"Hi, gorgeous. How has your day been going?"

"I'm not sure how to answer that. Some good. Some interesting. Some not so good." I smiled in spite of myself though. Hearing Luke's voice, despite my misgivings about our relationship, was making me feel better. "I think the day is taking a turn for the better though." I was flirting. It felt good.

"I hope so. Care to tell me all about it over dinner tonight? I'm buying."

I dreaded having the conversation I knew we needed to have but I also wanted to see Luke so much. I knew being with him would make so many things more bearable. My need for him won out.

"Sure. Where and when?"

"I know a nice Italian place right in Fountain Hills and I can pick you up at seven. I've been running around all day. The office was busy today and I need time to freshen up."

The next few hours dragged by. Finally, I heard Luke's car in the driveway. So did Sam and he greeted the sound with lots of barking. I held Sam back as I let Luke in the door. My arms were occupied, and Luke took advantage of that. He closed the door and swept me into a big Luke hug and kissed me.

"We'd better go eat now or we never will," he said, his voice gruff with emotion.

"Just let me grab my purse and we can go."

Dinner was everything I needed. Good wine, good food, and Luke who wouldn't take his eyes off me. We held hands in between courses, and I told Luke everything that had happened – my possible job loss, Peter's call and his offer on the house, Bianca's pregnancy. It felt so good to let it all out. Talking to Luke was even better than talking it all over with Hannah. I felt my world getting calmer.

Finally, after the waiter had brought dessert and refilled our wine glasses, Luke looked straight into my eyes and said what I had been dreading. "Let's finish that conversation we were having last week."

I put down my spoon. "Okay. You first this time."

"Look, I know what I'm asking. And I know I hurt you – us – a lot. I did what I did because I thought I was doing the right thing. And I'm not proud of this but I think part of me thought that somehow you and I would get together again. I didn't expect things to last with Cathy. We didn't make it work the first time and building a relationship on a pregnancy is no way to start again. I figured I would stay until the baby was born and then see where things stood. Then Darcy was born and I just couldn't leave. So, I let the fantasy of us go. Soon after that Camille and I found each other. She told me you were married. I was happy for you. I threw myself into my life at that point – the baby, Cathy, my work. Then Cathy died and thoughts of you came back. When Camille told me you were getting divorced I knew it was our chance."

Luke took both of my hands in his. The look in his eyes made me melt. It was as if all the years in between had vanished. Luke – my Luke – was in front of me and he wanted me. I thought of the kiss from just a little while ago. I knew I wanted more.

"I know I hurt you. I'm sorry. Please give us another chance. I love you, Charlotte. I never stopped loving you."

I brought one of his hands to my mouth and kissed it.

"Let's go home."

Luke immediately signaled our waiter and within minutes we were parked in front of Auntie's house.

We kissed again as soon as Luke turned the ignition off.

"Do you want to come inside?"

"Do you want me to?"

"Yes. I could make coffee." I smiled. Luke knew I was teasing him.

"I would love some coffee."

But we didn't have coffee. As soon as the front door was locked Luke took me in his arms again and kissed me as if he was never going to let me go. And I didn't resist. It felt as if we were back in New York in my old apartment and nothing had changed. We made our way to my bedroom, shedding clothes along the way.

The next hour was pure bliss. Tender at times, purely lustful at others. I was hungry for Luke and he for me. It felt as if no time had passed since the last time we had made love together. I couldn't believe I was finally in his arms, touching him, remembering places my fingers had caressed so long ago. When he entered me, it felt as if all the bad pieces of my world disappeared, and peace was in their places again.

Later, we just held each other, both of us out of breath. "Charlotte, I love you so much."

"I love you, too." It was true. It was stupid to continue to deny it.

"I've waited so long to hear you say that."

Then, Luke picked his head up. "Do you have to go out?"

"What? Out? What are you talking about?"

Luke laughed. "I was talking to the dog. He's whining. I think he has to pee."

I started to get up.

"Stay in bed. I'll take care of it," Luke said. He put on his pants and slipped his shoes on and then kissed me on the nose. "Don't go anywhere. I'll be right back. I want some more."

We made love again when he returned and then both of us fell asleep, Luke spooning me.

Chapter Thirty

 C8

I woke up frequently during the night. Several times I reached out to touch Luke, still unable to believe that he was really there, that we were us again. I felt as if I were finally home.

Safe.

Loved.

Once again with the only person I truly trusted with my heart. Yes, I had loved and married Peter and we had had a life together but knowing now how I still felt about Luke, I was painfully aware that I had never given myself over to Peter completely and maybe to some extent I bore some of the responsibility for our breakup.

I awoke for the last time as sunlight was streaming through the window shade. I checked the small clock on the bedside table and saw that it was after seven. I instinctively reached out for Luke, but his side of the bed was empty. I felt a stab of panic.

I sat up and called out his name but there was no answer.

Why would he leave without even saying anything to me?

I sat at the side of the bed and put on my slippers and robe. I heard Sam barking outside and thought that strange. How did the dog get outside? I quickly walked through the kitchen and noticed the coffeepot was on and a full pot had brewed. As I neared the deck door, I distinctly heard humming.

Curious, I opened the door.

And then I smiled.

Luke hadn't left. Or rather he had and had already returned. There on the little rattan coffee table Luke had set out a morning feast – table linens, cups, cutlery, plates, and a basket of bagels accompanied by two kinds of cream cheese.

Luke heard the door open and looked up, a huge grin on his face.

"Remember our first morning after our first date?"

"Yes, I do. You woke me up at the crack of dawn with bagels and cream cheese."

He made a sweeping gesture over his surprise. "Ta da!"

He pulled out a chair for me. "Sit. Enjoy. I even found the cream cheese with salmon bits in it like we had that morning. I'll bring our coffee out."

I couldn't believe it. Whatever will power I had left to put the brakes on our relationship vanished then and there.

Luke was so proud of himself. And with good reason. He could not have picked a better way to wake me up after our night of lovemaking. He knew if he could get me to remember how we had been in our early days that any misgivings I had would melt.

He was right.

And so the weekend went – filled with more attention and love than I had experienced in a very long time. Life once again felt good. All I wanted was Luke and thankfully, he wanted me as much, if not more.

We did take time out to visit Auntie. The first time was that afternoon during a break in Auntie's therapy schedule. I was feeling encouraged by her level of alertness. She was busy showing me how she was able to use the walker. It pained me to see her having to use the device but her enthusiasm at being independent again was infectious. At one point, Luke left us in her room while he went to the nurse's station to look over her chart. Auntie took the opportunity to grill me. She was sitting in a comfortable lounge chair and I had scooted the wooden visitors chair over to her side.

She grabbed my hand and with a twinkle in her eye said, "Okay, what is going on? And don't lie to me. Something's changed." It was obvious her speech pattern was also improving. My old Auntie was coming back.

All I could do was smile.

She patted my cheek. "I'm so happy for you."

Just then, Luke returned.

"Good news, Camille. They think you can go home the first part of this coming week." He sat on the edge of the bed and faced her. "But I know you. You're going to try to do too much. You still need rehab but they're going to start you off with therapy at home for a few days and then you can attend an out-patient clinic. And I want you in my office in a couple of weeks too. How does that sound?"

"Wonderful." Then her face clouded over.

"Auntie, what is it?"

She looked at me. "Are you going back to New York?"

"No. I'm going to take time off from work. I already spoke to my supervisor. I'll stay here as long as you need me. Besides," I looked at Luke and winked, "I'm pretty sure New York is a thing of the past anyway. We'll work this out."

And we did.

On Monday, I called my supervisor and told her to put me on a leave of absence. I was sure that this was just a formality and my time in New York was over, but I wasn't quite ready to burn all my bridges yet. I also called my attorney and told him to notify Peter's attorney that I was willing to accept the offer on our house provided it was reasonable, at least fair market value. I also asked for some time to go back and pack up my things. Whether I put everything in storage or moved it all out here was a story for another day. One thing at a time.

Auntie was discharged home on Tuesday and life fell into a routine. Home therapy was set up for her to start at the end of the week and continue for a couple of weeks. Assuming she did well, she would graduate to out-patient for a while. Her left hand was stronger, but her left leg was still weak, and her balance suffered because of it. She could not be left alone, and this worried both of us but there seemed to be an unspoken rule not to discuss it. She still had occasional word-finding issues but that too seemed to be improving. The sparkle in her eye was slowly returning and seemed to be encouraged every time she saw Luke at the house – which was every day.

We decided to have a welcome home party that first weekend. I invited Hannah and Sean and the twins. Of course, Luke was going to come. Then, because I knew it was the right thing to do and because the inevitable had to happen sometime, I made sure he understood he was to bring Darcy. I was nervous about it and discussed it with Hannah the day before the party.

"What's your biggest fear?" Hannah asked. I had called her when Auntie went in for her afternoon nap. I didn't want her to overhear how I felt.

"It's not so much a fear as it is a resentment. And I know it's not logical. She had nothing to do with our breakup. I mean, technically, yeah, she did. It was because Cathy was pregnant with her but that's not Darcy's fault."

"No, it's not. And she's really a good kid. And not so much a kid, either. She's only a few years younger than Beth."

I felt a stab of sadness at the mention of Beth's name. I hadn't heard a word from her since she and Peter had called with the offer on the house.

"It's just that when I see her, I see Cathy."

"I know but she's all Luke. You'll see. Once you get to know her, you'll love her as much as we all do. The twins are crazy about her. And she adores Luke."

I sighed. "I know you're right. And if I want this to work out with Luke, I must make peace with how I feel about Darcy. I certainly can't be with him and resent his child."

"Did I not tell you this trip was going to be awesome?"

I laughed. "Yes, you did. You and Auntie are a pair, for sure. So, let's talk food. Can you bring a fabulous dessert? We'll have everything else here."

"Sure can. It'll be a surprise."

After we hung up, I checked on Auntie. She was sound asleep, her loyal dog on the bed keeping her company. Sam raised his head when I opened the door but didn't move from Auntie's side. I quietly closed the door and let them both sleep.

I grabbed the book I had been reading, poured myself a glass of iced tea and headed out to the deck to read and relax. I laid down on the swing and opened my book. I was barely two pages in before sleep took over.

I woke up about forty-five minutes later to the feeling of Sam licking my face. Auntie was sitting in a lounge chair opposite me. Her walker was parked next to her.

"Hey, sleepyhead," she said.

"Hey, yourself. How are you feeling? "

"Pretty good, actually. I was thinking we could go into town for dinner. I'm getting tired of your cooking."

"I am too. That sounds like a wonderful idea."

"Do you think Luke could join us?"

"I'll ask." I dialed Luke's cell and he answered on the first ring. "Hi, Charlotte. I can't talk right now. I'm between patients and I'm behind schedule."

"Okay, I was just calling to see if you

wanted to join me and Auntie for dinner in town tonight."

"Sorry, hon. I think I should stay home. I haven't spent much time with Darcy this week. Besides, I'm bringing her to the party tomorrow so it makes sense that I stay home tonight."

I was surprised at the amount of disappointment I felt but I understood.

"Okay, see you tomorrow."

"Tomorrow. Love you." And he hung up.

I looked at Auntie. "Sorry, Auntie. I guess you heard. He can't. It's just us."

"Oh, well, that can be fun too."

Chapter Thirty-One

ॐ

I spent the better part of Saturday getting ready. The morning was filled with cleaning. The early afternoon shopping for last minute items and food preparation. I knew I was not going to be able to compete with Hannah's skills and I didn't even try.

Supper was going to be simple. Grilled hamburgers, potato salad, coleslaw, things to nibble on beforehand, and Hannah's dessert, whatever that turned out to be.

And wine. Lots of wine.

I was very nervous. I wanted the evening to go well. I also wondered how Darcy and I would be with each other.

And I wasn't sure what she knew about me. I had never discussed with Luke if he had explained our relationship. I assumed he had, and I wished now I had tried harder to find out. Well, the time for finding out was fast approaching.

Hannah, Sean, and the twins arrived before Luke and Darcy. I positioned Auntie on the deck in the most comfortable chair with strict instructions not to go anywhere without me. I was afraid the rambunctious twins would topple her over. I needn't have worried. The girls were very careful around her and gave her lots of attention which Auntie enjoyed. They were falling over each other in their attempts to take care of her. Sean busied himself getting the grill ready and Hannah and I retreated to the kitchen. She had already put her dessert – red velvet cupcakes with cream cheese icing – in the refrigerator.

She poured us both a generous glass of white wine.

"Nervous?" she asked as she placed my glass in front of me. I was at the breakfast bar, slicing cheese for the cheeseboard.

"Yes. I always get this way when I entertain. Peter and I did a lot of it in the early days and it never got any easier. But this makes no sense now. We're all friends."

"Yes, we are except for Darcy. For you, I mean. You really don't know her but trust me. After tonight, you're going to wonder why you made such a big deal out of this."

And then a few minutes later Luke and Darcy arrived, and the noise level went up a few decibels. After the usual hello's all around, the twins immediately transferred their attention to Darcy. Luke wandered over to the grill at the far end of the deck to keep Sean company and Hannah and I spent the next few minutes bringing trays of food to nibble on out to the deck.

The evening went well. Hannah had been right. I was foolish to have worried. Everyone enjoyed themselves and Auntie just glowed from all the attention. I was so glad I had decided to celebrate her homecoming.

Darcy and I had a chance to sit together while we ate dessert. The sun was starting to go down and we watched the colors change.

"I'm so glad I have this chance to get to know you better," she said. "I've only met you a couple of times and neither of those times allowed us to say much to each other. I have to admit, I was afraid you didn't like me."

I felt a pang of guilt. "I'm sorry I gave you that impression. I was just surprised that you knew everyone so well. Especially Auntie. But she explained everything to me. It was wrong of me to feel anything but warmth toward you. I hope we can be friends."

"I would like that. Especially now that you and Dad are getting so close. He told me how he feels about you. I have to admit I was surprised at first, but I know how lonely he's been since Mom died. It's great that he has a friend that he knows. I think the best relationships can spring from friendship."

I must have looked puzzled because she hurried to go on. "I hope it's all right that I say this. Dad told me how you and he were friends who worked together back east before he and my Mom got together."

I focused on my cupcake, unsure what to say. It was painfully obvious that Luke had given Darcy a very watered down – if not outright false – version of events. It was not my place to tell her otherwise, but I needed to talk to Luke about it. And soon.

I excused myself under the pretext of setting up the coffee brewer. I caught Hannah's eye and motioned for her to follow me back inside.

"What's up?" she asked as soon as we were in the kitchen. I busied myself with mugs and coffee pods while I tried to control my emotions.

"Charlotte, what's wrong? You look awful."

"I don't know how I feel. I was just talking to Darcy."

"Was I right? Isn't she sweet?"

"Yeah. Sweet. And terribly misinformed." I told Hannah what Darcy had said.

"Wow. I guess I can understand why Luke would want to break it to her gently."

"This isn't about gently. This is a flat out lie."

"Maybe he plans on telling her everything eventually. Let it go for tonight and ask him about it next time you're together."

I didn't meet Hannah's eyes.

"Charlotte. I know that look. Don't you do something you'll regret. Let it go. If you say anything to Luke tonight you run the risk of going someplace you can't come back from."

I sighed. Hannah knew me too well. "You're right. I'll talk to him tomorrow."

I managed to hide my feelings better than I thought I would. Luke and I hardly had any time alone together anyway. Soon, everyone had departed, and it was just me and Auntie. And Auntie looked worn out. I helped her to bed and then sat on the deck for a while. The night air was still warm. My phone pinged and I looked and found a text from Luke.

The evening went great. Thank you for making friends with Darcy. Love you. Talk tomorrow.

Yes, Luke, we definitely will.

Chapter Thirty-Two

ରଓ

But we didn't get a chance to talk as soon as I had wanted. One of Luke's patients had an emergency the next morning that kept him occupied most of the day. It was right around suppertime when he finally called. He had just arrived home and sounded beat.

But it wasn't from work. While he had indeed been kept busy with his patient, that was resolved by early afternoon. No, Luke was sounding tired because he had been out riding with Darcy for the last couple of hours. I was upset at first and then encouraged. Maybe he was telling Darcy more of our story.

But no.

"I want to break it to her in stages, Char. And, honestly, does she really have to know the whole story? What's the point? She knows about us now. Let her get to know you and love you. Telling her about our past might jeopardize that."

"Does she know her mother was pregnant before you were married? How did you explain all that?"

"Yes, she knows. She knows Cathy and I had dated and had been a couple several years before but then we broke up. And then we got back together when I traveled to Philly that weekend. And she knows Cathy got pregnant and we decided to get married. But she thinks there was more love than there was at the beginning."

I couldn't respond to that. This conversation was hurting. It was obvious that Luke was telling me he came to love Cathy after a while.

"Charlotte, say something."

"Say what, Luke? It hurts to hear you talk about your life with Cathy."

"I know and I'm sorry. But we're not virgins. You had Peter, too. And I cared a great deal for Cathy whether you want to hear that or not. I was a good husband, and I was head over heels in love with Darcy. It was really hard on us when Cathy died. Especially for Darcy. She was a teenage girl who had lost her mother. I'm glad I'm here for her. I wouldn't want to be anywhere else. Can you understand that?"

"Yes."

"But now life has given us another chance. I owe it to Darcy to do what's best for her. And if shielding her from part of her mother's story is best, then that's what I'm going to do. You and I are grown-ups. We can handle this. She can learn to love you now. As far as she knows, you and I worked together back in New York, and we dated. She knows we were involved for a while but that changed when I got back with her mother. Now, you and I are picking up where we left off. She knows how I feel about you now. That's how I have explained us to Darcy. I haven't told her that you and I were engaged. That I cheated on you with Cathy. I'm begging you to back me up."

"Luke, I don't feel comfortable with ..."

"Oh, shit!" Luke yelled.

"What's wrong?"

"Look. I've got to go. Darcy was standing in the doorway. I think she heard everything."

And he hung up.

Chapter Thirty-Three

cȝ

I waited for Luke to call me back, but he
never did. I kept checking my phone for a text
hoping to hear any shred of hope but there was
nothing. I tried to tell myself that maybe that was
good news. That maybe now that the truth was out,
we all could start fresh. But I knew in my heart that
was foolish. If Luke's relationship with Darcy was
threatened by his feelings for me, I would lose.

I felt bad for Darcy. None of this was her
fault. She was innocent. But Luke had lied to her
about us and there might not be any coming back
from that.

I barely slept that night. I kept waking up
and when I did sleep my dreams were full of
anxiety. My mind kept finding ways to make me
realize I was in real danger of losing Luke again.

I finally got a text from Luke the following
afternoon.

Darcy is very upset with me. Trying to make it right. Give us time. Miss you.

It was short but I clung to a little bit of hope.

Early the next morning, Auntie had her visit with the nurse overseeing her physical and occupational therapy. I gave them privacy while they worked and busied myself in the kitchen. When she was finished with her evaluation, the nurse sought me out.

"Hi, can we talk? Camille has given me permission to discuss her with you. I'd like to give you an update and go over her plan."

Over the next few minutes Lisa explained Auntie's therapy plan. She was optimistic that Auntie would recover almost all function, but she was hesitant to say if she believed Auntie could live alone again.

"Does my aunt know this?"

"Yes, we talked about it. But I think that's not something we need to decide just yet. Let's reevaluate after she's got more therapy under her belt. I think a couple of weeks of in-home therapy followed by out-patient is the way we should go for now. I understand she's already had some sessions and the notes are promising. Then after a few weeks we can revisit all of this."

I looked at the stack of records she had placed on the kitchen counter.

"Are all those Auntie's records?"

"Yes, it seems like a lot but these are from the hospital as well as her primary doctor."

Luke's office had called that morning while Lisa was doing her evaluation and asked me where Dr. Kramer's records were. They had requested Auntie's latest reports from her primary doctor – the records from just before she had seen Dr. Farrell - but had not received them yet. I was surprised Farrell's office hadn't sent them over to Luke. Didn't they share files? Who knew at this point? The more I knew about Farrell the less respect I had for him and his PA. But I saw a solution to this mix-up – and my personal problem - sitting right in front of me.

"Dr. Andrews' office is looking for Auntie's labs and EKG reports from Dr. Kramer and they haven't received them yet. If we could just copy those from you, I could drop them off at his office this afternoon. Auntie has an appointment later this week and it's important they have those." I had no idea how important it really was, but I didn't want to let this opportunity slip by me.

"I guess that would be all right. Let me just clear it with Camille."

Auntie of course said yes. I gave the nurse access to Auntie's printer/copier and a few minutes later I had the needed paperwork in my hand and my plan hatched.

An hour later I called Luke's office to let them know I had the requested paperwork. I asked as casually as I could if he was available later that day and was surprised to find out he had called in that morning and cleared his schedule. He was not in the office at all that day. My adolescent plan wasn't going to work.

The receptionist transferred me to the person in charge of medical records when I mentioned having Dr. Kramer's records. "Thank you so much for going to all that trouble but we found out that Dr. Farrell had the records we needed, and he gave us copies."

I thanked the medical records manager and hung up. I was frustrated but there was nothing else to do now except wait for Luke to make the next move. He had texted a couple of more times. They had been nice but short. I had no way of knowing what was really going on with him and Darcy right now. I was reluctant to call him and there was no way I would go to his home. Absent ambushing him at his office, I had to wait. And waiting was awful.

I busied myself for the rest of the day taking care of Auntie. She had therapy right after lunch and then was very tired and took a nap in her room.

I took that opportunity to look over her records to see if anything in there might be useful. Several pages in I was struck by the obvious disparity between two EKG's. When I looked closer, I realized that the one with the abnormalities was from Dr. Farrell's office. The nurse had mistakenly copied *all* the EKG's, not just the ones from Dr. Kramer's office. The one taken just prior to seeing Dr. Farrell was normal for a woman Auntie's age. Some minor heart block but nothing grave. The EKG from Dr. Farrell's office looked like an EKG from someone entirely different. There was no way this was Auntie's record. It could have been just a filing error but the name on both records was clearly Auntie's and the abnormal EKG was dated correctly for when she had seen Dr. Farrell.

Was it possible that records had been actually falsified to justify a cardiac catheterization? Would Dr. Farrell – would any doctor – go to such lengths? It didn't seem possible but what other explanation could there be?

I thought back to the day at Hannah's house when she told me she had heard Farrell was being sued by a patient. Then there was that conversation Hannah overheard between Farrell and Vince. Something about complications and records. Could that have been Auntie's case? It was right around the time she had had her stroke. Was I looking at evidence?

My hands shook. I didn't know what to do. Call Luke? Make a crazy accusation against his partner without any real proof?

I did what I normally did when I had a problem. I called Hannah. I hadn't even told her what was going on with Luke and Darcy, so this was a perfect excuse. Somehow, I would work the EKG record into the conversation and try not to sound like a conspiracy nut.

She had texted me Saturday morning and warned me she would be unavailable the whole weekend because she was preparing for another big party later in the week. But now I needed her. This couldn't wait.

"You caught me at just the right time. I have some stuff in the oven and I'm taking a break. Talk to me while I'm drinking my coffee."

I filled Hannah in on my horrible weekend.

"Damn, Charlotte. This is awful. Luke must be devastated. Darcy is his life."

"I know. I feel so guilty. I didn't want this to happen. I want Darcy to know about us but not this way. She may never want me in her life now. And I have no idea how she feels about Luke. I have to make this right."

"How?"

"I have no idea, but I have to talk to Luke." I explained how I had thought to use some files he needed.

"That was awfully Lucy-like."

"I know. It's probably better that it didn't work out. And he took today off anyway. But there's something else." I explained about the two disparate EKG's.

"Are you sure about this?"

"Hannah, I'm a cardiac nurse. I know how to read an EKG. No way both belong to Auntie."

"Maybe the first one is an error."

"I hadn't thought about that."

"See? You're letting your imagination run away with you because you don't like Dr. Farrell."

"I guess that's possible."

"Why don't you just tell Luke your thoughts and let him figure it out."

"You're right. That's probably best. If he calls tonight, I'll bring it up. This waiting is killing me."

"I know, Sweetie. But Luke is very methodical. You know that. He has to work things out in his own way. He'll come around." She was quiet for a minute, then – "Look, I hate to ask you this, but do you think you could do me a huge favor tomorrow?"

"Sure. What do you need?"

"The twins are bugging me to go see their friend. I told them they could go tomorrow but now I'm falling behind and I really don't have the time to drive them there and back. Their friend lives in Rio Verde. It's just the next town over. Could you drive them over tomorrow morning and then pick them up in the afternoon?"

"It's okay. I don't mind."

"Great. I really appreciate it. They're climbing the walls and I can get so much more done if they're occupied elsewhere."

We made plans for me to pick up the girls the next morning and then hung up.

Auntie woke up a little while later and thoughts of Luke and EKG's vanished while I spent time with her. We had a light supper and watched television. Auntie started to doze off and I suggested she go to bed which she did.

I sat in the living room with a glass of wine trying to read but with nothing else to occupy my mind, my thoughts drifted back to worrying about EKG's and about Luke and Darcy – and us.

My phone rang just then. Caller ID told me it was Luke. I couldn't help but smile as I answered.

"Hey you," he said. "I've missed you."

"I've missed you too. I was worried when I didn't hear from you."

"I know. I'm sorry but I wanted to spend as much time as I could with Darcy and fix things with her."

"And how is that going?"

"Pretty well, I think. I want to talk to you about it, but you need to answer the door first."

"What? There's no one -"

Just then, the doorbell rang.

I raced to open it and found Luke standing there, phone in hand and the biggest grin on his face. I grabbed him and pulled him into the room.

Chapter Thirty-Four

ೞ

Luke held me with the same intensity I remembered from our early life together. He kissed me over and over. His lips and tongue awakened a lust in me I had long ago thought I would never experience again. I knew there was no way I would let him out of my life. This is where I longed to be. This is where I needed to be.

Forever.

How foolish I had been to doubt it for even a minute.

Luke finally released me, and we stood there, looking into each other's face.

"I have missed you so much," he finally said.

"I missed you too, Luke. I love you. I never stopped. I know that now."

Luke smiled. "I'm so happy." He hugged me again. I put my head on his chest and just listened to his heartbeat. It was a sound I never wanted to be away from. This was what all I wanted and needed.

But we needed to talk, too.

"Want some wine? I want to hear what's going on with you? How is Darcy? Is she still upset with you? With us?"

Luke followed me into the kitchen. He kept touching me – my hair, my back, my cheek, as I grabbed a wine glass and poured wine for him.

We held hands as we walked back into the living room and sat on the sofa where just minutes before I had worried if we would ever be back together again.

Over the next few minutes, Luke told me how Darcy had been both angry and upset when she learned the full story of her birth. She felt that Luke and her mother had lied to her.

"And of course, we had," Luke said. "But it was to protect her. We didn't want her to know the full extent of what Cathy's pregnancy had meant. Especially for me. That's a horrible thing for a child to know. Especially after Cathy died. I didn't want her to ever know. And before we became us again," Luke was drawing circles on my hand, "I didn't expect that she would ever have to know the whole story."

I touched Luke's hair. "I'm so sorry, Sweetheart. How did you fix it with her?"

"I didn't. Not right away. Darcy was so angry. I've never seen her like that. I worried about her after her Mom died. She seemed to handle it almost too well. I think this was a catalyst for her. She finally let it all out. She simply exhausted herself. We didn't resolve anything that night. She just went to bed. But she must have done a lot of thinking after she was alone. That's how she is. She retreats and then sorts things out. The next morning, we talked like two adults and she seemed to come to peace with it. She forgave me. We spent time together and she had lots of questions."

"What about?"

"About my real relationship with Cathy. If I loved Cathy. Why I stayed. She had questions about you, too."

"I was afraid of that."

"Why? You didn't do anything. You're a victim too."

"I know but I feel so much the other woman in all this."

"Don't be silly. It's going to work out. Trust me."

Luke took the wine glass out of my hand and placed it on the coffee table in front of us. "Come here." He pulled me into his arms again and kissed me. I knew where this was headed.

And I couldn't wait.

He stood up and led me into my bedroom. As we undressed each other, I couldn't help but feel giddy knowing my life was about to change forever. New York was definitely history. My job there was gone, and I didn't care. Peter would never be part of my life again and that was a good thing. My life was here now.

With Auntie.

With Luke.

I knew if we were together, we would work out whatever was ahead of us.

We tried being quiet as we made love. We succeeded for the most part.

Afterwards, I lay in Luke's arms, my head

on his chest while he stroked my back.

"You don't think she heard us, do you?" I asked.

"Only if she's hard of hearing."

I giggled.

"It's so good to hear you laugh. I've missed that laugh." Luke kissed me again and I could feel that he was getting ready for round two.

I sat up. "Not that I'm not up for doing this all night but there's something I want to show you?"

"Oh? Is there something I haven't seen yet?"

I poked him. "Stop it. I'm serious."

I told him about the discrepancy in Auntie's EKG's.

"Let me see the records."

I went into the living room and retrieved the records and brought them back into bed with us. I watched Luke as he looked them over. I saw his forehead furrow as he realized what I had seen just hours before.

"What do you think?"

"I don't know what to think. At first glance, this could just be a clerical error. At its worst, it could be something more serious, but I find that hard to believe."

I reminded Luke of Farrell's pending lawsuit.

"That doesn't mean anything, Charlotte. It's not proof. It hasn't even gone to trial yet."

I told Luke about what Hannah had overheard at the party, when Vince and Farrell had been talking about "records".

"Again, that could mean anything. I know you don't like Mark, but this is a serious accusation if you think he falsified the records. That's career ending. Not to mention criminal. And it might put me at some potential risk too."

"I hadn't thought about that. What's the extent of your relationship with him?"

"I am not close with him personally. I knew of him about a year before we joined our offices a couple of years ago. We have a quasi-partnership. We share expenses and staff, but our practices are separate. Even our records. I refer to him if I need an interventionalist. It doesn't usually work the other way around. He rarely refers patients to me. But it works for me because I sometimes need his services. And sharing the office saves me money."

"Who does Vince work for?"

"He's employed by Mark. Mark pays his salary. Mark brought him along when he joined. Mark rents the space from me and his rent covers his portion of the office and the use of the staff. But he's independent from me. His records are his records. His patients are his patients. So, I guess I might be okay legally if there is something sinister going on. I'll have to talk to my attorney and insurance company. But first I need to know what we're dealing with. This is only one record and there could be any number of reasons why this is off."

"Do you have any way to look at his records?"

"No, only if the patient comes back to me from him."

"Has that ever happened?"

"Rarely. He usually follows them after they are referred. I took over Camille's case because she's a friend. And because of you."

Luke had pulled on his pants and was now pacing around the room.

"What about the current lawsuit? Do you have access to those records?"

"No. They asked for my records as part of discovery but it's Mark's lawsuit. There is no way I would be able to see the entire case. I'm not a party to it."

"There's got to be some way to know if there are other cases like Auntie's."

"Let me go home and think some more. If I stay here, I'm afraid thinking won't be a priority." He kissed me and grabbed the rest of his clothes.

"When can I see you again?" Now that we were back together, I didn't want Luke away from me for a minute.

"How about lunch tomorrow? Come to the office about 11:30."

"I have to drop Hannah's kids off at their friend's house first. But I should be at your office on time."

I walked Luke to the door. We hugged and kissed and then he was gone.

I took our wine glasses into the kitchen and jumped when I heard a voice behind me.

"Hey, Charlotte."

It was Auntie with a horrible case of bedhead.

"What are you doing up?"

"Who could sleep with that racket going on in the next room?"

Chapter Thirty-Five

❦

I was reluctant to leave Auntie alone the next morning. This was going to be her first time on her own since coming home from the hospital, but she assured me she would be fine. She reminded me she had her phone with her at all times and she was actually better than I was giving her credit for.

"I'm fine. Stop fussing. I'm just going to hang out here and rest. I'll read, watch TV, nap. Nothing exciting. Go. Have a life. I'll see you when you get back. And give that man a big kiss for me."

I reached Hannah's a few minutes early. The twins were getting dressed. I could hear laughing coming from their room.

Hannah looked tired. "I can't thank you enough for doing this for me."

"No problem. You look like you need a break."

"You have no idea. Have you decided what

you're going to do about Camille's EKG?"

I gave Hannah a big smile and she immediately knew something was up.

"Get out! I knew something was different about you this morning." She poured herself a cup of coffee and sat at the break bar. "Tell me everything."

Hannah listened while I told her about Luke and Darcy and about Luke's thoughts about Auntie's EKG.

"And? Okay, so things are working out in those two areas. That doesn't account for that shit-eating grin on your face. I know that grin. You've finally made up your mind. Haven't you? Tell me."

"Yes. It's official. We haven't talked about details yet but I'm not going back to New York. Except to pack. I'm staying. I'm moving to Arizona. I'm staying with Luke."

Hannah screamed and jumped off the bar stool and hugged me so tight I thought a rib would break.

"I am so happy for you. You have no idea. We have to celebrate. Maybe this weekend?"

"Slow down. Please. Yes, we'll do something, but I don't want to commit to anything yet. Let me talk to Luke. I'm meeting him for lunch."

By this time, the twins were standing in the kitchen doorway. Each had a backpack and I saw a bathing suit sticking out of Gloria's.

"We're ready to go, Aunt Charlotte."

Hannah gave me a piece of paper with the address on it so I could program the GPS on my phone.

"What time do you think you'll be back in

town?"

"I don't know. Not too late. I imagine Luke and I will be done with lunch a little after one. I don't want to leave Auntie alone for too long. I'll probably be back here in town about 1:30 give or take. Why?"

"Do you think you can pick the girls up around two-ish?"

"Sure. No problem. I'll call you when I get close and we can confirm in case anything changes."

"Great. Okay, girls. Give Mommy a kiss. Be good. Listen to Angela's mom and have a good time."

"We will," they said in unison and ran out the front door.

Hannah rolled her eyes and we hugged good-bye.

Minutes later, the GPS was guiding me to Angela's house. The twins were in the back seat, each of them texting their friends and giggling.

We arrived at their friend's house about twenty minutes later. The car had no sooner come to a halt when the girls grabbed their things and ran out to their friend who was waiting for them in her driveway. I waved good-bye and headed to Scottsdale. I had about forty-five minutes before I was to meet Luke. Just enough time barring traffic.

Chapter Thirty-Six

ଔ

I arrived at Luke's office suite right on time and told the receptionist I was there to meet him. She called back to his office and after he answered, she instructed me to go on back.

I stood in the open doorway to Luke's office. He was seated at his desk, frowning, reading something intently on his laptop. But he looked up and smiled as soon as he heard me. He motioned for me to wait in the doorway. He read for a few seconds more and then logged off, closed his laptop, and put it in his desk drawer which he then locked. All of that made me very nervous for reasons I couldn't identify.

"Let's get out of here," he said. He closed his office door behind us and taking my hand, we walked through the empty lobby. I was acutely aware of Luke's staff looking at us. He didn't seem to notice.

"Pam, I'll be at lunch for the next hour or so. Page me if you need me but only if it can't wait."

"Sure thing, Dr. Luke."

We walked to Luke's car in silence. I noticed Luke's jaw twitching and knew that meant he was very upset. The knots in my stomach that had started yesterday afternoon were getting tighter.

"I know a nice place nearby," he said as we got settled in. "It's not fancy but we can talk."

"I'm getting the distinct impression we need to."

"Yes. We definitely do."

The restaurant was just a few blocks away and we reached it in no time. The restaurant was Italian, and I immediately thought of our first date so many years ago – the quiet little restaurant that was just blocks away from where we both had lived. The restaurant where it all started. This didn't have the romantic flair that that restaurant had though. It was brightly lit. Several tables lined the walls while others were in the middle of the room. Two tables along the left wall were occupied. One with two gentlemen. The other by a teenage couple. The kitchen was along the back wall and was open to view. A cash register counter was by the doorway. A middle-aged woman stood behind the register.

And just like in that restaurant of years ago, the staff recognized Luke.

"Just sit anywhere, Dr. Luke," the hostess said as she grabbed two menus.

Luke chose a table along the right wall halfway between the front counter and the window. The hostess followed us to our table and placed the menus in front of us.

"Can I get you two anything to drink?"

"I'll have iced tea, Greta," Luke said.

The hostess looked at me. "I'll have the same," I said.

"Great. I'll be right back with your drinks. Take your time. Although I suspect you know what you're having already," she said to Luke.

Luke laughed. "Yeah, I think I have the menu memorized."

Luke grabbed both of my hands in his as soon as we were alone.

"I'm so happy about us."

I squeezed his hands. "Me, too. But you seem upset. What's going on?"

Luke sighed and opened his mouth to speak just as Greta returned with our drinks and a basket of Italian bread and pats of butter.

"Have you decided?" she asked as she took out her order pad.

Luke let go of my hands. "I'll have the linguini with clam sauce." He handed his menu back to Greta. She then looked at me. I hadn't even opened my menu and had no idea what I wanted. In all honesty, right at that moment I didn't even care.

"Same for me," I said. "Thanks." I handed her my menu, too.

As soon as she was out of earshot, Luke said, "I talked to Mark this morning. It didn't go well, as you can imagine."

"Wow," was all I could say.

"After I left you last night, I did some research. As I told you last night, Mark moved to Arizona about a year before he joined with me. Pretty much right when I first met him. We had talked at medical society meetings and he seemed nice enough. His reputation was good. His resume was impressive. So, at his suggestion, we joined up. Like I said, it was a good deal for me. It lessened expenses. I didn't know anything about Vince and didn't feel I needed to. He was employed by Mark. Vince isn't my favorite person, but we only interact in the office when necessary. He seemed okay. Nothing that raised any flags.

"A few months after Mark joined my practice, I started hearing rumors about him gambling. It didn't affect our work and I felt it was none of my business. Then that lawsuit was filed. Again, I felt bad for him. Lawsuits happen. That's why we have malpractice insurance. Most times, they amount to nothing. I was concerned when I heard the allegations, but I had no reason to think anything of it until yesterday. The cases are eerily similar. But without access to Mark's records, I'm stuck. One case did come to me from him last year and I looked at those records and they looked fine to me.

"So, I called my attorney this morning and told him about Camille's chart just to see what he thought. He told me to notify my insurance rep. I did that. And just as I suspected, nothing can be done unless we know more. All we know is that we have a record discrepancy. I really felt it was a leap to think anything nefarious was going on."

He stopped talking because Greta returned with our lunch. She placed both plates in front of us. The aroma was heavenly. Lots of garlic. Just the way I liked it.

"Enjoy," Greta said and left.

Luke picked up his fork.

"Eat before it gets cold. The food here is exceptional. The rest of the story can wait."

I didn't think I could eat without knowing what else was upsetting Luke but after one forkful I decided he was right. The food was too good to waste.

Just as we had finished, Greta reappeared. She must have been watching us. I couldn't blame her. Business was slow.

"Anything else?" she asked as she removed our plates.

"No, that will be all," Luke said.

"I'll come by with your check."

"No rush, we're going to sit here a while if that's all right."

"Take your time."

Luke sighed. He looked back to make sure Greta couldn't hear us and then continued.

"On a hunch, after I talked to my attorney and insurance rep I decided to dig deeper. I did some research to see if I could find out anything about Vince. I don't even know why I thought to check him out. Just a gut feeling, I guess. But that's where it gets interesting. Apparently, he has a sketchy past. If what I found is correct, he has had some legal problems. Nothing major – cashing bad checks, petty theft. But enough for me to feel uncomfortable with him around. I should have researched more before I let either of them into my office. I don't know how he's licensed with that history. But again, that's on Mark. Maybe it wasn't the smartest thing to do but I confronted Mark about everything."

"You did? Wasn't that risky? What did he say?"

"He was immediately defensive. Said I was wrong. That I didn't know what I was talking about.

That he and Vince go back several years and everything is fine. When I told him about the EKG discrepancies, he got angry. He demanded to know how I was in possession of the EKG's. Maybe it was a mistake, but I told him. I wanted him to know it was an innocent discovery. That I was open to an explanation. But he exploded. Accused me of setting him up. I just left at that point and went back to my office.

"Soon after that, Vince arrived. He went into Mark's office and I could hear them arguing but not what was being said. I heard doors slammed and Vince left. I haven't spoken to Mark, but he emailed me a formal letter saying he would be vacating the office at the end of the month. Then he told the staff to cancel his appointments for the rest of the day and he left, too. We may never know what happened but at least he'll be gone. I told my attorney and he said he would handle it from now on."

"Oh, my God, Luke. How do you feel? Do you think you're safe?"

"Why wouldn't I be?"

"You just accused them of falsifying records."

"You've been watching too much *Law and Order*. Nothing is going to happen to me. Mark's the one in trouble and he knows it. It was obvious that he's covering up something. I don't know what his relationship with Vince is and I don't care. Vince might be pissed off but he's not my problem. That's for Mark to deal with. It's my office space. I have a right to have whoever I want or don't want there. And I don't want anyone with a criminal record handling patients. How do I even know he's a real PA? Mark's word? That leaves a lot to be desired right now."

I thought back to when Vince had performed Auntie's admission process and had taken her vital signs. I felt my pulse quicken at the thought of it. Luke was right. People had to be protected.

Greta came by with our check just then. "It was nice seeing you again, Dr. Luke."

She turned to me. "Nice meeting you, too."

Luke handed her some bills. "Keep the change, Greta. Lunch was great as always. We'll be back soon."

Back in the car, we sat there for a few seconds before Luke put the key in the ignition and started the car.

"How could I have been so stupid?" he asked as we drove back to his office.

"Don't beat yourself up over this. How could you have known?"

"I keep thinking about Camille and how badly this could have gone. If they falsified records and she had that cath for no reason which caused her stroke that's even worse..."

"Don't go there. I know I can't. She's going to be all right. And we still don't know anything. All you have are suspicions."

"And lots of suspicious behavior. I have a bad feeling about this. I just hope this is the end of it."

"It probably is. Let your attorney take care of this if anything more comes up. It's out of your hands now."

We were back in his parking lot now.

"I need a ladies' room," I said when we got out of the car. "Can I come back to your office? I should have gone at the restaurant. Too much iced tea."

Luke held my hand as we walked back to the lobby elevator.

"Your staff is going to think something is going on between us if you keep doing this," I teased.

"Then they are very smart." After looking around to make sure we were alone, Luke kissed me. We separated just as we heard the elevator chime its appearance.

Once inside his office suite, he directed me to the staff ladies' room.

"Come back to my office before you leave."

Luke was behind his desk when I entered his office. He had a chart open on his desk and was intently reading. I was happy to see he was back to work. He looked up as I entered.

"Close the door."

I did and then gave him a quizzical look.

"Vince is back," he said. "He told Pam he's packing up his things and I just don't want either of us to run into him unnecessarily. What are your plans for this afternoon?"

"I promised Hannah I would pick up the twins at their friend's house in Rio Verde on my way home."

"Ah, yes. The twins from hell."

"Don't say that. They're good kids. Just a little boisterous."

"A little? Their energy level is overwhelming. I guess I was spoiled by Darcy. She was a very easy kid. And quiet."

He rose and walked around his desk. "Do you have water in the car?"

"What? Why?"

"Honey, this is Arizona, remember? In the summer. It's 115 degrees outside. What if the car breaks down and you have to wait for a tow? You need to carry water. Here." He reached into a small fridge he kept in his office. "Take this." He handed me a bottle of water. "Keep something like this with you at all times. I worry about you."

He kissed me lightly on the mouth.

"Okay. Go. Now. I have work to do and you're distracting me."

He opened the door and looked down the hall. It was empty.

"Scoot. I'll call you later."

As I opened the car door a few minutes later, I heard a noise. I turned to see Vince exiting the building, carrying a box I assumed contained things from his office. He stopped when he saw me. He was several yards away and wearing sunglasses so I could not see the expression on his face, but I felt his glare. He shifted the box to one arm and raised his free hand to me, making a gesture of a gun with it. I got the message. He blamed me for his job loss. I turned away and quickly got in the car. I saw from my rear-view mirror that he had walked to his car. I couldn't see which one was his and didn't care. All I focused on was getting the car started and getting out of there as fast as I could. I knew I had to tell Luke about this as soon as I got home.

Chapter Thirty-Seven

CB

I exited the highway on Shea Boulevard and had gone a couple of blocks when I remembered I had told Hannah I would call her on my way back home.

I made the call while I was stopped at a red light. "Hannah, I'm in Scottsdale on Shea. I'm about twenty-five minutes out from home. We still on schedule for me to pick the girls up about two?"

"Yes, I'll call them and remind them. And by the way, Frances told me she left her phone in your car. Make sure she picks it up."

"Are you sure? How do you know it's in my car?"

"Because I checked my spy app and her phone has been sitting in Luke's parking lot for an hour and a half." Hannah giggled. "I hope you had a nice lunch." She emphasized the word *lunch*.

"Don't be cute. We really did just have lunch. But we had a very interesting talk. I'll tell you about it when I see you. Ok, gotta go. Light's changing."

I slowly accelerated and drove through Scottsdale into Fountain Hills but instead of turning in the direction of Auntie's house I kept on, letting the GPS guide me back to where I had dropped off the twins earlier that day.

Traffic was disappearing as I got closer to Rio Verde. The road in either direction was empty except for the occasional car or truck. I noticed one black pickup truck that had caught my eye at one of the red lights in Scottsdale was now behind me but a few car lengths back. I thought that odd. What were the chances of two identical cars following along the same route for that length of time?

But my mind soon drifted back to lunch with Luke and what he had told me. Despite his apparent bravado, I was worried. And the thought of someone deliberately putting Auntie at risk infuriated me. And seeing Vince in the parking lot had totally unnerved me.

The black truck was now directly behind me. I couldn't see who was driving. The cab was higher than my line of vision, but he was definitely following too closely. I tried to swerve to my right to let him pass but he stayed behind me and got closer. I looked around. There was nowhere for me to go. The lane to my left was for oncoming traffic. To my right was a wash at the bottom of a slight embankment.

My pulse quickened. I was afraid he was going to hit me. Maybe he was drunk. I had no idea what was going on but feared the worst.

Then, seconds later, he rammed the rear end of my car. I swerved and he hit me again.

Then he came alongside on my left. At that

point, I saw who it was.

Vince!

He smiled and swerved to his right, hitting my car on my side.

I overcompensated and had trouble staying on the road. He hit me again, harder this time.

I lost control. My car went down the embankment.

I screamed just before I felt the impact.

Then everything went black.

Chapter Thirty-Eight

ɔঽ

Consciousness erupted in my head like a gun going off.

Where was I?

What was that smell?

Senses started to come back one by one. I opened my eyes and saw the Arizona desert as far as I could see. The car was upright but angled to the right and slightly downward. To my left was the embankment and to my right the large wash below.

The deployed air bag was in my lap, powder all over me.

My head hurt and I tried to think. Where had I been going?

I was going to - to get the twins.

Memory slowly returned. The truck - the black truck – Vince! - that was following too close and then ramming me repeatedly until I went off the road.

Losing control.

Going down an embankment.

The boulder.

The impact and then nothing.

Until now.

How much time had passed? I had no idea how long I had been unconscious.

I immediately looked myself over. No bruises were visible. No bleeding that I could see. I moved my arms and legs, and everything seemed to be working. In addition to my head, my body ached but nothing I couldn't handle. Yet. But I knew it was just a matter of time.

I had to get help.

I turned the key in the ignition. The car sputtered and promptly died.

I looked for my cell phone and found it on the floor in front of the passenger seat. I checked it. One bar. Barely enough and the battery was low. In the red. I scolded myself. I had meant to charge it this morning. Should have.

I turned the key again. It barely clicked this time. That meant no air conditioner.

A tear ran down my cheek. This was not the time to waste bodily fluids I told myself and I smiled at my poor sense of humor.

But I was scared. Very scared. I remembered the woman who had sat next to me on the plane ride over here telling me about immigrants and coyotes and people dying who got lost in the desert. I didn't want to be one of them.

And it was getting very hot in the car. I needed to get out but where to go? Wandering around was as bad as staying put. And I wasn't sure I could make it up the embankment by myself.

Then I thought of snakes and scorpions.

Crap.

I tried the key one more time. Nothing. Obviously, the battery was dead.

And if I didn't get out of this desert soon, I would be, too.

I opened the door on my side to get some ventilation. That's when I noticed the bottle of water Luke had given me. I had placed it in the cup holder in the console. It had fallen out but was still intact. I grabbed it and after twisting the top open, took a swig. The water was warm but welcome. With shaking hands, I called Luke.

It went to voice mail. Shit! He was probably with a patient.

I left a message telling him I had had an accident but how would I even know if he got it? And how could I tell him where I was? I had no idea where I was. Somewhere between Fountain Hills and Rio Verde. Judging from the angle of the car and the fact that I couldn't even see the road, I doubted I was even visible if you didn't know where to look.

I tried calling Hannah but just as I tried clicking on her number, the battery died, and the phone shut off.

I took another swig of water.

The heat was really getting to me now. I felt dizzy and my headache was worse. I knew I had a concussion.

I slowly made my way out of the car. I walked around to the passenger side and saw that the car made some shade on that side. I opened the passenger side door and sat on the seat there. It wasn't much cooler but felt a little better. With both doors open now the heat wasn't quite as oppressive.

I put my head back and I prayed and passed out again.

Chapter Thirty-Nine

CB

I went in and out of consciousness. For how long, I had no idea. Every time I woke up, I took a drink. I knew the heat was going to kill me if I didn't.

Then I swore I heard my name being called. I knew things were probably getting bad. I was hallucinating.

There. I heard it again. It was a woman's voice.

"Charlotte!"

I wasn't hallucinating. That was real.

"Charlotte! Answer me!"

I slowly stood up and screamed as loud as I could. "Help! Somebody help me!"

Far above me, where the road should be, I saw a woman on horseback.

Darcy!

She had her phone to her ear. "I found her! She's alive!"

"Stay there," she yelled. "Help is on the way." She spoke again into her phone, but I couldn't hear what she said.

"Rescue is coming to get you," she called to me. "They'll be here any minute. Are you hurt? Anything broken?"

"No, I'm just banged up. Concussion, I think."

"Okay, stay put. We have people coming to get you."

I cried with relief then. It was going to be all right. I sat back down in the car and waited for my rescuers.

Chapter Forty

C3

Despite my claims that I could walk, the rescue team, after affixing a neck collar on me, strapped me onto a stretcher and carried me up the embankment to a waiting ambulance. When I saw how difficult it was for them to make it back up, I was glad for the stretcher and for the rescue team. Up until that point I didn't have a full realization for how much trouble I had been in.

And Darcy! I felt so much remorse for all the bad feelings I had ever had toward her. She had literally saved my life. How could I possibly repay her?

For starters, I vowed to make sure Vince got what was coming to him.

Once we reached the road, I was transferred from the emergency carrier onto the ambulance stretcher which was then slid into the back of the ambulance. An attendant was already inside, and he immediately strapped a blood pressure cuff on my arm and started taking my vital signs. I tried to sit up and look out the open door, but he gently pushed me back down.

"Take it easy. Everything is going to be okay."

"Where's Darcy?"

"Who?"

"Darcy. The woman who found me."

"The woman on horseback?"

I nodded.

"As soon as they started to bring you up, she left. She said to tell you she would see you later and that her father would meet you at the hospital."

I lay back down and felt immediately at peace. Luke was going to be with me at the hospital. And it sounded like Darcy was okay with that.

"Let's roll," the attendant called to the driver. "BP is steady but low. Lights and sirens."

I could feel the ambulance turn around and I assumed we were headed back to Scottsdale and the medical center where Auntie had been.

"Starting an IV," the attendant whose name tag said Ted yelled out over the sirens.

"Slowing down," the driver said. I felt the ambulance slow a little bit.

"I'm in." The ambulance picked up speed again. Ted taped the IV in place and hung the bag of fluid on a hook above my head. "You should be feeling better soon. You're pretty dehydrated. Lucky for you your friend found you when she did."

I felt my eyes getting heavy, but Ted shook my arm. "Stay awake for me. You have a head injury. No napping until you see the doctor."

Ted tried to keep me occupied with friendly chatter and within about twenty minutes we were pulling into the ambulance bay.

An attendant was waiting for us and as they rolled me into the Emergency Room I listened while Ted gave out my information. It was surreal knowing he was talking about me. How often I had transferred patients in emergency situations and done the same thing. Overall, I thought I wasn't doing too badly. My vital signs were low but stable and I was definitely feeling better after getting the IV fluids. I decided I was going to be all right and just wanted to get through the next few hours and go home.

I looked around as best as I could as we rolled through the hallway to a curtained off cubicle in the ER. I was hoping to see Luke. Just when I was feeling disappointment, Luke's face loomed over me.

He kissed me on the forehead.

"You scared the crap out of me," he said. He grabbed my right hand and squeezed it.

"I scared the crap out of me, too," I answered.

By then nurses were coming in and starting their assessments. A new IV bag was hung, more vital signs were taken, and one of the nurses holding a clipboard addressed Luke.

"Hi, Dr. Andrews. Is this your patient?"

"No," Luke said. "I'm family. This is my fiancée." I looked at Luke and he winked at me.

"Okay, Dr. Macchio is the ER doc on today. He'll be in in just a few minutes."

As soon as we were alone, I pulled Luke down toward me. "Fiancée?"

"Yes. What do you say? I don't want to be separated from you for another minute."

"Well, this must be the weirdest proposal on record!"

"Is that a yes?"

"Yes. That's a yes."

Luke started to kiss me and stopped abruptly when we heard the privacy screen get pulled back.

A tall thin older man with silver hair stood next to my gurney. "Hi, I'm Greg Macchio," he said to both of us. He smiled but was all business. He looked at my chart.

"Mrs. Hobson, can you tell me what happened?"

"I was driving to Rio Verde to pick up my friend's children when a truck started following me very closely. Then he deliberately hit my rear bumper. After that, he came alongside me and hit my car on my side until I swerved off the road and went down the embankment. I must have hit my head and passed out then because the rest is fuzzy. I know I tried to call Luke. And I was able to get out of the car and drink some water. But that's all I remember until Luke's daughter found me."

I watched Luke's face change from concern to anger as he listened. It was then that it dawned on me that no one knew that I had been deliberately run off the road. Everyone had just thought I had had an accident.

"Did you see who did this?" Luke asked.

"Yes."

Luke turned to Dr. Macchio. "We need to get the police involved."

"I'll have the nurse call but let's take care of Mrs. Hobson first."

Dr. Macchio did a neurology assessment and wrote some orders on the records on his clipboard. "I think we're just looking at a concussion, but we'll know more after some studies. We'll get you out of here as soon as we can."

As soon as the doctor left, Luke turned to me. "Who was it? Tell me who it was." I could see he was getting angrier by the minute.

I hesitated to answer. I was afraid what he would do. "If I tell you, will you promise to let the police handle it?"

"Never mind. I think I know what you're going to say."

He started to leave the cubicle, but I held onto his hand. "Please don't leave me alone."

The nurse who had done my initial assessment returned.

"Dr. Macchio ordered a head CT and some cervical x-rays. The orderly will be here in a minute to take you over to Radiology. And I also want you to know I notified the police, and they will send an officer over to take your statement."

True enough, she had hardly finished when a young man appeared with a stretcher to take me to Radiology. I was afraid to leave Luke to his own devices but had no choice. He promised me he would stay and be there when I returned.

He was. And he was talking to a young policeman in uniform.

Officer Mullin was a good-looking young man who hardly seemed old enough to be a policeman. He and Luke seemed very comfortable with each other.

"I know Dr. Luke very well," he said when I asked about their relationship. I thought I saw his cheeks blush.

Luke laughed. "Tim and Darcy have started dating."

Officer Mullins cleared his throat and took out his notepad. Clearly, he wanted to move on. "Please tell me what happened."

Over the next few minutes, I told Tim my story, giving him the details as well as I could remember them. I watched Luke's face when I identified Vince as the perpetrator.

His jaw twitched but his voice was even when he spoke.

"You need to know, Tim, that Vince worked for my partner – my ex-partner now. His full name is Vincent Ashford, and he has a history of some petty crimes out of state. And he was let go today."

"Okay, good to know," Tim said. He wrote a few more notes and told us he would be in touch as soon as he had anything to report. Then he left.

Two long hours later, I was released. No broken bones. No head or neck injuries that were discernible on x-ray. I was probably going to be very sore tomorrow from soft tissue injury but there was nothing that could be done for that except anti-inflammatory medication.

"I don't think you should be alone right now," Luke said as soon as we were in his car. "Camille is in no shape to monitor you."

"Do you want to stay over?"

"I have a better idea. How about you stay with me at my place?"

I wasn't expecting this. I hardly knew what to say. And I wasn't sure I was ready to see the home he had had with Cathy just yet.

Luke seemed to sense my reluctance and the reason why.

"Don't feel awkward. This isn't the house I had with Cathy. After she died, I wanted a complete change of scenery for me and Darcy. The house we had before was farther out of town and I thought it would be better for both of us to be closer to friends. My house is actually pretty close to

306

Camille's, just this side of Scottsdale."

"What about Auntie? I don't want to leave her alone."

"Not to worry. Darcy is already with her. She's going to stay with her tonight and then we can go over there tomorrow after you're feeling better."

"You had this already planned, didn't you?"

Luke's smile gave him away. "I might have."

We arrived at Luke's house a few minutes later. It was a beautiful home, like Auntie's in style but larger. However, nothing like the monster house that Dr. Farrell lived in. This home was warm and cozy. Very Luke.

"Make yourself at home," Luke said. "I'll get you some juice and we can sit outside."

I wandered around the great room, looking over the photos on end tables, touching the wood of the furniture, trying to picture Luke and Darcy's life. Happy to be part of it now. Grateful to have survived. I looked out toward the backyard and opened the sliding glass door. The desert air was warm but not too oppressive.

I sat in one of the deck chairs just as Luke followed me out.

"Here you go." He handed me a glass of cranberry juice. I saw his glass had wine in it. I wished mine did. "How are you feeling?"

"Pretty good, considering. I have a headache though. And I'm tired."

Just then, the doorbell rang. Luke put his glass down on the table between us. "Be right back."

A few minutes later, he returned followed by Officer Mullins.

"I'm on my way home but I wanted to give

you guys an update in person."

Luke motioned for Tim to sit. He took a chair opposite both of us.

"A couple of hours ago we answered a call about shots fired. The address was Mark Farrell's house." Luke and I both opened our mouths to speak but Tim put his hand up. "I know you're going to have questions. Just let me finish. As I said, we got a report of shots fired. Farrell's girlfriend called it in to 911. Seems Ashford showed up and he and Farrell got into a fight. Over what isn't entirely clear yet. According to the girlfriend, she overheard Farrell saying he wanted to sever ties with Ashford. Ashford demanded money from Farrell and threatened him. The girlfriend said things got heated and she heard shots. Then, she saw Ashford leave. That's when she called us. When we got there, we found Farrell shot and bleeding. Not life threatening but he was taken to the hospital. We put a BOLO out on Ashford and caught him a little while ago. He's being held on aggravated assault. Other charges might follow. So, you can rest easy tonight. He won't be hurting anyone anymore."

"Thank you, Tim. We really appreciate you telling us," Luke said. He saw Tim look around. "Darcy's not here. She's taking care of Charlotte's aunt. But she might enjoy a phone call."

"Thanks, Dr. Luke. I'll do that." He stood up. "Well, I'll let you guys get some rest. I know I need some."

Luke shook Tim's hand. "Thanks again for stopping by."

After Tim left, we just looked at each other. I was at a loss for words. Vince running me off the road. Shooting Dr. Farrell. Now, Vince in jail. It was too much to comprehend. I was really wishing I could have some wine.

Luke pulled his chair closer to me and put his arm around me. "I'm so glad you're safe. I don't know what I would have done if you had been seriously hurt today. I was going crazy until Darcy called me and told me she had found you."

"Let's not think about this any more tonight. I just want to sit here and enjoy being with you."

That night I snuggled with Luke and fell asleep faster than I thought I would. The day had worn me out. I awoke a couple of times during the night. Each time I reached out to Luke and felt him melt toward me. It was the best feeling.

Chapter Forty-One

ଔ

The following morning, I woke up and reached across to Luke's side of the bed. It was empty. As my head cleared, I smelled coffee and heard humming coming from the direction of the kitchen.

I threw on Luke's T-shirt from the day before that he had thrown on the floor and followed the sounds and smells of breakfast.

"Good morning, Sleepyhead. I was wondering when you were going to get up."

I looked at the kitchen clock. It was ten-thirty. I never slept that late.

Luke put a mug of coffee in front of me, milk and sugar in it just the way I liked it.

"I thought we'd head on over to Camille's after breakfast. I called her and she's fine. She's expecting us around Noon. That should give you enough time to eat and get presentable." I put my hand to my hair. I definitely needed freshening up.

A little after Noon, Luke and I parked in Auntie's driveway. I was surprised to see Hannah's car parked at the curb behind Darcy's SUV.

Just as I approached the front door, I heard one of the twins yell "They're here!"

Hannah yanked the door open before I could even grab the handle.

She pulled me into a bear hug. "I was so worried about you."

"I was too, believe me. Everything is going to be all right now though."

The girls fawned all over me as soon as I was inside the door. They escorted me to the sofa, arranged some pillows around me and then ran into the kitchen to get me something to drink. Auntie was sitting in a recliner opposite the sofa, and I could see the concern in her eyes.

"I'm okay, Auntie. Please don't worry." She nodded.

Luke sat on the arm of the sofa and held my hand. "I know what will make you smile, Camille." She looked at him expectantly. Luke kissed my hand. "We're engaged." Hannah jumped up from the chair she had been sitting in and whooped.

I groaned. "Please, no loud noises. My head hurts."

She hugged me again. "I'm sorry but I'm just so darn happy."

The twins walked back into the living room followed by Darcy holding a pitcher of lemonade. One twin (I will never be able to tell them apart) was carrying a basket of chips and the other was carrying napkins and paper cups. Chips and napkins went on the coffee table and Darcy filled the cups with lemonade and passed those around.

When she was done, I motioned for her to

311

come over. I patted the sofa next to me.

"Saying thank you is not enough. You saved my life. But how did you find me?"

"When you didn't pick up the girls on time, the girls called Hannah and she called your cell. It went straight to voice mail. That's when she got worried. So, she called Dad. By that time, he had listened to his voice mail and he knew you were in trouble. He was already calling me. We had Hannah check Frances' phone and it gave her the general location of your car. Dad notified Search and Rescue and I headed out on horseback to help. I know the area pretty well. I had a good idea where you were. You weren't out there that long but, in this heat, any amount of time would be dangerous."

I hugged Darcy and felt relieved to feel her hug me back.

"And, Charlotte, I'm happy for you and Dad. Please don't worry. We're good. Welcome to the family."

I looked at Luke and he was beaming.

Hannah raised her glass of lemonade. "To Luke and Charlotte."

We all clinked glasses.

Auntie smiled through tears. The little stinker had gotten her wish.

And I was so glad.

Joy Collins trained as a nurse at well-known Bellevue Hospital in New York City and then went on to receive her BS in Business Administration from St. Joseph's College. In addition, she studied Reiki with Susanne Wilson, a medium and Reiki Master in Carefree, Arizona and is now a Reiki Master herself.

She started her writing career penning non-fiction articles. Then came two contemporary novels in the women's fiction genre – *Second Chance* and *Coming Together* (co-authored with Joyce Norman). Those were followed by *I Will Never Leave You*, a memoir Joy wrote after the sudden death of her husband John.

A transplanted Easterner, Joy now calls Arizona home. In her spare time, Joy enjoys mothering her four furbabies - energetic goldendoodle Bella and marmalade kitties Riley, Chaz, and Sean.

Follow her at www.joycollins.com